ALSO BY WILLIAM STORANDT

Outbound:
Finding a Man, Sailing an Ocean

THE

SUMMER

THEY

CAME

THE SUMMER THEY CAME

A NOVEL

William Storandt

VILLARD BOOKS
NEW YORK

Copyright © 2002 by William Storandt

All rights reserved under International and Pan-American Copyright Conventions.
Published in the United States by Villard Books, a division of Random
House, Inc., New York, and simultaneously in Canada by
Random House of Canada Limited, Toronto.

VILLARD BOOKS is a registered trademark of Random House, Inc.
Colophon is a trademark of Random House, Inc.

Library of Congress Cataloging-in-Publication Data

Storandt, William.
The summer they came : a novel / William Storandt.
p. cm.
ISBN 0-375-75909-3
1. Seaside resorts—Fiction.   2. Rhode Island—Fiction.   3. Teenage boys—
Fiction.   4. Gay men—Fiction.   I. Title.
PS3619.T69 S86 2001
813′.6—dc21   2001055922

Villard Books website address: www.villard.com

Printed in the United States of America

2 4 6 8 9 7 5 3

First Edition

Designed by Jo Anne Metsch

For Brian,
for lighting my fire

ACKNOWLEDGMENTS

I'd like to thank Tim Farrell, my editor,
for asking the questions whose answers
so enriched this tale, and Stuart Bernstein,
my agent, who apparently can walk on water.

THE

SUMMER

THEY

CAME

ONE

THE HELICOPTER rattled along, a thousand feet above the arrow-straight beach. Artie Kinzie stared down at the sparse scattering of beachfront homes, solitary dog walkers. "Just can't picture it!" he yelled over the roar, pushing his sunglasses up on his forehead.

"Give it a chance," shouted Mike. "We're not even there yet."

For fifteen more miles the Rhode Island shore unrolled beneath them, a ribbon of sand hemming a skirt of dune grass, salt marsh, and scrub oak.

Finally the pilot shouted back at them, "Can start to make out the village." Silhouetted in the haze a few miles ahead was an abrupt rise, topped by a cluster of gables and turrets. Artie peered intently.

Mike motioned to the pilot. "Take it low and slow."

They began to pass over more and more large homes, small estates really, with pools and tennis courts worked into the terraced gardens. Artie's stomach flip-flopped as the helicopter suddenly ascended, following the abrupt, ledge-pocked noggin of Signal Hill, every inch of it manicured and studded with ample summer houses, their proud bulks rising to busily elaborated white-trimmed peaks and dormers, and stepping off seaward into porches, pergolas, and patios.

They crested the promontory, passing over the mammoth, sagging Ocean Hotel, held together by thousands of gallons of legal-pad-yellow paint. Mike grinned. "We'll have to keep the boys from smoking in bed."

Directly below them, a dense little business district fronted on a cozy harbor bobbing with yachts. But beyond that stretched the key to the plan.

"Wow," said Artie, staring off ahead of them. "I see what you mean."

"Yeah, isn't it amazing?" said Mike. "Long Spit."

A pristine sand spit, topped with a ridge of dune grass, projected another mile beyond the village, into the busy waters of Fishers Island Sound. On the seaward side, a flawless white beach lay in a gentle arc; on the bay side, a scattering of yachts rode at anchor.

"Incredible," said Artie. "Why is it so deserted?"

"I have no fucking idea." Mike grinned and rocked back and forth in his seat. "But that's just what I told you. I've been going by on the boat for years, and it's always deserted. Check out the ruins at the end."

On a low hill at the tip of the spit, almost hidden in a tangle of undergrowth, were the rust-streaked, crumbling remains of concrete artillery emplacements.

"Perfect," said Artie.

"I don't know who they were expecting the enemy to be," said Mike.

"Right," said Artie, "but they're about to find out."

TWO WEEKS later, Artie held a meeting at the offices of his venture company in a former billiard parlor overlooking West Twenty-first Street in Chelsea. The six around the table ranged from Brooks Brothers and J.Crew to engineer's boots and a smattering of bondage accessories.

"Mike here told me about it," said Artie. "We took a look a couple of weeks ago. Setting couldn't be more perfect. Halfway between the city and Boston, isolated beach not too far from town, antique shops, art galleries, B&Bs, a big old hotel ripe for rehab . . . 'Course, this sort of thing has never been done from a standing start. Guess we have to figure how to get it moving on all fronts at once."

The others pushed photos around the table. "So what goes on there now?" asked Leo Robbia, the owner of the Snake Pit, a venerable leather bar in the meatpacking district.

"Pretty quiet," said Mike. "Old-money summer houses, an unbelievably fucked-up plywood-beach-cabana club right at the edge of the village, fucking thing blocks the view out to sea for half the village. Then, you know, the T-shirt shops, the yogurt window, the usual crap. But what's cool is that there are these time-share units with balconies down the whole second floor of the main street, and a couple of other small hotels, and the street—I think it's called Front Street—has buildings just down one side. It runs along a park right on the harbor. Could be like desperate parade after tea dance."

"Well, you can't just declare it open and throw a party," said B. J. Gelson. "You've got to have the buzz going already, word-of-mouth thing, the right people seen there." B.J. was an events planner who, when he wasn't organizing the Dalai Lama at Madison Square Garden, was promoting giant circuit parties for AIDS charities.

"Exactly the problem," said Artie. "We don't have years for that to happen. We don't own the venues, the accommodations."

Leo spoke up. "Maybe we should get it going with the nature dykes first. They could do their bird-watching thing, you know, not piss anybody off too much."

"No way," said Artie. "They already bought up P-town while the boys were busy worrying about their tans. We gotta watch it, keep a head start."

"But Leo's right," said Mike. "We're not even probably welcome. It's not like those B&Bs are exactly advertising in the gay papers." Then he got an odd smile on his face, and let out one low grunt of a laugh.

———

HELEN BOOTHROYD pushed aside the crocheted curtain in the front sitting room. She sighed at the sight of the brown, spent daffodils among the tulips along the front walk. At seventy, she just couldn't get to everything anymore. Too late for any last fussing, though: the guests who had booked her honeymoon suite were due. She shifted sideways to scan the street, her modestly but carefully groomed head held just back from view. But there was no one down front except the two big guys getting out of their black Jeep. They were dressed in ripped cutoff shorts and giant work shoes. Probably, she thought, from a lawn service.

She went back in the kitchen and resumed knitting baby hats for the hospital. It was just two years ago that Helen had taken the step—her grown kids were appalled—of turning her house into a bed-and-breakfast called the Lilac Bush. Since her husband of forty years had died, her social life had dwindled to nearly nothing. Couples were easier to seat at dinner parties. So now her guests had become her companions. She'd exchanged Christmas cards with a number of them, traveled to visit one couple in Maine. But she still felt a tremor of nerves before each new guest arrived, a trace of Yankee reserve. What will they think? There was a knock.

She opened the front door and reared back. The two men from the Jeep loomed in the doorway, blotting out the sky. As pumped as linebackers, they could have been twins. Both had boot-camp buzz cuts, tiny goatees, and cheeky grins. One had on a heavy, hammered-silver collar, the other a piece of bent rebar around his vast, puffy upper arm. Collar put out his hand.

"Hello, I'm Derek, Ritter?" His voice was a surprisingly light tenor. "This is Tracy."

"Derek and Tracy. Oh . . . I see, I thought—" Helen put a finger to her lips. "I'm sorry. I'm Helen Boothroyd. Come right in."

Derek and Tracy shouldered their matching black ballistic-nylon duffels and followed her through the foyer. Derek stopped in front of her pride and joy, an oil painting of the house her husband had commissioned for their twenty-fifth anniversary. "Wow," he said. "This is great."

"Oh yes, thank you," said Helen. "She's an artist who lives out on Cape Cod."

"I know," said Derek. "We sell her in our gallery."

The honeymoon suite consisted of a sitting room and bath, and spiral stairs up to a large square cupola with panoramic ocean views and a four-poster bed.

"Uh—I can bring in a cot—"

"No, no, this is terrific," said Tracy, flicking a frisky glance at Derek.

HOLLIS WYNBOURNE nursed his coffee over the morning paper. The small iron breakfast table in the glassed-in porch overlooked the algae-choked pond—once, it had held golden carp—and, in the distance, the arc of Long Spit. Surrounding him were stacks of old photos, engravings, and clippings, boxes of mildewed books and rumpled documents, heaps of worn-out shoes, odd scraps of clothing, and a few dusty but neatly arranged displays on card tables—manacles, whips, leg irons—all just an intimation of his collecting obsession: slave memorabilia. In the years since he had retired from the recital stage he had managed to infuriate all his siblings by gradually selling off the family heirlooms from the house to acquire ever more head scarves and slave-ship fittings. None of the family ever came from Pittsburgh anymore. Hollis squatted there, stocking his antique shop down on Front Street with family treasures, closing off rooms in the winters to save on heat.

He was a tall man, whose height varied with his mood, from proudly erect to moderately stooped. Both dated from his years as a baritone. The proud bearing he would have presented to an audience when performing Schubert lieder, the diffident stoop for greeting the cultural matrons afterward in the green room, so as not to make them feel towered over. His long-fingered hands moved with a measured stiffness, from years of having to behave themselves in front of audiences. His face had a strong-boned, large-featured quality, handsome from out in the auditorium, with an expression that tended, when he was under observation, toward a well-bred, cautious optimism, but in private toward a scowl.

"Not very goddamn likely," he said, finishing an editorial on the state budget. "Run by jackasses." He muttered bitterly, with cramped swipes of his hand, as though there were a valet at his side to nod assent.

Though Hollis had been a fixture in the village on and off all his life, and steadily for the last thirty years, he kept to himself, never had any visitors at the house, at least none from among the townspeople his own age. He was easy enough, if a bit reserved, with people who came in the shop, polite with the tourists, got on with the local regulars, but simply never partook of the elegant, if rather fevered, social life of the town. The house, Ledge Knoll, had been a regular stop on the summer round of dinner parties in the years when his brothers and sisters took their three-week turns using it. Now it had become merely a second-string subject of gossip, as more and more sideboards and armoires were lugged down the front steps, and large wooden crates were dollied up the front walk with stenciled return addresses in Mississippi and Liberia.

It was ten to ten; he put his cup in the sink. With a visage less stern than usual, he started down the lane to the shop. He would close an hour early today in order to give young Anthony Giannini his voice lesson.

Hollis took a roundabout route these first warm mornings, enjoying the greenish spring light, the intervals of faint heat between the early stirrings of the day's breeze. The daily progress of the village's flower beds lent some movement to his life, which seemed stuck in a kind of waiting. This morning he chose the several blocks of Front Street.

Although the village had the usual beach resort shops—snacks, swimsuits, sunglasses, lotto tickets—and even an antique carousel, there was no feeling of welcome about the place, especially not right now, as the long quiet season began to show signs of giving way. Rather there were signs everywhere of the residents taking their share of the place in private. The mansions, though somewhat densely situated, peered over hedges and from behind ironwork fences, or hid behind artful kinks in their driveways. The juncture between the village and the sand spit was paved with asphalt, a parking lot running the length of the unmarked Pequot Beach Club. This was a startlingly ugly three-hundred-foot-long structure on pilings, presenting a blank plywood wall to the village. It housed several hundred private changing booths for members, who parked in assigned spaces. To get to the sand spit, one traversed the parking lot to the start of the dunes beyond, where a trail led through the grass to the beach. At the other end of the harborfront park, the town pier was blocked by a gate with a sign forbidding entrance to all but berth holders and recommending against a paragraph of other behaviors. Even the yacht club was set on pilings out in the tiny harbor, accessible only by footbridge.

Aside from this atmosphere of reserve, the setting was flawless. The shops down Front Street looked directly onto the harbor and toward the sunsets. The prevailing southwesterly breeze, which had fueled the town's nineteenth-century flowering as a sea-air escape from the summer heat of a particular set of Midwest cities, slid in off the sound and discouraged the mosquitoes from venturing out of the vast marshes to the east.

Most of the shops occupied space in a long, arcaded building, surprisingly seedy for such a wealthy and picturesque setting. Above the shops were the several dozen balconies of weekly rental units. It was as though the wealthy had, as ransom for their privacy, ceded the little business district to elements they had no intention of associating with. The walls, fences, and hedges began just a couple of hundred feet up the lanes behind the shops.

Passing the Yankee Gulch boutique, the last shop in the arcade, Hollis nodded a greeting to Dot Bradley, the owner.

"It's beginning all over again, Hollis," she said.

"Oh well, what can you do," he said.

"Stick 'em while you can," she said. "Season gets shorter every year." Dot was tall, imposing, with a sensible shock of white hair. She ran the merchants' association from the Yankee Gulch, which specialized in Southwest housewares and clothing.

Hollis touched his forehead, not breaking stride. Once out of earshot, he muttered, "Unbearable idiot . . . probably gives to whales," the venom delicious in his mouth, like a lemon drop.

His shop was clustered with several other antique and clothing shops a block north of this arcaded strip, just beyond the barely surviving Signal Hill Inn. He unlocked the door and stepped in among the familiar jumble, breathing the familiar aromas of orange oil and mildew, and feeling, as he did every day, that he had reached both safe haven and prison.

THE NEXT morning, Helen Boothroyd sat on her bed, halted midway through folding a tea towel, listening with some concern to the sounds from the honeymoon cupola. She wasn't born yesterday; it had occurred to her that they might be homosexuals. She had perhaps let them down last night when Derek had asked, "So, where are the hot spots?" and she had said, "Oh, gracious me, not many of them, maybe a few in Westerly." They'd come in late. Now a rapid rhythmic creaking in time with a tinny rhythm (a Pet Shop Boys CD, as it happened) was interspersed with what sounded very much like hard slapping noises. Were they fighting? At any rate, the fresh scones were now cold, and she did have things to do besides wait all day to serve them breakfast.

Since her first suspicions the night before, she'd been examining her attitudes. They seemed nice enough, but, if they were in fact homosexuals, it was worrisome that they were so big. What if they ever got out of control? And was she now bound to tell honeymooning couples what may have gone on in their room? Of course not, but just the fact that she would know was bad enough. Would she have to start washing the mattress pad after every guest? And she had some regular guests by now. Would she seat them with this sort of person at breakfast in the sunroom, with their rivets and all, and introduce them just as if they were the most normal people in the world? And if they told people in the village, like Dot Bradley, where they were staying, would everyone think she had gone after this type of clientele?

When they finally did come down for breakfast, Tracy had on frightfully ripped jeans and a tank top with a neckline that plunged nearly to his navel. Helen was not one to stare, particularly at a strange man's body, but she was at first appalled, and then oddly fascinated, by a chrome chain that appeared from beneath his shirt on each side yet somehow was not hanging around his neck, but rather bridged the chasm between his pectorals, appearing somehow to hold him together—she certainly had no idea how, or for that matter why, nor did she want to know.

Derek lifted one of the poor scones with his thirty- or forty-pound arm and said, "I'd better just have a half, or are these low-fat?"

"Oh, there's not much to them," said Helen, wondering if he was pulling her leg. "A big fellow like you must have quite an appetite."

"That's the trouble," said Tracy. Derek shot him a smile that said: *Bitch*. "That's why we have to go to the gym so much."

"Oh, I see, yes," said Helen. They turned down the omelettes, and she had already beaten the eggs.

They all labored to make a success of breakfast chat, Helen gingerly interviewing them. She knew this was expected of the B&B hostess, but it didn't come naturally to her.

"I believe you mentioned a gallery?" she asked. "And is that—your living?"

"Yes," said Derek, who, though he deferred to Tracy in body language, seemed more the spokesman. "You've Been Framed, we call it, a lot of posters, prints, sort of a cross between a gallery and framing shop, but we do shows, like of Ilda, who did that oil of your house."

"Basically, we tried to figure out a business we could start together," said Tracy, "and that would leave us enough time to work out together."

"The eternal competition," said Derek, playfully flexing his biceps alongside Tracy's. Helen smoothed the tablecloth. Derek added, "It's one of our hobbies."

"Well, I suppose that's nice, to be able to do so many things together," Helen said tentatively, reminded for a moment of her husband. She shook the thought and soldiered cheerily on to local sightseeing tips.

As they were getting up from the table, Derek asked if they could take a sunbath in the front yard. "You know, watch the passing scene."

Helen stammered, "Oh well, actually there's a patio around back that's more out of the wind. You'd probably enjoy that more. More private for you, you see."

JIM HORNSWICH zipped shut the pouch under Marie Hazel's eye. Normally the meticulousness of his craft was engrossing enough to hold at bay the larger questions, such as What are you doing as a gay, single plastic surgeon, practicing in a no-account town in the part of Nebraska where you can see the church steeples from five miles away? But the endless procession of dewlaps on his operating table in recent weeks—everyone wanting a summer tuck—was wearing him down, and this morning he was distracted, badly in need of a break. Over his morning coffee, he'd been idly going to bed with a few dozen men in the *Advocate* personals when he realized that his normal dreamy percolation of arousal had escalated to an insistent, feverish rut with no hope of relief. Suddenly the prospect of solo release in the shower for the twenty thousandth time howled with inadequacy.

A quarter-page ad in the back had caught his eye. "Find him in the dunes." It was for a bed and breakfast called the Lilac Bush in a gay resort town he'd never heard of called Long Spit, "for the discerning male traveler who's had enough of the same old same old." It spoke of pristine miles of beaches in a major yachting center and whispered of boys being "left alone to get up to whatever boys will get up to."

All morning Jim had been dogged by reveries of beachfuls of men and now, as he tidied up the smeared, bruised terrain of Marie Hazel's cheek, a sharp memory waylaid him: the last time he felt truly alive, that day in Provincetown, his first visit, the time he was arrested by the park police in the dunes. He had been at a phase in which the idea of offering yourself on display to passersby, from a perch up among the poison ivy, was so surreal that he had lost touch with the necessary cautions. Having sex with living, nonvirtual men was still utterly novel for him, to say nothing of tumbling in the sand with one, both of them greased with sun oil, until they looked like a pair of cinnamon crullers. When the officer suddenly loomed above them on horseback, Jim had at first reacted with a mildly guilty smile, as though he'd been caught eating a grape at the supermarket. This had gotten him off on the wrong foot with the officer, and the incident had taken up much of the next several days.

Despite this setback, or perhaps because of it, the idea of meeting a man in the dunes had retained its magic for Jim, and images of abs glimpsed through dune grass now tugged him away from Marie's oozing lids. He told her to rest for a few minutes and ducked into his office to make a phone call.

"Hello?" Helen Boothroyd's voice sounded more elderly than Jim might have expected.

He asked, "Is this the Lilac Bush Bed and Breakfast?"

"Yes."

"Good. I'm calling from Hinton, Nebraska. I want to find out a little about your place."

"Gracious. So far!" Who might have told him about her?

He inquired about the selection of rooms, was startled to hear that she only had two rooms with double beds.

"Most of my people these days seem to want the twin-bedded rooms," she responded. "Not so much kicking, you know." She tittered agreeably.

"Do you get a lot of young guys coming through?"

"Well, funny you should ask. I've got two right now upstairs. Nice young fellows . . . huge, I must say."

"Hmmm . . ." said Jim. "So, let's see, do you have a weight room?"

"A waiting room? I'm not sure what—"

"I guess not. A hot tub?"

"Oh no, nothing like that," said Helen. "This is just a comfortable old house, nothing too fancy."

"Sounds great. I hear there's a good beach scene. Are you near the part where all the boys like to go?"

"Well now, I don't know. You mean the local boys?"

"Them too, I guess. I was picturing more of a visiting crowd, you know, a hot scene?"

"Oh well, no, it's pretty quiet, and of course we've always got the breeze. Picks up later on, you know."

"I gather it's not quite so tacky as Provincetown, more sort of upmarket, off the beaten track?"

"Well, I've never been there, but I'm sure it's lovely. We're not putting on airs or anything, but we have our old families."

"I'm going to go ahead and give you a try," said Jim.

IT WAS almost noon by the time Derek and Tracy, bored with backyard sunbathing, ambled into Hollis's shop, taking a first look at the shopping before heading out to the beach. Tracy was wearing a one-piece black Lycra combination tank top swimsuit with an eight-inch-wide weightlifter's belt. Derek had chosen his stainless-steel collar for the salt air. At the back of the shop, Hollis peered out from his desk, which was camouflaged behind a display of patent-medicine bottles. A greeting rose nearly to his lips. Hollis had the sense that greeting his patrons somehow conferred his approval on them, and, after he had drawn breath to speak, something told him these men were dangerous to him. He had certainly seen their ilk in big cities, but there was something unsettling about having them here in his oddly motivated little preserve.

Derek and Tracy were not particularly interested in antiques, their style leaning more toward industrial chic. But they couldn't resist bins of old prints. Framing good ones on spec had become a mainstay of their business.

"Honey, did you see these?" Derek asked, with a significant arch of an eyebrow. Tracy joined him at a bin full of turn-of-the-century photos of Connecticut private school athletic teams. Hollis had helped dozens of prosperous geezers recover such ephemera from their younger days, and in the process had skimmed the cream, gradually acquiring a portfolio of the lean, innocent musculature of privilege. This had a place of honor at home in his study, alongside another folio containing posters for Golden Gloves boxing tournaments.

Tracy approached Hollis. "Nice stuff," he said. "Do you have any more of that sort of thing?" His eyebrows gave a slight co-conspiratorial bounce.

"No, not really." Hollis's tone was curt. "Got into it originally as a service to some of our local men."

"I'll bet," said Derek brightly. Hollis gave him a tight smile.

A few minutes later they were heading out the door. "Thanks a lot," Derek called. "Take care now."

"Do come in again," Hollis replied. The latch clicked. "Ludicrous fucking nitwits." He expelled a snort. "You look like a pathetic goddamn circus act." He stopped to straighten the print bin, leaving a War of 1812 naval battle showing.

Back on Front Street, the day was turning into a steamer. Derek and Tracy wandered along the arcade and into Angleton's Tea Room to get a sandwich for the beach. At several tables, older patrons stared quietly over afternoon tea. Lattie Teachout looked up from the cash register. "I'm sorry, sirs? Sirs! We can't allow you in here like that."

Tracy turned. "Like what?"

"No swimsuits." She looked nervous. "Anthony! You want to come here a minute?" She turned back to Tracy. "It's Health Department."

"This isn't a swimsuit," Tracy said, getting a twist out of one of his straps. "If you want to know the truth, the catalog described it as pajamas."

"Well, I'm awful sorry, but I don't think we ought to chance it," Lattie said. "We could get in a lot of trouble."

Anthony Giannini had appeared from the kitchen in his waiter's drip-dry white shirt and black vest. He was tall, slim, eighteen, with black longish hair, on the cusp between pretty boy and handsome young man.

Derek glanced at him, started visibly, and let his gaze linger. "Well, we certainly don't want to get anybody in trouble. All we're after is a couple of sandwiches to go. Think we could just wait outside for them? He could bring them out?"

"Sure," said Anthony. "What are you having?"

A few minutes later, Anthony brought out their lobster rolls. Derek was sitting on the windowsill. A rip in the crotch of his cutoffs displayed a generous swatch of his black leather bikini briefs. He took the bag. "Thank you very much."

"Oh, no problem. Anything I can do to help," said Anthony.

Derek looked at him, weighing Anthony's delivery a moment. He got a sly smile on his face. "What time do you get off?" he asked.

"Excuse me?" said Anthony, his eyes fleeing Derek's.

"Oh, that's okay," said Derek. "Hope we see you around town."

"Well, 'bye now," said Anthony.

TWO

OME EARLY from work, Anthony peeled off his shirt and regarded himself in the mirror over his dresser. The black polyester pants hung loosely at his waist, showing a bit of hip bone on each side. He had long held the nonconformist view that his slimness was okay but, in the face of overwhelming consensus to the contrary—from the taunts of high school peers to the pity of relatives—he kept his views to himself. He struck a couple of lanky poses, considering what to wear to his voice lesson.

Anthony had been studying with Hollis Wynbourne for two years, ever since the night he had sung the tenor solo in a Stephen Foster medley with the Long Spit Community Chorus. Afterward, Hollis had made some rather extravagant remarks about Anthony's gifts, the "imperative of a career," and so forth, and had offered him free instruction.

This overture had startled both of them. Anthony had never taken his singing very seriously, and Hollis had never allowed himself in any way to act on his veiled yearning to befriend certain young men.

The lessons had proceeded for several months before Anthony first detected a whiff of inappropriate ardor in Hollis's pedagogy. Those first inklings—a hand lingering on the tummy to assess the progress in diaphragmatic breathing technique, fingertips venturing about the throat and jawbone to trace the proper path of the sound column—had given Anthony the creeps, yet, at the same time he had found them oddly thrilling: it was the first time anyone had ever noticed him the way he craved to be noticed. He had acted oblivious, first because he didn't want to spook Hollis and make him too self-conscious to continue, but mainly because his pleasure derived only from receiving these attentions; finding Hollis far from attractive, he wanted to offer him no hope of reciprocation. But he had started giving more thought to his choice of clothing.

A month had passed since the iron pumper had taken the carry-out order from him in front of Angleton's. The memorably bulky man had dug in his cutoffs for some time looking for a tip, which he'd then pressed into Anthony's hand while fixing him with a split second of eye contact and a flicker of a smile that had left Anthony feeling found out. Time and again he'd caught himself replaying that moment in his daydreams, as though it were insisting he examine it.

In the intervening weeks he'd had the strangest sense that there were suddenly gay men everywhere in town. He couldn't be sure whether something not entirely welcome within him was awakening from long dormancy, demanding that he see things which had been there all along, or whether the pairs of handsome young men window-shopping on Front Street, the single men loitering, hips cocked provocatively against bench backs and street lamps, were actually a new presence. At Angleton's, where the menu leaned toward steaks and chops, the one or two menu items containing sun-dried tomatoes or arugula had sold out midway through his dinner shift three times in recent weeks. And, for the first time ever, Anthony had noticed a distinctive sort of man—youthful from a distance, surprisingly mature up close—sitting on the curb in front of Frankie's Slice by the Sea Pizza. These men dressed like laborers, stage hands, even like skateboarders; some had traces of mascara. It seemed strange to Anthony that they saw nothing odd in just sitting there on the sidewalk for hours. This was new.

After trying several possibilities, Anthony settled on a blue oxford-cloth shirt and old khakis, pausing first to switch from Jockeys to boxers. The pose was: boy who's never given much thought to what he wears, doing his generic moderately dressy look, a grade above jeans and a T-shirt, below sport jacket. As he went out the door, he added a beaded wristband.

HUMMING ALONG, top down, in the Miata he'd picked up at the Providence airport, Jim Hornswich offered his forehead to the sun as a sort of toast to being on holiday. After all, he described such behavior to his clientele as a sin. He was impressed by the approach to Long Spit, the glimpses of the river along the road down from Westerly, here and there yachts on moorings, then the road narrowing and winding between high hedges and stone walls as he hit the outskirts of the village proper. A far cry from the miles of scrappy by-the-week bungalows on the way into Provincetown.

Helen Boothroyd's house was much nicer than he had expected. It looked like a family home rather than the sort of shabby one-night-stand pads he'd tried up on the Cape. Helen answered the door with a bemused look. "Hello? Now, you'd be Mr. Hornswich?"

"Yes, hello. It's Dr. Hornswich, actually, but Jim is fine."

"And you've come all the way from Nebraska, did I get that right?" Her voice was friendly but wary, as though she were coping with a game whose rules she didn't quite understand.

"That's right, ma'am."

She ushered him into the front hall. "Well, I'm so glad you've come, but really I can't get over how you thought to call me. I've had others, well, right now I've got another—I guess you'd call them a pair—of young men upstairs, here for a second visit, and, of course that's just fine and all, I just don't understand where you're all coming from. Do you have friends here?"

"No, but I hope to pretty soon," said Jim, jaunty but a bit puzzled. "I saw your ad in *The Advocate*."

Helen started. "Well now, I've never heard of that. What's it called again?"

"Here, I'll show you." He dug in his bag and produced the magazine. "It was here somewhere, in the back, in the travel classifieds." He flipped through pages of phone sex ads depicting muscular young men entwined in phone cords or licking their receivers. Helen's eyes darted nervously.

"Yeah, here it is." He handed her the magazine. Helen's lips moved, her brow furrowing: "'Where boys can be left alone to get up to whatever boys will get up to'. . . . Well, this just has to be a mistake." She glanced at the cover: "We Do Hot Berlin." "What is this magazine?"

"It's the biggest gay magazine in the country," said Jim. "You mean you don't know anything about this?"

"Why, no. Nothing at all," said Helen, beginning to understand a couple of things.

"I just thought this place looked like something a little different and I'd give it a try," said Jim.

Helen continued to scrutinize the travel page. "Well, I'll be," she said. "Here's Nancy Jenkins's place up the street. Hmmm . . . 'Could he be waiting for you beside our pool?' This is most peculiar." Helen looked up. "Oh, I'm sorry. I'm not being a very good hostess, am I. Let me show you to your room. May I borrow this for a few moments?"

When Jim was installed in his room, Helen put the magazine in a brown paper bag and strode up the street toward the Gull and Rose Guesthouse. Nancy's husband, Sam, had been a hydraulics engineer at the Electric Boat plant in Groton, but had been downsized into early retirement, so she had started taking in guests at about the same time as Helen. They were each other's confidantes in their new ventures. From the start, Sam had been prickly about the guesthouse, perhaps feeling it called attention to his humiliating idleness.

Helen gripped the folded magazine so tightly her arthritic knuckles throbbed; she felt queasier by the minute, as though her house had been broken into. It had been a leap for her to open her home to strangers in the first place, but somehow she'd gotten used to it. She'd done a bit of advertising, really just the small ad in the back of *Yankee* and a corner of the placemats at Angleton's, so she'd never really thought much about where her clientele came from—"word of mouth" had a cozy, safe feel to it. But discovering that unknown forces were reaching into her life this way was disturbing.

At the Gull and Rose five young men lounged on the front porch. She nodded to them with an apologetic smile and stuck her head in the front door. "Nan? It's Helen."

Nancy Jenkins arrived at the front door, glanced at Helen, at the men, and back at Helen. "Come on in the kitchen. I'm just cleaning up." As soon as they closed the kitchen door, Nancy said, "Do you have any idea what is going on? Where are they coming from? Lois has them, too. My husband is having a fit. I mean, they're nice enough young fellows, very clean actually, I barely need to touch their rooms, but—have you got them too?"

"Yes, I do," said Helen, "and one of them just showed me this." She glanced around cautiously and produced the magazine from the brown paper bag.

HOLLIS SAT on his sunporch, awaiting Anthony's arrival. He always felt a mild agitation, almost pleasant actually, before these lessons. First would come the appetizer: watching Anthony come up the walk. Anthony's walk was a beguiling mix of shyness and jauntiness; it combined the bottomless unease of adolescence with a charming openness to whatever the next moment held in store. And those endearingly hesitant strides would deliver him to these rooms, where he would be close at hand for at least an hour. Hollis's determination to observe proper decorum gave a certain tingle of the forbidden to the routine touching of the young man that was, to be sure, necessary for assessing his developing vocal technique. Sometimes, though, he was so caught up in fine-tuning his pose of nonchalance that he not only neglected to enjoy the information coming in through his fingertips, he also failed to note whether the vocal technique was improving. He couldn't very well repeat the pressing of the tummy or the gentle grasping of the bony shoulders to correct the posture, surely a giveaway. So he would be forced to make some noncommittal response, compounding his erotic frustration with the concern that he was a pedagogue of worryingly low integrity.

As he idly scanned the porch's commanding view of Long Spit, something caught his eye and propelled him to the telescope on its tripod nearby. It was a very good one, a Carl Zeiss that his father had acquired for spotting enemy bombers during World War II. It was one family possession Hollis had not sold off, handy as it was for inspecting the occasional jogger passing in the lane below.

He brought the dunes, a half-mile or so distant, into focus. What had caught his eye was a figure the unmistakable color of skin standing in the tall grass at the crest of the dune. He located the figure and fiddled with the focus knob. "What in the . . . ?" Sure enough, the figure was a naked, rather well-built man, standing utterly motionless. He was positioned so that, while Hollis had a clear view of him, anyone glancing up at him from below on the beach would have glimpsed just a suggestion of his nakedness through the waving grass.

Hollis traced the ridge of the dune with the lens and came upon another figure, slightly more hidden, also standing still as a sentry, also naked but for a black military cap and black straps crossing his chest like bandoliers. He stared, muttering to himself in the "confused idiot" voice that he often used to vent irritation. "People never stand that still. Are they playing statues? Maybe they're mimes."

With a start he became aware of Anthony, tapping insistently and looking in at him from the screen door at the end of the porch. "Oh, hello, Anthony, sorry, come in!" He jumped up, swiveling the telescope toward the wall. "A thrush, lovely, the first of the season." Anthony padded across the porch, understanding that he was not expected to pursue the topic.

They went into the front parlor where the ancestral rosewood Chickering grand piano reposed, its lid bearing a display of slave auction handbills, each illustrating the sort of vigorous merchandise that would be on offer. They took their places, Hollis at the keyboard, Anthony standing at his side, and Anthony began his vocalizing. As always, Hollis encouraged, admonished, indicated diction for Anthony to parrot ("Nay, nay, nay, nay, nayyy . . . Noo, noo, noo, noo, noooo . . .") corrected intonation, vibrato, ordered hard consonant attacks ("Tut, tut, tut, tut, tuuuut") and legato arpeggios—but couldn't quite keep from glancing out the parlor windows, across the porch, to the barely perceptible figures off in the dunes.

He had Anthony run through a scale in long tones, normally one of his favorite moments, since he had leave to perform the breathing check: one hand on the small of Anthony's back, the other on his deliciously flat tummy. Normally, this was the moment that posed the most exquisite test for his studied reserve; though lost in pondering the effortless leanness of youth, he must remember to furrow his brow and chide, "Support the air column!" Yet even in that moment he couldn't resist shooting another look out the window.

Anthony was instantly aware of Hollis's distraction, and surprised by his own reaction to it. He had convinced himself that he was magnanimous in allowing this pawing, and even permitted himself, before each lesson, an inward groan at the prospect of it. Surely he had every right to find it presumptuous, and without a doubt he had no interest in ever reciprocating the impermissible longings made plain by the moment that he knew, each week, would come: the long, bony fingers, the dreaded, lecherous invasion. He would brace for it, stiffen slightly—but also make sure everything was held just so, arch his back slightly, because, for all the unease, there was a sense of power in drawing Hollis's touch, for the first time a hold over an adult. This power needed to be skillfully, subtly put in play. But this time Hollis was not even paying attention. What's out that window? Have I held him off for too long, has he given up the chase?

The lesson played out in a slightly chillier atmosphere—Hollis uncharacteristically distant, Anthony resistant to the other small touches. Each felt his way on new ground, a tit for tat of small slightings, infinitesimal, stubborn delays in response. In the space of just a few minutes, this new atmosphere made clear by contrast what had been tacitly understood before: that each was getting something from the encounters, something that needed to remain unexpressed.

After the lesson ended, Hollis watched Anthony go down the walk. He had completely missed the weekly pleasure of watching his student come up the walk, and now he noted a subdued quality to the departing figure, nearly a pout. He mulled over why the lesson had left him so thrown off balance.

Hollis had spent years evolving his timid routines, lovingly expending thousands of hours on his peculiar archival passions, his erotic flights rigidly restricted to the realm of fantasy. These last months of teaching Anthony had been a crack in his armor of self-discipline. He'd told himself this foray was not a departure because these touches weren't headed anywhere, rather were a destination unto themselves, one he could be satisfied with. But having settled for an exclusive diet of the imagination for so long, he'd been astonished by how much libidinous fuel could be concentrated into a second's touch of fingertip to collarbone, enough to keep a week's worth of fantasy smoldering dangerously, like a fire in a wastebasket. Although he had convinced himself that his purity had remained uncompromised, he'd become quite simply addicted to this weekly crumb of taboo. He'd avoided thinking about the certainty that this idyll would end, possibly badly; he persisted in regarding it as an indulgence just as harmless, just as divorced from reality, as his dreamy leafing through his folios of slave boys. But now, having Anthony in range of his touch against the backdrop of the men in the dunes confronted Hollis with a connection he found deeply unnerving.

Anthony, for his part, was amazed at the intensity of his reaction. All that had happened was that his weekly scrap of approval in what he'd convinced himself was a minor arena had been snatched away, and yet there was no denying that he felt utterly rejected, devastated. He had taken Hollis's attentions for granted, had settled for them as his total exploration of that hazardous region of his soul, and now had been summarily kicked aside. Suddenly the whole setup seemed preposterous. How could he have let something so important, mysterious, and fragile hinge on such a haphazard, unacknowledged arrangement? He felt set back to zero, a perilous state with his village newly populated by handsome young men, roaming the streets, sitting on the curbstones for hours on end, waiting.

THE NEXT afternoon, Leo Robbia rumbled into the village and double-parked his giant battered black van in front of the Signal Hill Inn, a tired-looking white clapboard mishmosh of colonial shutters and aluminum picture windows that stood facing the harbor on Front Street between the arcade and Hollis's shop. Each door of Leo's van bore the logo of his New York bar, the Snake Pit: a cobra emerging from an unbuttoned fly. He plunged his hand into his paint-splotched black leather pants and pulled out the real estate agent's name. From her Camry, parked a few spaces away, Kit Honeycutt took in the greasy denim vest, the bandana tied around his head.

"Oh boy," she muttered to herself, opening the car door. She straightened her silk jacket and ventured forth to meet him.

"Hi. I'm Kit, the Property Shop?" She extended her hand.

"Yeah. So this dump's it, right?" Leo fired his cigarette butt into the gutter. They stood on the sidewalk, squinting.

"Yes, it's been a landmark here for a good many years. It's had constant updating, as you can see, to, you know, take advantage of the view." Leo didn't reply. She simpered nervously.

"My mom and dad used to bring us here for Sunday dinners sometimes when I was growing up."

"Right . . . right," Leo said absently, scrutinizing the haphazardly expanded building, its grandiose touches, like the porte-cochère, at odds with the cheesy ones, like the prominent kitchen exhaust fans on the roof. "Yeah . . . I gotcha." He started to head inside, Kit trailing behind. She saw the alarm on the face of the desk clerk and signaled *It's okay* with an uneasy smile.

"They've tried to keep the old-fashioned-fishing-village sort of feel to the dining rooms and all? . . . With the real fishing nets and those are actual lobster pot floats from our local boats . . . and that all stays, of course."

Leo let out a sharp bark of a laugh. "Yeah, right."

They viewed the upstairs rooms, the kitchens, the cracked pool; completed their tour under the peeling porte-cochère. Leo had some questions about fire exits, noise regulations, liquor permits. "And what are they talkin', a million two?"

"Yes, that's right," said Kit. "I'm sure there's some wiggle room there."

They headed down the drive toward Leo's van. A police officer had just pulled up behind it and was getting out of his cruiser.

"Yo, I'm outta here," Leo shouted to him. The officer waved and moved off. Leo turned to Kit. "Cops leave you alone around here?"

"Oh yes," said Kit. "It's a very safe town."

Leo stuck a screwdriver in the empty door-lock hole, climbed into the van. "Awright, be talkin' to ya." He drove off.

THE AFTERNOON had the soft focus of hazy sun, more like an August than a June day, except that the early-season water temperature was still giving the breeze a refreshing nip down by the water. Jim trudged along the beach, heels digging into the sand, tendons getting stretched, at first annoyed at the laborious pace, then remembering: You're on vacation. He adjusted himself in his Speedo to most flattering effect, and squared his shoulders with a nice buzz of anticipation, pleased that at least he had used the paralyzing boredom of life in Hinton to head off an incipient paunch with frequent trips to the gym. There was no one in the gym, to be sure, perhaps no one in the county, to take note of his work. He'd had to settle for the personals, and for endless online chatting and exchanging of pictures. Perhaps because of his profession, the best of these left him suspecting digital surgery, and the worst, truly off-putting images of large pasty men proffering singularly unappetizing equipment, propelled his cursor to the "sign off" box. But now here he was, prepped in the tanning beds of Millerton, the town next to Hinton, where he sent his patients (the one time he allowed them UV) to prepare them for first seeing their friends after a lift or a tuck. It was his first time on a gay beach since his fateful encounter with the park police in Provincetown.

But where was everybody? Here it was, a sunny Saturday in June and the whole, gorgeous beach was nearly empty, just a few joggers, beachcombers, dog walkers, a sprinkling of readers on towels a hundred yards apart. This was hardly the coconut-oiled mass of boys humping to disco boom boxes that he had expected. But wait—there, on the crest of the dune, out toward the end. One guy? Two guys. Hmmm, yes . . . Jim picked up his stride, cupped himself to set some voltage in motion, felt a wave of butterflies pass through. This could be just fine.

From his vantage point atop the dunes, Derek, naked but for a piercing that at times served as a sort of towing hitch, studied the lone man approaching along the water's edge. He appraised the pattern of shadows across the torso . . . promising . . . thighs of substance, perky butt, and . . . well now, fluffing himself up a bit, just as plain, and arranging it to the left—interest shown. Derek felt himself coming to attention. He glanced over at Tracy, posted on the next dune, and gave him a conspiratorial smile. He advanced a step so that his growing arousal could be appreciated from below.

Thus they entered into the dance, wordless and subtle, with the potential to lead, if the signals clicked, to acts still considered felonies in twenty-three states. It was all still new enough to Jim, and set off such tremors, that he delegated his body to proceed while he observed, detached. All such presenting in the animal kingdom, it seemed, whether the audience was man, mantis, or peahen, amounted to the same edging farther and farther out on the limb, looking for encouragement at each perch. But here in the outdoor meat pursuit, a choreography of lust prevailed that was singularly efficient, amoral, and heartless. The hierarchy was inflexible, selection thinkable only within the narrowest of bandwidths either side of one's own rating. Jim's calves warmed from putting a bit of extra spring in his step. Let's see . . . perhaps, straining to be charitable, it's the presumption of being entitled, by the suffering entailed in coming out, maybe that's it, to refuse to be constrained by any other straight mores, including consideration for the feelings of others. Perhaps the absence of the battle-of-the-sexes, oppressor-victim aspect allows the parties to view themselves as two (or more!) equal, penis-driven entities who have entered the fray with eyes open, each at his own risk, and deserve no further coddling. Yes, this is closer to it. Whatever the underpinnings, the meeting can be brief as a swat, frank as a goat sniff—or it can be the beginning of a life together. Yes. He pumped his chest a notch, not too obviously.

Advancing along the water's edge to the point closest to

Derek, Jim crouched to pick up a particularly fascinating shell, making sure the angle of the sun was just right to throw his thigh tendons into sharp relief. He examined the unremarkable shell, barely able to support its weight in his straining arm, then tossed it casually in Derek's direction. Derek seemed suddenly bitten by a bug on the back of his head and reached up to grip his scalp, boinging his biceps to the size of a generous papaya and twisting his torso into a spiral that threw several hundred other chiseled muscles into full flex. Jim glanced his way for a split second, then gazed earnestly out to sea for several moments, apparently reflecting on how insignificant it made him feel. Then, with a here's-as-good-as-anyplace kind of saunter, he chose a patch of sand directly below Derek to spread his towel and sprawl fully stretched, legs apart, on his back. Derek advanced to the top of the sloping dune, turned to adjust the fall of light across his pectorals, and stood absently and slowly stroking himself, staring intently across toward Tracy, who was doing the same. Jim busied himself applying sunblock to his abdomen, now and then allowing his fingertips to plunge beneath the waistband of his swimsuit. His interest in the occasion was now plainly visible through the glossy fabric; Derek's was sufficient to get him arrested had law enforcement been present.

After an interlude of this leisurely crescendo, Jim popped up from his towel as though he were just not really a sunbathing sort of guy, struggled ostentatiously to confine himself within the few square inches of pouch available, and bounded up the slippery slope of sand to have a look at the dune grass and maybe take a pee. In the hollow behind the first rank of dunes, Derek and Tracy converged on him with quiet, naughty smiles.

THREE

FROM HER office in a corner of the baronial kitchen, which had originally been designed for a staff of ten, Betsy Haring peered out through a stand of mature oaks at the harbor directly below. She was drawing up the agenda for the Landmarks Preservation Commission meeting at four o'clock. Her work as chair was tiresome at times. The landmark owners were all friends of hers. At dinner parties they would rhapsodize about "our" town, its architectural heritage, blah, blah, It's what makes Long Spit so special, we must hold the line, no condos, especially not on Signal Hill. Then, one by one, they would come to her, wanting to put in some godawful sunroom like the worst side of a Burger King ("We've never had enough sun in the dining room—well, you've seen the mildew—and now that Lucian's doing the bonsai") or enclose their beautiful broad porch, or worse, just half of it, with jalousie windows

("Well, I know the porch is symmetrical the way it is, Betsy honey, but with the winters so cold and us not managing the stairs so well, we've been wanting more of a parlor, keep everything more on the one level") or bulldoze an ancient perennial border to throw up a prefab garage for their sports car collection ("It's just a garage, Betsy, doesn't need to be fancy, and it's around the back, and Evelyn's just been letting the garden go anyway") or subdivide their property to put the kid through Yale. Why did they always have to make her the villain? But she kept plugging away at the work because she believed that the town's housing stock—perhaps the most important concentration of Shingle Style architecture on the entire East Coast—was absolutely the equivalent of a priceless art collection. Her own house, one of several Stanford Whites on Signal Hill, had the distinction of being the only design he'd done locally in stone. Its generous, busily divided windows commanded the harbor, like a discreet sentry tower; cloistered wings surrounded a serene private courtyard and pool that might have been in Tuscany.

Today's grief was Polly Dickson, who was casting Betsy as the force driving the family out of town after one hundred and ten years because she wouldn't approve an addition with more bedrooms for the proliferating Dickson grandchildren. The house was a perfect jewel box of a gambrel-roofed cottage, on a knoll at the juncture of Signal Hill and Long Spit, overlooking an unbroken sweep of the lighthouse and Long Spit Passage.

Betsy really wouldn't have minded if the Dicksons did leave town—with their endless calling the police on trespassers sniffing "our" beach roses—but unfortunately Polly wouldn't go quietly; she would first bray about the injustice of it at every cocktail party of the summer. Betsy would not, of course, stoop to rebutting these charges. Rather, she had a way of intimating

that her view of the town was informed by decades spent privy
to layers of connections—ancient feuds, nominally settled but
still embedded in the social terrain like unexploded ordnance;
pragmatic, loveless marriages that often gave rise to unexpected outbursts and alliances; petty jealousies that simmered
like a thick New England stew, occasionally burping to the
surface in a repressed exchange of snub and counter-snub—
connections unfathomable to the parvenu, but, she let you
know, perfectly clear to her. Further, she conveyed that her
Charleston upbringing had imbued her with a complex and ex-
acting view of the morals and manners appropriate to such sit-
uations. One got the message that, from her vantage point,
there seemed just one suitable path through the thickets of
guest lists and listed homes, a path that oughtn't to need explaining. So if Polly carried out her threat to pull up stakes,
and did it noisily—insisting that hostesses take sides in drawing up their seating plans—Betsy would just have to hold herself above the fray until it subsided. But it would make the
summer season less fun.

She tapped out Ray Hardman's number.

"Salt Air Estates, Ray speaking. May I help you?"

"Ray, honey. Betsy."

"Darling! I will get the iris to you, I'm so sorry. I—"

"No, no, that's not why I'm calling. Don't worry about that.
You've given me an excuse not to clog my fingerprints with
loam." The two rattled on with the requisite small talk: gardening, cat tricks, the chamber music series at the Willoughby
Gardens ("Schoenberg," Betsy tsked, "was perhaps not the
most sensible programming to kick it off "), the need for an alternative caterer in town ("If I taste one more peanut sauce,"
Ray moaned). Known for his discretion, Ray was the real estate agent in town who invariably handled the muffled, rarefied transactions involving the homes of the historic district.

He could be counted on to provide an invisible but rigorous screening process in violation of entire chapters of equal opportunity statutes, without ever troubling his starchy, church-going clients.

At the correct moment, Betsy said, "Well, must scoot, dear. Got a commission do this afternoon . . . see what Quonset huts the best families have dreamed up. Any certifiable preservation fanatics lurking in your Rolodex at the moment?"

"You know I save them for you, my dear," said Ray. "Why?"

"Oh, nothing really. Polly and Ben are chafing again, could be getting a bit fed up."

"Hmmm, interesting . . . Well, 'bye for now."

AFTER A morning of genteel restlessness at the kitchen table, Helen finally went upstairs and tapped gingerly at Jim's door. She had learned with these men not to crack the eggs in the bowl till they came downstairs, but they didn't make it easy for her to be a proper hostess. She just wanted to let Jim know she'd be weeding out back whenever he was ready for breakfast, but there was no answer. How odd. They'd definitely all three come in last night—at the same time, actually, very late. After that she'd drifted back to sleep with the upstairs floor-boards creaking as they got off to bed. Could he have gotten up early to go for a walk or something? Other folks did that, the couple from Virginia, the bird-watchers. But it's quarter to twelve. I've been downstairs all morning. Well, I did go down in the cellar for a jar of pickle relish, but just for a minute. Anyway, I'll just clear his place.

She was still a bit intimidated by Derek and Tracy, even on their second visit. They were perfectly polite and all, but the odd things they adorned themselves with, the bent nails and bits of chain, and the clothes that always needed to be a bit bigger or mended, or at least tugged down to cover better. And she kept remembering the images from the back of that magazine Jim had showed her. She wondered if these young men might not be part of some sort of cult, maybe somehow connected with telephones. Now Jim, on the other hand, seemed like a very pleasant young man. He'd sat on Helen's porch with her a couple of times, asking her lots of questions, nothing improper mind you, about the different neighborhoods, a little of the history. He seemed really taken with the town, kept exclaiming how "neat" it was, that there was nothing very old in Hinton, Nebraska, that he loved antiques and this was "heavenly."

She had even found herself telling him about her husband, about his last, long illness and how cut off she had felt from everybody in town while she was caring for him, and how nobody had made much of an effort to pull her back into the swim afterward. She had never said any of that to anyone from town, of course, because it could come back around. She even told Jim how hurt and cross she'd been at the way her grown kids, who lived in Colorado and Washington, D.C., for goodness' sake, had shaken their heads at her taking in guests. They didn't understand what it was like for a sociable older woman to find herself alone. Jim had said he certainly understood that.

Finally she heard footfalls on the stairs. She went into the dining room to say good morning and there were all three of them. "Oh, well, gracious, good morning," she said. "I'm afraid I got a little mixed up and thought you were up and out already, Jim. I've gone and taken away your plate. Now that's not very nice, is it? I'll just . . ."

Jim blushed and reached down to straighten the silverware. "Uh, no, I was in, uh, visiting with Derek and Tracy."

Helen glanced about in confusion, feeling color creep up

the back of her neck. "Oh, I see . . ." Derek's bright good morn-ing smile looked slightly raffish. "Dear me," murmured Helen. "I'll just fetch your setting and, oh, coffee?" She fled.

Later, she left them on the porch with their last coffee refills and went upstairs to tidy up the rooms. She finished the bath-room, let herself into Jim's room with the skeleton key she wore on a long ribbon around her neck, and was brought up short again: the bed had not even been slept in. "Well, now that makes it pretty plain," she fretted to herself as she fluffed the dent in the comforter where he'd sat to pull his sneakers on. As the picture sank in, Helen grew more and more flus-tered. What on earth would she have done if there were other guests in the house, with this secret barefoot traipsing going on at all hours? She'd just been lucky so far. It was one thing to tolerate these other lifestyle choices, as they put it on the tele-vision, but did she now have to make sure she *never* mixed these men with her other guests? And how was she supposed to know who was what anyway? She couldn't very well ask them on the phone, could she?

Then she unlocked Derek and Tracy's room, climbed the stairs to the honeymoon cupola, and gasped in shock: connect-ing the four posts of the bed was an ominous network of black nylon straps connected by metal rings and harness buckles, with a shallow leather seat suspended in the middle and leather and Velcro cuffs at the four corners. She felt her heart thudding. She might need to sit down. It *was* a cult. This was very serious. No question but this must be some sort of torture device. How could this be? Jim was up here with them, but still, at breakfast they were all smiling, just as friendly . . .

She heard them coming up the stairs and panicked. Was she next? Derek and Tracy came in. Helen turned, at bay, flapping her dust rag in distress. "Oh, I'm sorry, I was just seeing to your room, I can come back after . . ." She let out an involuntary whimper. "I was just so . . . taken aback by this . . ."

"Oh yeah, sorry, we should have taken that down," said Tracy, climbing the spiral stairs. "We were afraid we were already too late for breakfast." He eased past her, released one of the corner buckles; Helen recoiled. "See," he said mildly, "it's got these padded cuffs, so it can't damage the finish."

Helen peered timidly but obediently from her corner. "But what—I mean, it's none of my—"

"It's for when we're traveling," Derek offered helpfully, joining them by the bed. "Fully adjustable, rolls up in a little pouch. We can hook it up to almost anything. Kind of a one size fits all?" Helen nodded dubiously.

"It's just a hobby." Tracy shrugged. "Just for fun."

"Well, I'm sure," Helen murmured as she edged past them and down the stairs. "I'll leave you alone, then."

Derek called down after her, "Oh, could you please make us lunches for the beach again? That was terrific. Thanks."

FISHERS ISLAND was partly shrouded in fog, Wesley Herndon noted as he motored his Hinckley 51 out of Stonington harbor. That meant visibility could be less than a mile out in Block Island Sound. A conservative sailor, he had two totally inexperienced crew aboard, the bouncer and bartender from a bar called Trik's in Providence. So perhaps the prudent thing to do would be to take a quick left outside the harbor and follow the winding Napatree Channel in behind Long Spit to anchor for the afternoon. They could have lunch aboard, buzz ashore in the dinghy for a look around; the channel was well marked even if the fog closed in. He'd never been in there, always heard it was a nice anchorage, but it had always seemed too close to his home mooring to feel like a destination. Jake and Ozzie would probably just as soon do that as spend the day fog-bound out in open water, staring at the satellite navigator screen to find their way home. And Ozzie had joked about being seasick-prone.

Much as he loved sailing, and particularly aboard his new *White Wings IV,* Wesley had to admit that she was a bit of a headache, really too big for single-handing. The constant search for crew led him to some fairly strange measures, like bringing these two along. In the run-up to closing time the night before, he'd heard himself, after a few too many drinks and after admiring Jake's shoulders all evening behind the bar, half-jokingly suggest they do a little "yachting" with him the next day. They had half-jokingly accepted, with a lot of teasing about not knowing any knots, or having any white ducks. Somehow the teasing ("You guys would probably attack the launch boy, I could never show my face around Stonington again"; "Ahh, you're bullshitting. You probably got a rowboat, or no, an air mattress") had escalated until the mutual dare had become a plan. So here they were. Wesley had actually relished the moment when they first saw her, riding so grandly at her mooring just off the dock at Dodson's.

Wesley was a compact, handsome man, well preserved for his fifty-one years, with salt-and-pepper hair and the requisite wild eyebrows of the yachtsman. He had the sort of looks that advertisers invoke to sell high-end khakis. Normally self-contained to the point of aloofness, he nonetheless had an appealingly self-conscious, mischievous smile at the ready when he felt safely ensconced among gay friends.

Jake and Ozzie had no idea who he really was. Wesley's taste in men had always led him to venture across the social chasm toward what he idealized as the rugged, uncomplicated, clear-eyed boys of the blue-collar ranks. These forays had limited objectives: although he protested otherwise to his friends, he was not really looking for Mr. Right; he was, in fact, constitutionally incapable of admitting anyone to equal partnership in his life. He had not become chief executive of a multibillion-dollar telecommunications conglomerate through a propensity for power-sharing. On the few occasions when well-meaning friends tried to set him up with someone more of his station, Wesley became about as cuddly as Ezra Pound until the hapless date retreated in dismay. On the other hand, he had ordered the trim outside his bedroom windows repainted three times, insisting it be done only on Saturday mornings, so that he could gaze, from his nest of costly French linens, at the sturdy thighs of the unsuspecting painter.

He asked Jake to take the helm for a minute so he could go forward to ready the anchor. Jake stepped behind the five-foot diameter, teak-rimmed wheel, Wesley at his side to make sure that he had the hang of it. "Give her a chance to respond. There's a delay; she weighs eighteen tons." Could he plausibly use this moment of instruction to touch that massive, tanned shoulder? Wesley was used to "entertaining" men—the best restaurant, best wine, a generous tip for a massage that ended up including the prostate, or that turned into a solo performance for the avid voyeur in him. But he'd never brought any of his sex objects into this other realm before. Did inviting these two scalawags aboard give him the same license as a fat tip? His hand danced in the air near the temptation, then settled for grasping the wheel to make a correction. "We need to stay right in the middle of the channel through here. There's barely enough depth for us."

"Oh yeah?" said Jake. "A tight fit, huh? We gonna be plowing the bottom? I like that." He reached back and gave Wesley's butt a playful squeeze. Wesley seized the moment to give both shoulders, and both upper arms, a scurrying once-over with his fingertips.

For an instant, Jake thrust out his chest and leaned back against Wesley. "Hey, this is, like, cool, Wes. Didn't know your pride and joy was so big."

"Oh, I'm full of surprises," said Wesley, and went forward, pleasantly flustered. How quickly a day could be switched into this gear.

They anchored in the bay sheltered by Long Spit, about two hundred feet off the beach. Ozzie took the binoculars up on the foredeck to inspect the surroundings. Wesley went below to make lunch, a matter of dealing out the cold marinated duck and walnut salad from the deli. He resented having to wait on these two, even to this small extent, but serving them was easier than ordering them to make lunch, and then having to hover over them, lest they run afoul of his fastidious regime in the galley. Always the same old trap.

He heard Ozzie let out a low moan. "Ooooh, look out! I do believe there is a beach *scene* happening. Hurry up with that lunch!" Wesley poked his head up through the companionway. Ozzie handed him the glasses. "Pervs, hot to trot," he said. "Check 'em out."

Despite the fingers of fog riffling through the dune grass, Wesley could make out the waiting men, three of them, spaced along the crest of the dune.

"And did you see the b.j. goin' on?" said Ozzie, pointing. Wesley scanned until he spotted them, in a cranny of the ruins at the end of the point, hidden from anyone on shore: two men sprawled on the concrete, one head bobbing up and down rhythmically.

"Requesting shore liberty, Cap'n," said Ozzie. Wesley

grinned; his lunch menu suddenly seemed too prissy. He was shocked; no one had ever told him anything like this was going on over here.

After lunch, they headed in and pulled the dinghy up on the sand.

"Joinin' us?" said Ozzie.

"Oh no," said Wesley. "Too racy for my blood. I'm gonna stroll in toward the village. Meet you back here in a couple of hours?" He set off, turning to gaze with a wistful pang at Jake's broad back and galumphing, bow-legged walk. Wary though he was of people angling to take advantage of him, he now found himself a bit annoyed that these guys didn't seem more susceptible to his wealth, more eager to please.

Wesley lived in Lyme, a town where pairs of stone posts marked long driveways that disappeared into the ledge-ribbed, laurel-studded hills, finally arriving at secluded mansions inhabited by genteel, desiccated folk of lengthy pedigree. He had had his house, an imposing, though not enormous, eighteenth-century farmhouse, moved from its original location fifty miles away to its present site, high on a hilltop where no one in the eighteenth century would have thought to build. Lyme was so prestigious, and the project had been so absorbing and staggeringly profligate—even the central chimney and its five fireplaces had been disassembled stone by stone, labeled, and reconstructed—that only after he moved in did he discover that the whispered reserve and sedate mores of the town made him want to put a gun to his head. For a while, he had kept busy hunting for sufficiently important antiques and rare, smuggled English perennials to grace his new surroundings, and indulging in lightly naughty, but ultimately frustrating whims like having his bedroom window trim repainted repeatedly. But when horniness impelled him to burst the town's prim bonds for nights out in the nearby cities, he found that even his local gay friends—settled, coupled, tamed—were stultifyingly disapproving, shaking their heads and worrying over what unseemly regression their friend could be undergoing. He had painstakingly assembled all the accoutrements of a pinnacle of Eastern Seaboard status, yet his appetites were griping, tugging him toward wickedness like four leashes' worth of heedless, big-balled dogs.

Wesley padded toward the village, first along the hard sand at the water's edge, then along the stone bulkhead encircling the compact keyhole harbor, where he scrutinized the bobbing fleet of proud but unassuming antique sailboats, each one maintained by a gruff old Yankee boatyard crew for generation after generation of gruff old Yankee owners. Wesley had always, when sailing past outside the spit, admired the confident jumble of Signal Hill's gables, turrets, and porches. Now he first saw how close those upper reaches were—albeit behind their hedges and fences—to the small, pleasantly bustling business district, with its antique shops, restaurants, and— what were these strolling pairs of cuties doing here? And that hot number lounging with a Walkman on that harborfront bench? And that one idling past on the phone in his little roadster? Wesley felt a dawning excitement; a smile played on his face. This was extraordinary. Why had no one ever told him there were boys on the loose here? Why—that meant that all the elements of happiness were here: houses with good bones, boats as understated and redolent of obscure connoisseurship as the best kneehole writing desk, a thrilling proximity of the snooty and the trashy. He sauntered along under the arcade of Front Street, feeling expansive, strangely at home, and stopped to peruse a real estate window.

His acquisitive reveries were disturbed by the sound of

raised voices several shops down from him. He edged to within earshot, feigning interest in espadrilles.

It was Sam Jenkins, Nancy's husband, whose tight voice carried over the others, "All I'm saying is, just because we open our doors to guests doesn't mean we should be sitting ducks for any weirdo outsider scum that drifts into town."

Dot Bradley glanced around, worried at who might be hearing this in front of her shop. "Get over it, Sam. They haven't done anybody any harm."

"Not yet, they haven't, but I don't know what they have in mind. Helen here is all alone in that place."

"Oh, for Pete's sake, Sam," said Dot. "They didn't lock her in the furnace room, they asked her to pack them a lunch. I don't think Helen is really worried—*are* you?"

Helen shifted uneasily, "Well, it did give me a fright, but then they seem like nice enough young men. . . . Oh, I don't know."

"Dot, they were three of them in one bed, engaging in some goddamn kind of ritual torture, for Christ's sake." Sam shook his head. "Why the hell you're defending them— Sometimes I wonder about you."

Nancy said, "Look, Dot, we just feel the Merchants Association should get to the bottom of who placed those ads, so that—"

"Why bother?" Dot interrupted. "The damage is done, if there even *is* any damage, and I doubt there's anything illegal about placing an ad for somebody else's business." Dot didn't mention the distinct uptick in sales of her "Scottsdale" line of table linens.

"Well, just so we would know what we're up against, is all," said Nancy.

"What we're up against is a goddamn faggot invasion!"

shouted Sam. "Are you blind, Dot? Just look up and down this street. Come over and look at our front porch. Anybody driving by would think it was a queer quilting bee."

"That'll do, Sam," murmured Nancy.

"They would!" he bellowed, turning purple. "We are watching this town go down the tubes!"

At this point, Lattie Teachout came out of Angleton's. She strode up to Helen and Nancy, brandishing a copy of *The Advocate*. "So, you're the ones bringing them all to town, are you? Placing these ads?" She shook the magazine at them. "So now I've got them holding hands in my window booths and—"

"No, it wasn't us," Nancy protested. "That's just what we're trying to figure out."

Sam had a what-did-I-tell-you smile. "And this is just the beginning," he said.

Wesley drifted away as Lattie continued with her complaints, "And I saw one pat Anthony on the behind, and . . ."

When Wesley got back to the dinghy, he found Jake and Ozzie lounging on the sand with a good-looking man in his thirties, his rugged body intriguingly at odds with his refined, intelligent hands.

"This here's Jim," said Ozzie. "We caught him looking at your boat, told him we thought we could get him aboard."

Jim got up and offered his hand to Wesley. "Jim Hornswich. Hi. It's true. I'm from Nebraska, a long way from the ocean, so she looks pretty exotic to me."

"Wesley Herndon. Pleasure." The two locked eyes an extra second. Wesley had never offered his surname in this sort of context. "Sure. Be delighted to show you aboard. Just had a very interesting stroll. Seems this whole gay presence here is kind of new. Overheard some of the locals arguing about it. Kind of funny, actually; one of them was ranting about what

sounds like some leathery stuff going on in one of the B&Bs."
Jim's smile tightened. Wesley turned to Jake and Ozzie, trying
to sound casual. "You boys okay on the beach for a while
longer?"

"Yeah, sure," said Jake. "We told him he might be able to
wash up out there too." Jim shot him a look, caught but game.

"ANTHONY, HONEY, leave some hot water," his mother called
up the stairs. "I want to put your laundry in."

Anthony stood in the billowing steam on one leg, lost in
washing between his toes. The summer's turn had brought
with it a new project. While he had always granted himself adequate marks for attractiveness, he had never before quite
given himself permission to break his body down into sep-
arately graded bits. He wasn't sure what had prompted the
change—maybe it was the minute details he heard being re-
viewed by the Angleton's clientele nowadays—but he found
himself newly analytical in his self-regard, and today it was his
feet that had captured his interest.

Never an athlete, he nonetheless had surprisingly strong
feet for a slight young man. They had rarely endured direct
sunlight, so they did have an otherworldly pallor, and his ankles did retain the imprint of his sock elastic more or less permanently. But the foot he now grasped and examined, the hot
water sheeting over it, had a strong arch, a nice busyness of
vein and sinew, long straight toes with a sturdy heft to them.
So long used to regarding them as mere conveyances, he now
let the question surface: where exactly does a foot's sexiness
reside? Raising his leg in slow motion, he placed the foot on
the rim of the tub, flexed his toes against the porcelain so the
foot looked poised to pounce. Up until recently, the only po-

tential his feet had held to affect his social life was as stink bombs; he recalled the time his best friend, Rain, had taken him to the rather formal Japanese restaurant. But now the thought first crossed his mind: they might, all by themselves, actually have allure.

"Anthony, there are other citizens who rely on that same reservoir!" His mother's voice pierced the fog. He shut off the taps and stepped onto the bath mat. Might have to take these out and let the wind hit them a little more often, he thought, rolling up onto the balls of his feet a couple of times, feeling the twinge in his calves, and that increasingly familiar, distinctive hum in his solar plexus.

FOUR

A S JUNE progressed, word spread rapidly in New York, Providence, Boston, and all through Connecticut of that potent spark of gay life, the New Place to Go. The pioneers returned every weekend, bringing their friends, who in turn went home pleased to have a fresh reply to "What have you been up to?" The "Hot Tip" section of the gay travel magazine *Out and About* called Long Spit a "banquet of delights; every element of a potential perfect gay resort town is there. All it needs is more boys." The *New York Blade* sent Bart Connors, its regional reporter, to have a look around, write a feature on the odd way the scene got started, and add Long Spit to his regular beat. The piece took a so-far-so-good tone, and the part about the B&Bs quoted Lois Crabtree saying, "Once we got over our surprise, it really hasn't been too bad. They sure don't eat very much breakfast." The buzz was on. From

Washington, D.C., to Portland, Maine, any self-respecting gay man stepping out to his local bar on a Tuesday night had to be able to say, "Oh, Long Spit—yeah, I've been down a couple of times already. Yeah, it's really cool." For guys from New York and New Jersey, the place seemed too good to be true: an unspoiled beach without the Fire Island prices and attitude, three hours closer than P-town. The Boston guys loved skipping the inevitable traffic jams heading out the Cape on the dreaded Route 6.

Sea Breeze Properties, the office that managed all the by-the-week condos with balconies along Front Street, was suddenly awash in business. Lonnie, the longtime employee whom everybody in the office had always quietly known about, came into his own fielding the flood of inquiries, offering to "keep you in mind if anything should come available," putting together groups of complete strangers to share the larger units, based on their preferred body types and the sound of their voices. When the twenty-year regulars called, thinking they were just making sure their usual three-week slot was going to be fine again this year, there was a note of triumph in Lonnie's voice as he said, "I'm sorry, Mrs. Pegrin, but we *told* you to reserve back in April."

The Ocean Hotel, leaning on itself atop Signal Hill, flickering near extinction for years, had suddenly made it into the databases of travel agents in gay enclaves across the country. The tired old giant, with its listing porches and listless management, had seemed caught in a slow but vicious cycle, as replacement of the claw-footed bathtubs and cracked, rust-weeping sinks was shunted aside by the increasingly frequent emergencies, such as the time a chronic leak that had stained the ceiling of the main dining room for years finally achieved sufficient sogginess to release several tons of plaster and rotted lath onto the Hunt Breakfast buffet one Sunday morning. Fortunately, on that occasion, as on all too many occasions, there were no customers to be injured. But now the Ocean had become the budget-priced option (it was known as "diving in the Ocean") for the impecunious young who might previously have had a sixteenth share of a plywood dormitory on stilts somewhere in the Fire Island dunes. The Ocean's front-desk staff had stopped raising its eyebrows at pairs of men sharing beds, and Marcia Pepitone, the manager, had approached the hotel's owner, Milam Sandermeyer, long since retired to Florida, about redoing the dinner menu for the first time since 1952.

Front Street sprouted its first rainbow flag, at a shop called the Beachcomber, as Stevie Lund made a business decision to expand her stock of beach gear, souvenirs, sunglasses, snorkels, and flip-flops to include condoms, some greeting cards featuring airbrushed hunks and suggestive messages of vague sexual orientation, a blow-up muscleman swim toy, some pink triangle decals mixed in with the tourist mementos, and a few other items to draw the new crowd. She hired a peppy gay college kid named Des who had a pierced chin and a selection of contact lenses in colors to match each of his pairs of high-top sneakers. Des was bright and saucy, happy to flirt with any and all comers; Stevie watched her gross receipts double over the previous June.

Leo Robbia bought the Signal Hill Inn and within days of the closing a rowdy building crew of giants arrived from New York wearing Canal Street Hardware tank tops, their massive legs bursting out of preposterously short cutoffs and plunging into ten-pound work boots. They hitched on their twenty-pocket rawhide tool belts and set to work with house music thumping, hauling out, in the first few hours, an entire Dumpster full of fishing nets, lobster-pot floats, seagull paintings, wagon wheel chandeliers, Early American chairs, Naugahyde banquettes, booth jukeboxes, dressers with seashell decals, mirrors with seashell frames, carpeting with seashell and sea-horse design. By the end of the third day, the building was gut-ted and the site rang out with the *scree* of power saws and the *thwap* of pneumatic nailers.

It wasn't long before the renovations were the hot topic at Sully's, the village's only bar, along Front Street beyond Hollis's shop at the end of the business district. State regulations forced Leo to hire local licensed plumbers and electricians, and they'd turn up at Sully's after work with stories of a laby-rinth being constructed in the back with no wiring for lighting, a wall of giant pigeonholes with vinyl-covered foam pads in them, a dance floor lighting grid fit for a football stadium, ma-chinery for suspending cages from the ceiling, a roomful of what looked like prison cells, and a whole separate bar area completely done in bathroom tile, surrounded by three walls that were being plumbed for urinals. At the same time, Sully's was becoming, for lack of any alternative, the place where a lot of the gay guys went to hang out. They were just as interested as the locals in finding out what sort of place was being cre-ated, and ended up in lively conversations with the regulars, trying to explain, with much nervous guffawing all around, how all these facilities might be used.

"It just doesn't seem very sanitary, is all," said Lou Russell, "you know, pissing right nearby where there are people drink-ing—smelly, too."

"Well, see," said a guy named Stan, just in from New York, "I doubt anybody will actually use those as urinals. What it's really about is—"

"That's a few grand worth of plumbing for nothing, then," harrumphed another regular.

Stan continued gamely, "See, the whole point of gay bars is

to meet people, and it starts with, we call it cruising, you know, checking each other out, same as goes on in any kind of a straight place. So this is meant as kind of a joke on the fact that, in certain sorts of bars, a certain amount of that checking out goes on, you know, in the men's room."

"Hah! Don't I know it from the Interstate," said a heavyset local fellow, snatching off his GMC cap and rubbing a pale forehead. "Got to head right for the last can and face into the corner if you don't want everybody tryin' to get a look at your pecker. Half the time I can't get my stream started." Here the gay listeners' smiles stiffened; there was a murmur of affirmation among the locals, with much shaking of heads, followed by everyone leaning in to hear more.

"Seems kind of rude, I know," said a guy from Boston. "But in a gay bar, we're all guys, we don't have to worry about some woman getting an attitude, unless it's some dyke—sorry, lesbian—who thinks you shouldn't be smoking so near her. Anyway, we know what we're there for, so we just, like, cut to the chase, you know?"

Through these and many other exchanges over recent weeks, Mickey Sullivan, the proprietor, sat bemused on his stool at the end of the bar, amazed at his regulars for mixing with this lot, happy enough that the place was so busy you couldn't even hear the game on the TV. His practice of staying open as long as there was anybody around had kept him there until the legal closing time every night for three weeks straight. He finally decided this wasn't just a fluke and he would have to hire another bartender. After asking a couple of the locals who had filled in for him from time to time and having them turn him down when he explained why it was so busy, he put an ad in the Westerly paper and ended up with a nice, friendly young fellow, a lumberjack sort of guy named Jed. After Jed had been on the job a couple of weeks, Mickey said to him, "Well, you seem to be working out okay, huh? Not too many problems with all these"—he glanced around significantly—"fairies?"

"Careful," said Jed. "You never know who you might be talking to." He winked.

Down at the end of the Front Street strip, Frankie's Slice by the Sea Pizza had been utterly transformed, as though Frank Della Souza's ambitious son Rocco had just been waiting for the invaders' instructions. Frankie's had been nothing more than a take-out window with a couple of white plastic tables and chairs teetering on the edge of the weed patch where two or three cars could pull in while people picked up their orders. The new patrons, though, were determined to linger with their slices, and kept asking for more tables and chairs, so finally Rocco lined up some cousins who owed him favors and spent a couple of weekends leveling the weed patch, covering it with brick, bringing in heavy wooden tables with café umbrellas, setting out whiskey barrels full of geraniums, and installing benches around the back perimeter. The boys rewarded his efforts by turning the place into a major hangout and a rendezvous for parties headed to and from the beach. For the moment it was the only outdoor place to sit and watch the passing show, so all day and late into the evening there was a wait for tables and, even after closing time, the tables and benches hummed, while men by the dozen sat on the curb. Frank wanted the police to keep them off the premises after closing, but Rocco understood that this crowd would not do the place any harm, that in fact they seemed to take almost a proprietary interest in it, pointing out to the waiters when the geraniums needed watering.

For the first time ever, there was actually a street scene. The locals and the straight tourists had always preferred to drive everywhere, climbing aboard their Buick Roadmaster Estate

Wagons with the wood-look shelf paper glued to the sides even just to go from their motel the three hundred yards to the ice cream window. The new guys, on the other hand, strolled and prowled and loitered all day and all night, their demeanor combining aimlessness with the disciplined, patient attention of a cat watching a mole burrow.

Angleton's Tea Room had never done so much business since it opened in the thirties. Lattie Teachout continued to fret about the new clientele, peeved when the boys held hands in the front window booths and so on, but gradually she saw that Anthony seemed able to talk to them and get them to behave without causing a scene, so she let him take over more and more as host while she retreated behind her chrome cash register. She had to admit that having people holding hands in the window booths seemed to be good for attracting at least this kind of business.

The month of June had given an unexpected jolt to Anthony's process of self-exploration. Besides his newfound appreciation of his feet, he was taking a budding interest in good posture, and not just during his lessons with Hollis. Suddenly, he was enveloped by an atmosphere in which, instead of feeling isolated because he was the only boy taking such a dangerous, lingering interest in other boys, he now felt isolated because all these men were taking open, high-spirited interest in each other, and in him, and he was the only one who seemed so blocked up about acting on it. He'd gone from accepting Hollis's once-weekly timid touches to maneuvering, every minute at the restaurant, through a nervous-making but titillating gauntlet of attention, ranging from lingering eye contact to flattering innuendo to pats on the butt to phone numbers turning up in his back pocket. And he'd gone from feeling like a freak for being slim and lean and proud of it, to realizing that, to a fair segment of this crowd, he was like catnip.

But this new atmosphere, in which the once most forbidden, secret yearnings were suddenly yawningly average, in which he'd been transformed from scrawny object of pity and derision to slender object of desire, didn't make it any easier to come to terms with himself. He was stuck on the cusp: he clung to the idea that, despite the countless hours he spent lost in reveries of some schoolmate's downy forearm, he wasn't gay as long as he never actually *did* anything. In his mind, "gay" was not an umbrella encompassing a million distinct characters; it was a blunt epithet that he had so far dodged. As he maneuvered among the tables with a hot turkey sandwich, a BLT, and a watercress salad with egg-white omelet stacked along his arm, he regarded the men who were conspicuously gay, camping it up or looking, in their leathers, as stern as prison guards, and thought, Well, that is definitely not me, so I must still be safely clear of the label.

So Derek's playful come-on several weeks back had triggered days of worry for Anthony, and nights of feverish masturbating. He had been so panicked at being found attractive by a complete stranger, especially one who could snap him in two, that he ceased bathing for two days, as though Derek's pass meant he had somehow been found out and therefore needed to add a layer of dishevelment and body odor to his disguise. And if Derek was what it meant to be gay, then Anthony was confirmed in his belief that he himself must not be; they might as well have been two different species. Derek had the crotch torn out of his cutoff shorts, revealing a bulging swatch of black leather bikini briefs; in his wildest dreams, Anthony couldn't imagine parading himself in such a lewd fashion. But after a couple of days he not only resumed bathing, he also resumed his speculations about exactly which parts of his body such a man might be responding to. And so, as he lay in his narrow bed by the attic window, images of that bulging crotch and those tanned, powerful legs danced before his mind's eye, and he succumbed to fantasies of being lifted in the arms of such a gentle giant and carried off to some wicked fate.

A couple of weeks later, a handsome, studious-looking guy of about twenty, just a bit older than Anthony, was sitting alone at a back table. He had been polite throughout the meal, even a bit withdrawn, seemingly unable to hold Anthony's gaze even for the brief interval Anthony was capable of. When Anthony brought the change, the young man took off his rimless glasses, looked up, and put out his hand. "Thanks very much. I'm Wendell."

Anthony was a bit flustered by Wendell's green eyes and startlingly long eyelashes. "Oh, uh, I'm Anthony," he said. "But I guess you know that." He pointed to his name tag with a lame smile.

"Are you from here in town?" asked Wendell shyly.

Anthony nodded, momentarily lost in those eyes. "Uh, yes. Yes sir," he said. "And you?"

"I'm from New London, pretty close by." Wendell started to get up. "Well, I hope I see you again."

A thousand times Anthony had replayed that brief encounter, for him so full of coded messages. Once again a man had reached directly through his fortifications and camouflage, but this time with respect and reserve. How did he know to make such an overture, if it even was an overture? Was it something Anthony was giving off? Wendell seemed so . . . regular. It began to dawn on him that legions of gay men, maybe even the majority, could walk right by him and he would never guess, and in fact, they were the ones he was most intrigued by. This time Anthony didn't go without washing. Rather he wondered for hours about what a day in Wendell's life was like, what his room looked like. He allowed himself a chaste wish to become Wendell's friend, and convinced himself that he detected the same wish on Wendell's part. But Wendell was over there, in that other realm, where Anthony couldn't go.

So he passed his days, threading among the patrons with sides of fries and slaw, in a state of befuddlement, tingling occasionally with electricity, occasionally with panic. Thanks to his adolescent need to appear worldly-wise, he developed an easy manner with the tables of men, joking, even mildly flirting in his light tenor voice—once, when a customer couldn't make up his mind, even planting a fist on his cocked hip in mock exasperation and quite enjoying the gust of amusement this drew from the table. He saw Wendell a couple of more times, never alone, and took pleasure in greeting him by name and noting the resulting exchange of looks among whichever of his high-school friends happened to be nursing a coffee in a booth nearby. He was toying with something mysterious and dangerous. It was that same intoxicating power that had been drawing Hollis's touch all this time. But here there was no revulsion mixed with the excitement, and so he was afraid to let it go beyond words, to touch.

HELEN BOOTHROYD was getting used to Derek and Tracy, really quite liked them. They'd been back several times, snooping out possible locations for a branch of their gallery. On the visit after the S&M gear fiasco they'd brought her a peace offering: a small watercolor by the same artist who'd done the oil of her house. She'd hired a chambermaid; she was booked to capacity most of the time now and was really getting too old to make that many beds every day anyway, plus this way she needn't concern herself with whatever these polite young men were getting up to behind closed doors. Derek and Tracy had helped her move a new queen-sized bed into the front room on the second floor to replace the twins that nobody seemed to want anymore. And then they astonished her by climbing the fold-down stairs into the back-wing attic and hauling down an armoire that had been there for fifty years and that she had despaired of ever using again.

Nan Jenkins's husband, Sam, was still trying to stir up trouble, grumbling at anyone who would listen about how the town was just rolling over and playing dead before this onslaught of perverts and pansies, and Was it going to take one of the local kids getting raped before anybody did anything about it? He wasn't managing to rouse much rabble, apart from a couple of the dock geezers who sat around Runcie's Bait and Marine. Most of the buttoned-up Yankees whom Sam tended to run into were more put off by his using such language in front of them than by the threat he described. Nan was getting thoroughly fed up with his smirking, sullen demeanor around her guests and lived in fear of what they might overhear him saying down on Front Street. He'd volunteered for years as a driver on the village ambulance and now got into a row with the EMTs when he demanded the drivers be equipped with masks and rubber gloves.

One day he came into the kitchen in a muttering fury: "Two of them are sitting all smootchie-cootchie with their arms around each other on the front porch glider. Are you happy now?"

"Oh, Sam, for God's sake, get a life," said Nan. "What on earth are you worried about, the neighbors? They know what's going on. People driving by? Nowadays anybody driving by is likely gay anyway. Could be good for business."

The next day at the supermarket, Nan came upon Sam in the soap aisle putting a two-gallon jug of bleach in the cart. "What in goodness' name—"

"You listen to me," he hissed. "That's our home we're talking about, in case you've forgotten. I have to live there too, and I don't want to be worrying about what's living in the towels."

"Dearie, the biggest medical hazard in that house is your gardening sneakers." Nan planted the jug back on the shelf.

Lois Crabtree, who ran another B&B near Nan's, received a mailing, sent to all businesses advertising in *The Advocate,* inviting her to extend the ad that who-knew-who had put in there in the first place. She called Helen, who'd gotten the same mailing, and declared that she was going to do it. "You know something, Helen?" she said. "I've never felt so safe in the house in all the time I've been taking in roomers. And these fellows have the most interesting stories to tell around the breakfast table. Why, I had a young man here a few days back who'd just got back from teaching a ballet company in Monte Carlo, telling all about Princess Stephanie throwing a reception, I swear . . ."

Derek and Tracy visited Hollis's shop again. He had no idea they were the same men he'd become obsessed with gazing at through his telescope, but he would have continued being chilly with them anyway, the more so when they proposed taking some of his prep school rowing-team photos and the like and selling them on consignment through You've Been Framed. "Could be a nice link-up for you," said Tracy. "We're right in the middle of the South End. We could display the stuff with your card on each piece. Could make for some nice advertising."

"Oh, well, that's fine," said Hollis, scowling at the floor, "but I think I'll just leave it." He was especially irritated by their offer to buy a twenties poster for YMCA Boys' Homes that he had displayed on the back wall, showing a group of handsome boys out in the snow, looking longingly in the windows of the cozy YMCA home, also full of handsome boys.

"How much for the poster?" asked Derek.

"Oh, uh, sorry, that's not really for sale," said Hollis.

"Oh, come on—every boy has his price," Derek persisted playfully.

Hollis gave him a wintry smile. "It's quite unusual; I'd just as soon hang on to it." He cleared his throat. "Adds a bit of color back there."

"No shit—oops," said Tracy. "I'd want to hang on to them too."

Sam Jenkins, collaring Hollis one day on Front Street, had rather unkindly gone on about how "everybody knows all these faggots are pedophiles." Sam, after all, knew as well as anybody else in the village the gossip about why Hollis had been teaching Anthony all this time. Hollis's unease at the new atmosphere had reached the point where, far from wanting to call more attention to his archival fetishes, he'd given serious thought to pulling the photo bins out of the shop. And lately his lessons with Anthony had gone through some sort of negative evolution, seeming less adequate—a bit pathetic, really—yet more dangerous. Anthony, for his part, had actually grown a bit cheeky, showing up one evening wearing a too-small orange T-shirt with the sleeves rolled up a couple of turns.

One incident in particular had tattered Hollis's nerves, and for reasons that had nothing to do with it being the first time a black man had ever stepped into his shop. He'd always kept a few items from his slave collection in the shop, generally just a shelf of engravings, a presence sufficient to add another flavor to the stock but not to proclaim his odd passion. He'd always known that someday he would be confronted with the potentially awkward matter of explaining such merchandise to a black customer, but he was nonetheless impelled by some deep urge to leave this signal in place.

The door opened one morning and Hollis was startled to see a very dark-skinned man in yellow-tinted glasses, wearing an orange fez and a cape made of African mud cloth, gliding into the store with an aura that suggested that, slight though he was, he might be an African king. He was accompanied by a tall, lanky, honey-colored man so exceedingly refined and handsome that Hollis was struck dumb, the sort of man you might glimpse glowing among the reflector panels of a photo shoot in Nice.

They drifted among the torchières and commodes, handling and regarding small items in a discerning fashion. It wasn't long before the regal figure came to a halt before a framed illustration of a muscular young man standing on an auction block.

"Hmmmm," he said at a stagey volume, with an inflection that, in its brief melody line, managed to touch on dismay, world-weariness, a connoisseur's spark of recognition, perhaps even a fillip of arousal. The other man approached for a look; Hollis moved toward them in an agony of regret. Why couldn't the first time have been an amiable working Joe? At the same time, he was transfixed by the second man, so preternaturally beautiful, and orbiting languidly around this powerful figure like a butterfly around a bloom.

The young man sidled near, glanced at the engraving. "Could I do with some of that," he muttered. The other slapped him on the arm and rolled his eyes. Hollis approached them.

"May I help you?" he said, in his most diffident, post-recital manner.

The man in the fez continued to gaze fixedly at the engraving. "Why is this here?" he demanded, in a challenging and rather too loud voice. Hollis felt the hair stand on his nape.

"Well, certainly it is a historical artifact," he said haltingly. "We must look at such things squarely, don't you think . . . not try to sweep them under the rug?"

The man gave him a look—his eyes obscured by the yellow lenses—that suggested he was puzzling over a language barrier. "Oh please. I mean, is this an interest of yours?"

"Well, I— Interest? Interest . . . I'm not sure what you're getting at." Hollis loathed this man, toying with him this way. "There are connotations there that I'm not sure I—"

"I am simply trying to establish"—the man spoke with pedagogical deliberateness—"whether you realize what you have here."

Hollis glanced at the cheerless, superior smile. "Once again, I'm sorry, I'm not clear. Are you speaking in political terms, or—?"

"This is one of perhaps only three copies of this handbill still in existence." The man spoke as though before cameras. "The Charleston rice worker series. Did you have any idea? You have no price affixed."

"No, well, it's really not for sale," Hollis blurted in confusion, wondering why he was getting himself in deeper. "Yes, I was aware of its importance."

"Do you know of a source for such material?" He extended his hand in a formal fashion. "Forgive me. Ellington Hazelett. And?"

"Well, yes, actually, I'm a collector. —Uh, Wynbourne. Hollis Wynbourne."

"You must show me." There was in the voice an utter certainty that this would happen, and Hollis submitted to it, proposing they stop by his house at five.

And so, late that afternoon, Hollis skittered about through his shuttered, seldom-aired parlors and anterooms, turning on clamp lights, pulling dropcloths off the tables of his collection, uncovering hundreds of faces, none of them happy. He felt he had been catapulted into uncharted territory. He'd shown his materials to only one or two people ever; now Ellington had represented himself as a trustee of the Schomburg Center of the New York Public Library, sitting on the board's acquisitions committee. Hollis had long known of the existence of this repository of manuscripts and artifacts of African American history, but had always regarded his own collecting as far too obsessive and freighted to even consider revealing it to strangers, especially possible fellow enthusiasts, as though it were some sort of plane-spotters' club. Anyone knowledgeable in these arcana would immediately understand the truly peculiar extent of his fixation. And yet here was not only an expert, but a black, gay expert, headed for that door, to view his hasps, binding thongs, manacles, and hundreds upon hundreds of images of young black men, his trove of trespass. And as though this weren't enough cause for agitation, Dr. Hazelett's friend Florian, who it turned out was a curator at the Studio Museum of Harlem, was coming along as well. And Florian was the most beautiful human being Hollis had ever seen.

Ellington and Florian rang at the front door one half-hour after the appointed time and, from the start, Hollis felt ensnared by his own eccentric ways. He had not used the front door since the last time a family heirloom had been carted off to the shop, and now he had unthinkingly blockaded it with a heavy map cabinet. He trotted around the side path to greet them, and, from the moment he laid eyes on Florian, he was filled with regret that he had so systematically refused to prepare himself for such a moment. He'd devoted his adult life to amassing a storehouse of glimpses of a certain realm, steeped himself in its sadness, when really the whole exercise had been camouflage, entitling him to surround himself with images of strong young men. And now, here was the flawless epitome himself in the butterscotch-colored flesh, with aristocratic bearing and the languid, loose-limbed grace of a leopard, waiting expectantly at his barricaded door. As he led them

back past the neglected flower beds and into the sunporch
stacked with the pointless reiterations of his collection, he
couldn't help but see through their eyes the pitiful recluse he
had become.

Florian eased himself through the narrow pathway, taking
care not to brush against anything with his immaculate jeans
and white sweatshirt. At seeing the size of the house, he had
been looking forward to a fine interior. He glanced around,
eyebrows arched, his expression falsely casual: he might just
start whistling a tune, he was so dismayed.

"Sorry for the mess," said Hollis. "I don't get many visitors."
Florian flashed him a brief smile, merely polite, with a shy,
downward glance that left Hollis reeling inside.

Ellington made straight for the tables of materials. Hollis
trailed him, pointing out various items, but mainly distracted,
fretting at what Florian might be concluding about him. Unaccustomed since his retirement from the recital stage to caring
what impression he made, he was now rueful at how rusty he
found himself. Florian wandered among the dusty tables, familiar from his curatorial work with the dreary singleminded-
ness of collectors, aghast anew at how they could trash their
very nests with the stuff. After all, one could rent storage
space; the solution was not so mysterious, but they never
seemed to get it. And the afternoon, he thought, was getting to
the end of the unwelcome browning rays and the beginning of
the late-day fun urgency of things at the beach. After what he
hoped would seem a decent interval, he beamed Hollis a smile
that he knew very well from long experience was disabling, and
said, "I'm gonna leave you two to poke through all this, while I
go do my dune *thang*." He offered his elegant, veiny hand. "Mr.
Wynbourne? Pleasure."

Hollis placed his hand in Florian's for an instant and then,
utterly flummoxed, watched it fly out to adjust one of the

clamp lights. He felt, as though in a dream, the fingertips burning on the hot shade, bobbled the contraption in a distracted spasm, hurling it to the floor, where the bulb exploded with a blue flash.

"Gracious," he said. "I certainly couldn't have made much more of a mess of that." Ellington stood frozen in recoil, as though waiting for the butler with the whisk broom. Hollis felt as though treasure were being wrenched from his grasp before he'd so much as had a glance at it. This was a final torture fate had devised. Florian, the paragon, was to be one of those figures in the dunes, and Hollis was to be trapped in this cobweb-draped room with these inert, bloodless stand-ins. He watched Florian maneuvering through the obstacles on the sunporch, saying over his shoulder, "Don't you have the view. My." Hollis thought the telescope might as well have been flashing neon.

FIVE

B Y THE end of June, the gay invasion had become the topic of nearly every conversation in the village, from the dinner parties on Signal Hill to the fuel dock at Runcie's Bait and Marine to the polished remove of the Yacht Club bar, out on its pilings in the harbor. Betsy Haring more and more often felt called upon to tamp down surprisingly harsh offhanded comments that she heard over cocktails. Her set was used to sniffing at the plebeian doings of the summer village, confident that none of it would wash up the lanes to lap at their hedges, but now there was a wariness in the air. Were they safe? The resurgence of the Ocean Hotel, for example, was a worry, placed as it was directly in their midst at the top of the hill.

At a cocktail party after the Napatree Club senior doubles

tournament, the retired ball-bearing tycoon Leverett Stahl announced breezily to Betsy that he'd seen a rainbow towel draped out the window of one of the Ocean's rooms. "That virus isn't mutating fast enough to suit me," he added blandly.

"Why, Leverett," said Betsy, giving him a politely quizzical look, "you're just not an adequate citizen of the planet, now, are you. Live and let live, and all?"

"I'm not a prejudiced person, my dear, in my actions." He stared off over the balustrade with a squinty smile. "But I do have my thoughts. Let's just say I haven't been rooting for the CDC."

Betsy herself was of two minds about the changes sweeping the village. A preservationist at heart, she was apprehensive at the slightest alteration of the status quo, even though barely a ripple had reached her heights. It was the tackier details— men with boom boxes sunning on the grass by the harbor— that troubled her, just as she'd never liked the racks of sunblock and flip-flops in front of Stevie Lund's shop. At the same time, she'd always had gay friends, regularly swapped perennials with Ray Hardman and his friend, Herb, and was keenly aware of how many gay men had rescued good houses from the jaws of vinyl siding in architecturally endangered enclaves across the country.

At a dinner party at the Coffeys', of the Rhode Island banking family, Betsy had to bite her tongue through more moaning from Polly Dickson. Now it wasn't just Betsy, fighting their plans for an addition, who was forcing the Dickson family out of town after umpteen generations, or was it umpteen and one? Now there were the intruders, as well, to grouse about. "The town just isn't what it was. You're not getting the quality of person that we had years ago. I like to have a cup of tea with Peggy Broadhurst sometimes on an afternoon. But you can't get near Angleton's anymore, with them all sashaying around. It's gotten so I scarcely go down into the village at all."

Betsy made a mental note and gave Polly a smile of apparent concern. "Oh, sure," she said brightly, "but we've always all skipped the village in season, anyway, haven't we. I'm sure Lattie will welcome you and Peggy come October."

On the first weekend of July, a flurry of interest attended the arrival, off Long Spit beach, of a small ship, the first of a series of gay weekend cruises from South Street Seaport that Artie Kinzie had been feverishly organizing and promoting. Expensive optics were trained on the vessel from broad porches all over Signal Hill's west face. The ship, which could accommodate eighty guests, was normally in service gentling retirees between New England and Florida on the Intracoastal Waterway. Artie had chartered it for six three-day sailings, leaving New York after work on a Friday, with a fancy dinner laid on in the western reaches of Long Island Sound, the return on Sunday evening capped off with coffee and liqueurs served as the vessel passed under the lights of the New York bridges.

With all eyes on the cruise ship, hardly anyone took note of the arrival, on the Saturday morning, of a rather severe-looking motoryacht: gunmetal-colored hull and superstructure, deeply tinted windows. *Nighthawk* grumbled into the harbor, not a soul on deck, pivoted in place with its bow thrusters, and eased sideways into one of the highly restricted berths at the town dock. Only then did several startlingly handsome liveried deckhands appear briefly to handle docklines. This boat was a far cry from the modest seventy- or eighty-foot classic Trumpys and Elcos from Greenwich and Oyster Bay whose captains normally reserved these few places months in advance to visit local folks for the weekend. For hours no one else appeared on deck; the dock geezers in attendance concluded that only crew were aboard and turned their attentions to the harbor's other comings and goings.

During the rest of Saturday, the cruise ship rested at anchor; her tenders trundled back and forth to the beach and to the harbor, depositing knots of boys, from the gym-buffed and tanning-bedded to the office-soft and pale, attired in painstakingly selected ensembles of denim, linen, leather, Lycra, and rubber—each boatload then dispersing to pursue whatever the favored pleasure might be.

By happy coincidence, that same Saturday saw the steady arrival in the anchorage of the two dozen or so yachts of the Long Island Men and Buoys, a gay sailing club. This visit resulted from an inadvertent connection made by Wesley Herndon, even though he was not a member—not a member of anything, actually, except the Princeton Club.

Shortly after returning from his first visit to Long Spit, he got one of his periodic calls from Herb Tate, a goodhearted but garrulous acquaintance who was forever prodding him to partake in some cornball camaraderie or other. They'd met when, in an uncharacteristically selfless mood, Wesley had taken pity on a solitary older man standing at the bar in Trik's, and had thus been the very first person to hear Herb's appalling story of coming out after twenty-five years of marriage, with all possible acrimony following, including estrangement from his grown children. Since then, Herb had not looked back. He had become a strenuous booster of all things gay, bringing to his fervor all the exasperating cheeriness of his career as a traveling salesman, quite oblivious to the way his conversational gambits were absorbed by Wesley's indifference like golf balls disappearing into tall grass.

This time though, Wesley was, for once, not merely fidgeting for an exit line, but had something of his own to say, filled as he was with his new discovery, which had culminated in

Jim's visit aboard, or, to be more precise, in the totally unexpected thrill of watching Jim pleasure himself, sprawled on the main cabin settee before Wesley's eyes, to the accompaniment of impatient, lascivious catcalls from Ozzie and Jake on the beach. This Wesley described to Herb only as "a bit of mischief," but he did work up some real enthusiasm telling him about the other features of Long Spit—so much enthusiasm, in fact, that Herb immediately said he would propose, in the LIMB club's weekly e-mail, that they make it the destination for the next weekend's cruise. In the end, Wesley even succumbed to Herb's urgings and agreed to show up with *White Wings IV,* unable to resist the temptation to invite Jim along and in every way put the rest of the fleet to shame.

But that Saturday didn't go exactly as Wesley had hoped. Jim was delighted at the invitation and picked up quickly on the routines aboard, but, shortly after they anchored, a notorious founding member of the club anchored right next to them with his stubby little orange boat with its chalky, unwaxed hull, the entire crew wearing stacked-heeled, open-toed espadrilles, halter tops, tennis skirts, and bad wigs. Wesley considered moving, but decided that would likely open him up to much of the sort of joshing that passed for bonhomie in this crowd. So Jim and Wesley sat in the cockpit with their backs to the affront, as though the boat were an unfortunate drunken street person that one oughtn't to stare at.

Jim went along with Wesley's huffing and groaning enough to be polite, but in fact he was still so amazed at how his two-week holiday was going that having a yacht crew in drag next door was hard to regard as a problem. Jim had hoped for some sexy fun this trip, and meeting Derek and Tracy in the dunes was certainly that. He'd never met men so lighthearted about playing with their bodies, and his. Derek, in the middle of a conversation, would reach over and, with a quick grin, give Jim a squeeze in the crotch. In a booth at Angleton's, Tracy once flipped up his shirtfront and flashed Jim a peek at his muscle-armored tummy. And they had fun sitting outside Frankie's Slice dishing the passing strollers, Jim describing the improvements that plastic surgery could offer each individual. Then Jim had no sooner ventured to the dunes on his own than Jake and Ozzie made a beeline for his perch and worked him over without so much as a how-do-you-do: handed him a joint, manhandled him, turned him every way but loose, and only told him their names when they were all drenched with sweat, catching their breath on his beach blanket afterward.

But meeting Wesley was when the experience began to deepen beyond frolic. It started as just more fun. Ozzie's dope still had Jim in a randy buzz when he first stepped aboard *White Wings IV,* and Wesley was so clearly wowed that Jim felt he had permission for a little showing off, something that was, of course, a commonplace in his video library but that he'd always been too inhibited to try. Wesley's approval was whole-hearted, to say the least, and he was skilled not only at dirty-talking Jim to liftoff, but also at continuing to speak matter-of-factly and admiringly afterward, heading off the danger that Jim might lapse into remorseful embarrassment the minute the last spurt was spent. All of this kindled a spark of exhibitionism in Jim that he'd never known was there.

Wesley, for his part, was used to talking well-hung louts through their paces; it was the most satisfactory mode, the only possible mode really, that he had discovered for having any sexual encounter at all with this sort of eager, muscular young man who would otherwise barely acknowledge his existence. He was only too happy to treat them to a cost-no-object evening in return for the privilege of watching them jolly themselves to moans. But Jim was his first experience of a delectable gym body conjoined with a sweet-natured intelligence, and Wesley had been feeling an apprehensive giddiness ever since, the hazard of connection in the air.

One day Jim jumped in his rented roadster and drove the forty minutes to visit Wesley at home. He was flabbergasted by the roomful after roomful of investment-quality furniture, some of which he actually remembered from auction notices and feature spreads in his *Art & Antiques* magazines back home. Wesley beamed at this unaccustomed discernment on the part of a sex toy, the enthusiasm so refreshing after his friends' bitchy, bored expertise. While crooning over the patina of the paneling around the reconstructed keeping-room fireplace, Jim spotted an ash bucket on the hearth and said, "Even the bucket is perfect. I can't believe this place." Wesley responded on impulse, "It's yours. Think of me whenever you throw a condom wrapper into it." He even served Jim a lunch and a dinner without any fits of grumpiness. The next evening Jim ventured to ask whether he might bring along a man he had met at the beach. "Now, you must be perfectly blunt about this. I don't want to hurt your feelings, but I think this guy and I might be into putting on a little show in the front sitting room." Wesley died and went to voyeur's heaven, watching the two of them wrestle, and worse, on his priceless Uzbek carpet.

Now Wesley and Jim sat aboard, twirling their cold fettucine with pesto and olives and considering the merits of the various houses nestled among the ledge outcrops and specimen plantings of Signal Hill. Wesley was unused to caring whether his hunk-of-the-moment showed any leaning toward deeper connection. With Jim, though, he kept looking for signs, although of course the need to appear invulnerable barred him from actually broaching the subject.

"Now see," said Wesley, "that one, with the corner turret, is fun for what it says about the original owner, but nothing I'd ever be interested in."

"Right." Jim nodded. "He sort of commanded the architect to create an exclamation point no one could miss."

"The point is, go ahead and show off outrageously, but do it by restraint and flawlessness rather than size and flash."

"We still talking houses?" Jim winked. "No, I know, you're right. I love to check out the real estate office windows when I'm traveling, see what's posted. You?"

"Could be a plan for the afternoon," said Wesley. "Maybe do a few stroll-bys. Can you tear yourself away from the dunes for a few minutes?"

"I'll try to be brave," said Jim. Wesley let him clean up the galley without supervision.

Ashore, they quickly found a few real estate storefronts offering a discouraging assortment of raised ranches and condo units on the outskirts of town, their charms described in terms of proximity not to the sea, but to the gigantic, Indian-run casino a few miles inland to the north.

"This is sure not what we're looking for," said Jim.

"No," said Wesley, "but there's always one guy who's got a lock on all the good stuff." They reached the end of Front Street, next to Frankie's, and started up the hill to the left, on Hartley Lane. A couple of doors up from the antique carousel stood a small mansard-roofed building with rather formal detailing, perhaps once a carriage house for a grand cottage. They were admiring its dentil soffit trim when Wesley noticed a brass plaque next to the door: Salt Air Estates. "Ah, here we are," he said. "No pictures taped to the windows. Very promising."

Ray Hardman looked up from his *Vanity Fair*, took in the yachty salt-and-pepper-haired gentleman with the handsome, fit, younger man, and said, "Why hello, I've been expecting you." He smiled. "In a general sense." Ray had been wondering when he would first benefit from the new infusion.

"Yes, lovely village, and getting lovelier in a hurry," said Wesley with a stiff smile, putting out his hand. "Wesley Herndon. Looks like some significant houses, too. Don't want to take a lot of your time, but—"

"Don't be silly." Ray shook Wesley's hand and gestured to the leather armchairs. "I'm Ray Hardman." He gave Jim an approving smile. "And you're . . . ?"

"Jim. Jim Hornswich. Yeah, neat town."

Out came the leather-bound presentation folios and, in a couple of cases, the video house tours. Soon they headed out in Ray's Range Rover to drive by a few places. "Not that there's ever all that much available in the sort of thing you're looking for," Ray said. "Most often, they don't actually come on the market."

"Yes, of course," said Wesley impatiently. He did not like being taken for somebody who didn't know that.

"But," Ray added, "I can still help out, you know, on an informal basis. Act as your ear to the ground, if you will."

Ray drove them past the Hollisters', the Van Gelders', and the Duncans', all the while subtly jousting with Wesley to establish who was the more rarefied house snob. Jim enjoyed the batting back and forth of obscure references to Eastern families, architects, other pockets of cossetted splendor along the New England coast ("Oh yes, didn't he do a similar entry on the Weston house in Northeast Harbor?"; "I think it was Little Compton") as though he were listening to one of those esoteric quiz shows on the BBC. After they had idled past several intricate, repeatedly expanded mansions, Wesley, as though revealing a character flaw, shook his head and said, "I can't quite bring myself to relax into the Shingle Style—not starchy enough, too ephemeral. It has an appeal visually, I suppose, but for me it conjures up, I don't know, dozens of Irish grandchildren spilling off the porches in their lace frocks, terriers

barking, just not my thing. Guess I'm just hopelessly formal."
He heard himself edging beyond the harmless look around
that he and Jim had intended. A good house here, right on top
of a supply of hot boys like Jim, hmmm . . .

Cautioning them that the house was only *possibly* becoming
available, Ray drove them by the Dicksons'. The house sat
among white and pink beach roses in all its fussy perfection,
the calm sweep of Block Island Sound shimmering in the heat
beyond. It was Jim who was transfixed. "Wow," he said. "That
is cool. Kind of an H-O gauge house. It's speakin' to me. . . . I
love the way they've done that wave pattern in the shingles on
the gable end."

Ray quickly said, "Yes—well, of course, that would have
been a later, more a Victorian touch. It's a good house, though,
1820." Jim understood that he'd just been lobbed like a small
grenade in the good-natured skirmish that was taking place.

Finally, a truce: Wesley and Ray each acknowledging he'd
met his match. "I'd like to show you one more place," Ray said,
portentously switching off the Schubert on the CD player.
"Normally I wouldn't bother; it's really beyond the means of
most people I take around. It's been semi on the market for
years, pie-in-the-sky price, in a family that can afford to say, 'If
anybody wants it, this is what they're going to have to pay.' But
really superb. From everything you've said, I think you might
appreciate at least a peek. It's just down here at the bottom of
the lane."

He had been descending from Signal Hill toward the opposite end of Front Street from his office, and now crossed Front
and turned onto Mussel Cove Lane. Gliding to a halt beneath
oaks that formed a leafy tunnel overhead, he said, "The Ferryman house, Fog Bells." The house was a haughty Georgian
block of brick, with a pair of gloss-black front doors crowned

with an unusually fine upper-hall Palladian window. The twin bronze railings of its granite-faced double-entry stairway dropped like garlands to the cobbled forecourt. "A ship captain built it, around 1840. Doesn't have the long views, but for a sailor, it could be quite special. It's a surprisingly deep lot; let me show you." He eased forward to where they could see along the side of the house: a walled garden, stepping gradually downward in formal terracing to a heavily constructed dock, ramp, and float. "It's a private cove, just three houses. The chart shows no way to get in, but there have always been deep-draft boats kept here. The families must have had friends in the cartographic office. Hurricane-safe. As a matter of fact, the Ostwald family yacht *Ariadne* survived the hurricane of 'thirty-eight on her regular mooring in this cove while every single house was scoured off Long Spit and hurled into the bay."

"There used to be houses on Long Spit?" said Jim.

"Absolutely. Cheek by jowl from end to end," said Ray. "That storm was probably the best thing that ever happened to this town. Cleared away all the crap, never to return. Just left the good stuff."

"This is really something," said Wesley. He wore the self-conscious, uncontrollable grin that normally installed itself only when he beheld a spectacularly constructed young man or a significant kneehole desk. After a few seconds, he mastered it and abruptly looked as though he were facing down a senator on an investigating committee. "What are they asking?"

"Three million two."

"Ouch," said Jim.

Ray idled to the end of the lane and turned around. "Come to think of it," he said, "there's somebody I'd like you to meet." He reached for the mobile phone. "Betsy, honey, Ray. Just fine, and you? Doin' anything? You sure? I've got a couple of gentle-men with me that I'd . . . Just down at Ferryman's. . . . Great. See you in a minute."

They climbed the spiraling drive to the top of Betsy's knoll, took the service fork, and came upon her kneeling by the garage doors, surrounded by flats of seedlings and sacks of de-odorized manure. She shucked off her garden gloves. "Begin-ning of July, already time to redo the pool urns, can't believe it." Over introductions, she took in Jim's open-faced friendli-ness and jaunty, rugged bearing and found herself taking on a coquettish air that allowed her South Carolina childhood to get the upper hand over the Vassar layer. There was nothing so carefree as a good flirt with a handsome gay man.

"Nebraska!" she said. "Amazing how you-all are finding our sleepy little village this season. Can you stop a minute for tea? I was just looking for an excuse for a break." She led them toward the back door. Wesley had the delicious feeling he got entering an important house. He was on overload with all this architectural feasting, but understood that something might be at stake in this meeting and so quashed any gushing and gawking. They passed through a suite of pantries and storage rooms for china, crystal, linen, and silver, and finally entered a sprawling kitchen intended for ample staff. Betsy's office was set up in a corner by the window. Though Wesley was busy act-ing as though the house were not the point, he was delighted when Jim said, "This is incredible. My house could fit in this kitchen. Do you think . . . It would really be a thrill to see some of the other rooms. Not a tour or anything, just maybe a couple of the downstairs rooms."

"Oh, by all means," said Betsy. "Since the kids left, I hardly live in most of it, just make my tight little turns back here in the scullery."

"These guys are definitely enthusiasts," said Ray. "They've

got it bad." He lowered his voice. "I took 'em by Polly's." He winked.

Betsy bounced her eyebrows, then gave Jim a slinky look. "Now, are you two, how shall we say, companions?"

"No, no, we just met here a few days ago," said Jim. "Been hangin' out together."

"Ah, hope." Betsy sighed. "Just kidding. And you're some sort of doctor?"

"That's right. A plastic surgeon."

"In the privacy of my home! We must talk. Come." She led them through the dining room—marble fireplace at one end, bay of windows at the other—into the living room, which occupied an entire projecting wing with windows on three sides, and ended up in the entry hall, with its dark oak staircase and portal leading directly to the cloistered courtyard around the pool.

"Very fine indeed," said Wesley, as Jim let out a low whistle.

"Yeah, but I'm such a ragamuffin," Betsy said, tiptoeing around a corner of Persian carpet. "Take today, for example. I'm so filthy that the only place I can sit down with you is out there by the pool, where I can hose down my chair after."

Over tea Ray steered talk onto preservation. "Oh yes," said Betsy, "I'm the wicked witch standing between all these old duffers and their beloved jalousie windows. I don't mind. I was always the class snitch, you know, hall monitor and all? Guess I've got busybody blood. But in the end"—she waved it away—"they all love to brag about the village."

"You must get to know everybody pretty well," said Jim.

"Honey, too well, too well." She pinched her throat between thumb and forefinger. "Can you imagine trying to get this turkey wattle cinched in a bit in this little gossip patch?" She laughed and gave Jim a light swat on the knee.

Not sure she was joking, he spoke of a motel near his practice in Hinton: "My receptionist calls it the Black and Blue Inn."

Later Betsy took Jim aside, ostensibly to show him the pocket doors leading to the study. "You know something? I wasn't kidding back there," she said, checking through the window that Wesley was still inspecting the astilbes. "I just blurted that out like any old joke, but ever since my husband left, I've been thinking about some tinkering, just, you know, to bring my face in line with the het-up schoolgirl inside. Not just the wattle, but these extra eyelid folds, and the dimples that used to be fetching till they turned into permanent dents. God, I can't believe I'm talking to you about this. The gossip-mongers would have a field day. Mind you, I could give you a list of the girls here in town who've confided to me that they've thought about it, too." Here she gave him a coy look. "I mean, you look at me and you see woman of a certain age, and you might forget that when I see a handsome, sexy man, I'm as eager as when I was seventeen. But if I'm ever going to meet Mr. Next Chapter, instead of all these pompous old farts who think I should be delighted to pour them another drink, I've got to tuck up the sags. Golly, I'm going on. You're probably thinking, What on earth is *with* this loony? But something about you just makes me feel, I don't know, kind of safe?"

Jim was a bit taken aback, but said, "No, no, that's okay. People often feel very self-conscious when they first come to me. But what you're asking about is all very easy. Any qualified plastic surgeon could take care of it." He reached out a clinical thumb and tested the elasticity of her eyebrow.

"No, I don't want just anybody," she said, leaning into his thumb with a hint of hunger.

"Well gosh, I guess I could write down my number back home, but Hinton's a ways away. . . ."

WHEN THE phone rang, Anthony leaped to his feet as though caught. He'd been on his back doing trunk curls for the first time ever outside of a gym class. He darted into the hall, grabbed the cordless, and retreated into his room.

"Hello?" He flopped on the bed, trying to keep his breathing quiet.

"This is your Christian dating service."

"Oh, hi." It was Rain, his best friend.

"Yes, it's that time again, the one concession a year to keep peace with Grace." For several years, Anthony had been Rain's escort to the summer potluck dinner put on by her mother's church. Things had been going downhill fast between mother and daughter lately.

Anthony groaned. "I just got the Velveeta off the roof of my mouth from last year."

"I know, I know. Think of it as anthropology," Rain said. "Let's meet up and make a plan. We've got to coordinate outfits, earrings, you know, everything has to be perfect."

"Uh . . . yeah, cool." The beat's hesitation couldn't be taken back. "I'm working tonight, wanna stop down?"

"Well, sure . . . but if you really want to know," she said, trying to keep her voice light, "I feel like a groupie when I see you down there anymore. Like I'm trying to get a word in while you're busy working the crowd."

"Oh, please, it's just that it's gotten so busy," Anthony protested, riffling his fingers over his warmed tummy muscles. "Come down late, after the dinner rush."

"When would that be?"

"Um, ten-thirty?"

"Angleton's used to *close* at eight!"

"Yeah, well . . . things change." He hadn't meant to sound reproving. "Hey, we got a nightspot now."

"Right. Okay, see you later."

Holding the dead phone, he had a wry flash of his father, who had always insisted on giving him advice about how to manage "people of the female persuasion," advice that Anthony could never picture him having applied to his wife. Anthony's mother was a guileless, self-described "homemaker," hardly a fitting opponent for his father's cynical playbook. Tony Senior had left two years earlier to move in with a croupier named Madeleine from one of the nearby casinos—he was always vague about which one—but evidently his wisdom was lost on her as well, because she kicked him out within a week and, out of embarrassment and maybe even guilt, he'd then moved to Florida. How, Anthony wondered with a smirk, would Dad have managed Rain?

He resumed his trunk curls. He had always hung with the poets, who distinguished themselves from the jocks by shunning exercise. But he was becoming more and more accustomed to the attention he'd been harvesting lately, and he was starting to acknowledge to himself that its continuation need not be left to chance. He could actually exert himself to fine-tune the magnetism. After he had crunched his abdominals to a fine heat, he uncurled slowly, using the only large enough patch of floor in the room to stretch to his full eight-foot reach. He felt the contracted muscles letting go, let out a contented groan, and thought what seemed an exotic thought: This is my body.

ARTIE KINZIE had prevailed upon Marcia Pepitone, the manager of the Ocean, to try a Saturday afternoon tea dance in conjunction with the cruise ship's visit. He even offered to supply a DJ and sound system free of charge to get it launched. She was inclined to try it but was nervous enough about the idea to want to run it by Milam Sandermeyer in Florida.

"W'now, what exactly has tea got to do with it?" he'd said. "Can you help me there? I just can't picture it."

"I'm not really sure what that means," she replied. "They tell me it's just for the couple of hours between the beach and dinner. Have a beer, run into your friends, decide what to do for the evening."

"And these are all fairies you're talkin' about? What about the rest of the guests? Are they welcome, too, or is it like a private party?"

"Well, quite frankly, sir, there *are* no other guests as far as I can tell. They all seem to be, you know . . ." In the end Milam had approved it on a trial basis. Marcia did not tell him it would be outside on the hotel's vast side porch and patio overlooking the sea.

Artie's crew had arrived on Saturday morning and spent the day setting up. Artie told Marcia she'd need a quick way to serve lots of beers. "You got some old bathtubs?"

She gave a rueful laugh. "Yeah, but unfortunately they're still in the rooms." She thought for a moment. "How about—we've got an old canoe down in back?" She added timidly, "We could paint it rainbow colors?"

"Now you're talkin'!" said Artie, giving her a thumbs-up punch.

There were seventy men staying at the hotel and nearly eighty aboard the cruise ship, and during the morning the gay telegraph spread the word through the B&Bs and time-share units, so four-thirty saw men streaming from all directions up Hartley Lane to the top of the hill, drawn like iron filings to the magnetic thump of the dance music. By five-thirty, a few hundred revelers were cruising, dishing, posing, dancing on the porch, whirling, waving their arms over their heads, shouting along with their favorite numbers, cheering the climaxes. The staff lugged more and more cases of cold beer through the crowd to the canoe full of ice.

The racket drew a few of the curious from the neighborhood: Edith Tiddle propelling her walker with her poodle, Jerome, tied to one of its legs; others in large sedans gliding to a halt at the curb, small boys peering out of the bittersweet tangles, all taking in the first-ever sightings of grown men dancing with each other, or whatever that was they were doing. Arnold Prendergast scowled out the window of his imposing house, which looked across a small ravine at the side of the Ocean. His jaw muscles worked: *Not bad enough this dump has been a fire hazard all these years . . .* And Bart Connors, the reporter from the *New York Blade,* patrolled the margins with his notebook.

Marcia was toting up the take from the cover charge (which by itself was more than the hotel's normal gross for a week) when Mickey, one of the busboys, told her she'd better come take a look under the porch. They scrambled down the hill in back to where they could look up at it from near the delivery entrance.

"Saw it when I was bringing up more beer." Mickey pointed to the main horizontal beam that supported all the floor joists of the porch. It was a massive timber mottled with moss and mildew, and it was bouncing a good several inches in time with the music. Mickey and Marcia exchanged a worried look.

"How long do you think it can hold?"

"Beats me," said Mickey. Just then, Cher reached the climax of "Believe" and the dancers began to jump, wail, stamp, whistle, and hoot in rhythm. Long, dark cracks started to open along the sides of the timber. They watched, paralyzed.

"Holy shit," moaned Marcia. "We've got to stop them."

"No, wait!" hollered Mickey. "Maybe I can get something under it."

"I'll help you," said Marcia. They crawled in under the porch and clawed at the tangle of scrap lumber, plumbing pipe, and broken cinder blocks.

Mickey shouted, "I think we can find enough whole blocks to stack under the lowest sag!" Working feverishly—Marcia kept picturing the headline announcing their deaths—they got the blocks stacked to within a few inches of the timber.

Mickey was hefting a bundle of lumber chunks to make up the last few inches when Marcia screamed, "Omigod! Hurry!" The bottom face of the timber had begun to part into long splinters. Mickey held a chunk of wood in each hand, poised to jam between the column and the beam. He took a moment to get moving in time with the music; then, on the afterbeat, in the split second the timber was moving up, he plunged the pieces into place. The next bounce of the beam acted like a pile driver, driving the column down into the soft ground, nearly tipping it over, shattering the top block. Marcia rolled another one through the debris while Mickey frantically straightened the column. Finally they got enough blocks rammed home to stop the bouncing.

By the time Marcia emerged, filthy and sweating, from underneath the porch, nearly all the boys on the dance floor had taken their shirts off and the dancing she beheld had deteriorated to a tangle of humping, butt-bumping, chest-banging, and slippery, slithering bodies, less like dancing, really, than mass rut. She had the uneasy sensation that she had abruptly brought the Ocean Hotel to a surreal and untenable pass. She noticed Artie Kinzie hovering around the fringes of the mêlée with a rotund man wearing a broad-brimmed black hat, sunglasses, and several thousand dollars' worth of Italian clothes. Artie was gesturing intently—pointing at something to do with the exterior of the building. With her smudged smock, Marcia thought it best not to approach just then, and shortly watched them get into a waiting taxi and head back down toward the harbor.

That evening the crew of the cruise ship ferried tables and chairs and all the passengers—with whatever additional boys they had met along the way—ashore for a clambake on the beach, presided over by Mel Cleveland, an amiable black man who, Artie discovered, had become a minor area legend as an impresario of clambakes and barbecues. Mel drove his bigfoot pickup truck out the fire access road right to the site, set up all his cooking equipment, ringed the table area with a white picket fence hung with pots of petunias, strung colored lights, and started playing CDs of sea chanteys.

All evening long, the jolly island of light flickered cozily on the broad, dim arc of the beach. After dinner, some of the boys returned to the ship and got their country two-step CDs. The tables were cleared away; everybody kicked off his shoes and two-stepped in the sand, half of the men teaching the other half, whooping and clapping in time, unaware that small groups of townspeople were making the pilgrimage to just outside the pool of light all evening, gazing from the hundred hopping men to the lights of the ship, shaking their heads, and trudging back to the village.

MEANWHILE THE crowd at Angleton's was finally thinning out. Anthony realized that he had spent his entire shift scanning warily for Rain and hopefully for Wendell, fearing most the arrival of both at once. He was leaning on the waiters' station when she came in, and he strode over to seat her. "Good evening, I'm Anthony and I'll be your waitperson this evening. That will be one for—frappes?"

"I'll give you a frappe," Rain said brightly, giving him a peevish swat. She swept past him to a booth in the back, shaking her long hair free from her fedora. Rain was quite tall and a bit on the blocky side, with square shoulders, but she carried herself with a bohemian flair, like a café habitué out of Toulouse-Lautrec.

She plopped into her seat and abruptly fixed him with a mock-hurt look. "So I can escort myself to this thing if it doesn't sound like fun—anymore."

"No, no, we'll do it," he said. "It's just—when is it?"

"A week from tonight, like always, the second Saturday in July."

"Whoa," Anthony said thoughtfully. He almost said That gets to be an expensive night off from work, but caught himself in time.

"Listen, what *is* it?" she demanded.

"Nothing, we'll do it, we'll do it . . . Coffee?" He brought them both coffees and sat down. "It's just—I'm not really your boyfriend. It feels weird."

"What on earth? Since when has *that* made any difference? You never were!" Her voice had escalated to mock astonishment, but the mock part was under strain.

"I was never anybody's anything," he said, not meeting her gaze, "so it didn't matter." He turned to face her. "Look, we're going, so don't worry about it."

"If you're sure," she said, unconvinced. She stirred her coffee a moment. "Then next is . . . accessories—gold or silver?"

SIX

OLLIS WYNBOURNE, through no effort on his part, had become part of the lore passed on to newcomers in the village. On rainy days, when groups of men would camp at Angleton's, stirring cup after cup of coffee, trying to keep their banter fired up, someone would always propose a stroll to Hollis's shop: "Have you ever been up to see that old thing in her closet?" "Her! She's a hoot. The more we mince, the more she scowls. Meanwhile, I'm talking *bins* full of boy pix. She's too much, that one."

Ellington Hazelett had summoned an archivist from the Schomburg Center to examine Hollis's private collection, all again without any encouragement from Hollis, who realized he should perhaps feel offended at this high-handedness, but allowed it to continue on vague grounds, sketched by Ellington, of "making scholars in the field aware of resources and their repositories." Actually some deep instinct in Hollis was allowing him to loosen his grip on this protective mass, the way a crab finds itself molting.

At times Hollis had a sense of emerging into the world after an illness, feeling shaky and stiff, trying out faculties he had temporarily given up on. Events seemed to be sweeping him along, sometimes leaving him behind. Anthony, for example, who had shown Hollis perfect deference since their voice lessons had begun, had recently started treating him with an irritating sympathy, as though he were hopelessly stuck, his real life over. That description would have suited him just fine only a couple of months before, when he'd been, if not happy, at least resigned to his reclusive existence with his mute family. Now he was like a hibernating beast being poked and prodded. He'd gone from providing Anthony's one, oblique glimpse of a realm neither of them was prepared to enter, to feeling paralyzed as Anthony proceeded to the gate and peered through, gathering himself to readiness.

Not that Hollis was *entirely* reluctant. His telescope, for years used to spot the odd grebe or guillemot, and only the very occasional jogger, had become a critical keyhole on this newly impinging reality. First it had been focused on the threatening presence of Derek and Tracy, so disquieting that it only mortared him deeper into his cave. But, in the last few days, it had brought him the lean, butterscotch figure of Florian, hips cocked atop the dunes, looking around with a hint of impatience, as if his date were late. Usually the image was just fuzzy enough to be tantalizing or frustrating, depending on his frame of mind. But occasionally he would have the good luck to catch Florian stretching, lofting his arms skyward with a dancer's grace that took Hollis's breath away. Or he would chance upon the young man reapplying, for perhaps the sixteenth time, his skin potion, compounded to order by an an-

cient French purveyor of elixirs on the Lower East Side from a
mixture of rare oils and SPF 45 sunblock. Hollis would be
frozen behind the eyepiece at his remove of nearly half a mile,
transfixed by those long elegant fingers, just out of focus, lovingly double-checking for coverage every sleek inch of that
gleaming torso. The telescope became a siren calling to Hollis
from the porch.

Even when Hollis wasn't actually peering through the lens,
he found himself thoroughly preoccupied with Florian. After
years of relatively effortless self-discipline, he was hard put to
understand, first, what had suddenly relegated his collection,
the painstaking labor of some two decades, to the status of
laughable stand-in, and second, what had, at the same time,
elevated this perfect stranger to the pedestal of obsession.
Hollis would abruptly come to, the butter knife poised over his
toast, and realize he'd been lost in pondering what Florian
might think to get up to when he was alone with that beautiful
body: what activity could possibly make any sense, other than
to gaze at it, sample the feel, the heft of it, tend to its needs?
How frustrating it must be in a way: on the one hand it is always right there with you, available for touch, obedient to
commands, yet you are it, trapped in it, and can never experience it as a lover would, from without, and yet beauty is beauty
and—just think: to exist as a definition!—simply to regard oneself if you looked like Florian would be so pleasurable and . . .
Oh, the toast.

The certainties by which Hollis had stitched together his peculiar routines: long-suppressed remembrances of the heart-
break in his conservatory years; the renunciation of the sensual
life in favor of the endless rehearsals and airports of a career;
the pleasantly familiar bitterness this renunciation afforded
him—all this was suddenly not seeming like an adequate
recipe for existence. And, old Yankee that he was, he was fur-

ther agitated by the speed of the inner changes, so rapid that he had little time to consider what public face to put on, never mind how to manage any change of public face in a village where steadfastness, even eccentric steadfastness, was the only way to avoid being shredded by the gossip mill.

On the Wednesday after he'd first been introduced to Florian, and burnt his fingertips on the lampshade, Hollis hung his "Back in 15 Minutes" sign in the door of the shop a bit later than usual and ambled up the lanes to his house for lunch. His ambling concealed nervous anticipation; he was late because, in the days preceding, he'd noticed that Florian didn't usually arrive at his perch until nearly two in the afternoon (after the worst of the darkening rays). He'd had to chuckle at himself that morning when he prepared his lunch in advance so he wouldn't miss a moment at the telescope.

As he entered the sunporch, he glanced out toward Long Spit: sure enough, there was the familiar, tall, honey-colored figure in the distance. Hollis fetched his lunch with a fumbling urgency, took his position on the stool that now had a permanent place before the telescope, and had the enormous good luck to bring eye to lens just in time to catch Florian retying his sarong. This he did in his distinctively provocative manner, too slowly and with calculated pauses and glances at the horizon, all of which gave Hollis the eerie feeling that Florian knew he was watching, even though, from Florian's vantage point, the audience seemed to amount only to a couple of dozen men putting on their own little shows on nearby towels below him. Florian grasped the two corners of the sarong and did a little shimmy, ostensibly to unwrinkle the cloth, but the motion looked as though he were buffing his splendid twin-melon butt. Hollis strove to glimpse between the riffling fringes whatever might be dangling in the shadows. Florian flashed the sarong tails open once, twice, of course merely to adjust them to equal lengths; Hollis was paralyzed but for the eyeball climbing into the barrel of the telescope. Florian overlapped the two tails, tied and tucked them; Hollis finally breathed. Then Florian checked whether his hipbones were showing properly, judged they were not, and flung the sarong open again. Hollis was frozen in mid-chew, locked onto this bonus, when—

"Well now, I didn't know bird-watchers got so excited."

Hollis felt color marching up his neck. He turned, a tip of bologna protruding from his lips, to see Sam Jenkins at the screen door. "Oh, Sam, yes. Did I not hear you knock? Yes, extraordinary—well, actually nothing, but, to me, something, a pecker—woodpecker that is, pileated, gone now." He made a show of peering out the window as though to be sure, then closed the blind in front of the telescope, then, realizing how absurd that was, opened it again, compounding the absurdity. "Please, come in. Can I get you anything? Iced tea?"

"Nothing thanks," Sam grumped, gazing around brazenly. "I'll just be a minute. Stopped by your shop. Thought I might catch you." He pushed back his Bulls cap and scratched his pale pate. "Hollis, I'll come right to the point. We need your help. This little town's got a big problem, I don't know if you noticed." This last was muttered; Sam had never liked Hollis and it kept slipping out. "I'm gonna put it to you straight. The village is overrun with queers, pardon my French, and nobody around here seems to want to do anything about it."

Hollis looked away and down. "Yes, well, I—"

"It's not bad enough they're smooching and grabbing each other right on Front Street—right in my own house, for Christ's sake. Now they've taken over a place you and I grew up eating Sunday dinner at, well, I did anyway, and they want to turn it into a goddamn sex club, and I say it's time to say *Enough.*"

Hollis cleared his throat. "I wouldn't, uhh . . . Sex club? Surely—"

"That's right, that's the God's honest truth. Right in the old Signal Hill Inn. Padded pigeonholes in the dark, a bar made out of a latrine, you can go ask Ernie Stambro, he did the plumbing. I wouldn't shit you about a thing like this. He told me right when you walk in, where the Louie the Lobster sign used to be, they put up a poster of some guy called Tom of Finland, looks like a biker, but with a dick the size of a loaf of bread poking out his jeans right in your face. I'm telling you, Hollis, this is not right. But we can stop 'em, or at least slow 'em down, tell 'em what kind of a town *we* want."

"I see," said Hollis, nodding his head warily. "And . . . how—"

"You see, they need a liquor license to open this cesspool, and the public gets to comment on it, you know, speak up." He hitched up his jeans. "I've got this committee going to write a letter to the liquor control board and I—we—thought it would make more of an impression if some of the older families in town were represented, people like yourself."

"Well, I'm not usually one for getting involved in that sort of thing," said Hollis, edging toward Sam to crowd him back toward the door. "Not really a joiner, I'm afraid."

"That's the goddamn trouble with this town!" Sam burst out. "Just hand it over, that's what everybody wants to do, hand it over. Turn it into some kind of a sex mecca for perverts. You don't believe me, go down and have a look at the sign they just put up. Goddamn picture of an asshole is what it is, hanging right over the street." He fluttered a limp wrist and simpered. "'Oh dearie, shall we go down to Front Street for a beer and a blow job, or a little doggie fuck?' Pisses me off, I'll tell you. You-all'll just grow your hedges a little higher. I still got to come and go around this sorry infested place." He planted his hands on his hips. "Listen, all I'm asking you to do is sign the frigging letter. I'll have a lawyer write it up so it's all proper-looking. What in Christ's name are you so afraid of?" Sam very well knew the answer to this, was taking utterly for granted the dependability of Hollis's closet.

"I'm not afraid of anything," Hollis said, his back up. "One needs to think—"

"So you'll sign."

"If you must, bring the letter to me, I'll take a look. Now I need to be getting—"

"I know, I know. Well, at least you heard me out. That's more than I can say for some of the other old snoots—oh, sorry—up here on the hill." He turned to go. "I'll bring that by next day or two."

"Perhaps you could just mail it," Hollis said frostily.

"No, I want to ride herd on this, keep things moving. You take care now." Sam hitched up his jeans again and strode pugnaciously down the steps.

Hollis waited until he had disappeared around the corner of the house before checking the telescope. Florian was talking animatedly to someone; Hollis felt a strange, jostling urgency, as though Florian were on the Charleston auction block and he himself a bidder. He muttered, "Just like a Venus flytrap, aren't you."

He passed along Front Street on his way back to the shop. Frankie's Slice by the Sea was humming, a high-spirited crowd filling all the outside tables; Sade crooned over Rocco's new outdoor speakers. The balconies above the arcade were draped with sunbathers; here and there a pair of manly feet projected through the railing; the tinny twitch of boom boxes shifted Hollis from one sort of music to another as he passed along the street below. A pleasant, summer-season density of strollers licked cones and window-shopped along the arcade, some flashing the shocking badges of missed sunblock. Still some

families in the mix, but, Hollis had to admit, fewer small children than in past years—no loss, in his eyes.

Dot Bradley was promoting a new line of distressed South-
western-style leather accessories—belts, totes, backpacks,
even a selection of collars. In the bottleneck in front of her
windows, Hollis came up against a male couple holding hands.
In an encounter spanning perhaps three seconds, he ever-so-
slightly planted himself in their path, requiring them to let go
their hands to pass him. As they did, he turned sideways, as
though letting them pass but annoyed by the crush, and
grunted peevishly, "Pardon me!" He glanced back to see that
not only had they already resumed holding hands but they
were giving each other a cheerful peck on the lips as well, so
relieved were they to be over their separation. He hurried on in
some irritation, stuck glaring through Sam's eyes.

Rounding the bend at the end of the arcade, he came upon
the object of Sam's apoplexy. The old Signal Hill Inn, now
painted dark gray with black trim, had "Coming Soon" banners
on the facade and a new sign hanging from a bracket, an oval
just a few feet across, done expensively in enamels and gilt, announcing THE CRAB HOLE, with an illustration of a crab,
rendered as a perky pink projectile, about to dart into a hole
that, true enough, smacked more of sphincter than sand. Hollis could not have said precisely why he felt such a rush of
anger at this. "Idiots!" he muttered. "Don't they know they're
not pink till you cook them?" He resolved to sign Sam's letter.

THE PEQUOT Beach Club at the root of Long Spit was certainly nothing fancy: a couple of hundred feet of windowless
gray plywood faced the village; a few tiers of so-called cabanas—actually nothing more than cubicles with two hooks
and a seat—faced the sea, the whole shabby structure on con-

crete stilts skirted with battered lattice. But it had, since the forties, stood quite apart from the vicissitudes of the village as the preserve of those longtime middle-class residents not privileged to own seafront property, but disdainful of the summer day-tripper element. There was a waiting list for membership, but it was a malleable one, entrusted to a cabal of matrons; even when members died, next of kin and favored canasta partners jumped the line in preference to johnny-come-latelys who had only been waiting, say, twenty years. Each family had its several assigned cubicles, some retained in hopes that progeny long since decamped to Raleigh or Paris might someday return. Each family brought its own padlocks, and, despite the waiting list, even a balmy Saturday saw only a quarter of the capacity in use.

By state law, access to the beach itself could not be restricted, but the club tried in subtle ways to make the stretch in front of the cabanas unwelcoming to the rabble. They raked the seaweed, set out color-coded sun lounges and umbrellas in neat rows, placed their lifeguards' surf boats at the borders, bow lines acting as cordons, and they taught the summer staff how to glare decorously at any settlers in the sand. The club had formerly included a snack bar at the far end but it was forever attracting the dreaded public up from the water's edge, with unpleasant scenes ensuing when they were refused service, so the committeewomen had finally deemed it a liability. The disused building, apparently designed by its general contractor in about 1959, combined elements of A-frame, Swiss chalet, and tiki shack, and now stood in cantilevered disarray, gradually disappearing under the guano of thousands of seagulls.

The peeling, delaminating partitions of the club's cubicles had sheltered many a torrid adolescent romance over the years. The children of the beach club set grew up knowing that you could do whatever you wanted in the cabanas as long as one or both of you stood on the seat so your mother couldn't look under the door and spy four feet. Undoubtedly even a few pairs of young boys had used the cabanas to conduct those experiments the books say mark the homosexual "phase." It was just a matter of time before the new presence in the village breached this redoubt and strained the seat planks with behavior less experimental. What was required first was an infiltrator.

He came in the person of Mark Blais, who had left many a pink wad of Dubble Bubble under the seat planks in his tender years, and now, on his summer vacation from college, was discovering with amazement and delight what had happened to his hometown. He was a wholesome young man of Iroquois and French-Canadian ancestry, an environmental studies major at the University of Vermont—tall, lean, with excellent posture, a serious mien, and the repressed Catholic child's bent for forbidden sexual pranks.

Mark had grown accustomed, in past summers, to making use of his family's beach club membership solely for the convenience of its reserved parking place. The days were long gone when his grandmother, sunning her arthritic knees while the rest of her sheltered under the umbrella, would press a coin into his hand and send him off to get them ice cream sandwiches. The last thing he wanted to do now was sit on a sun lounge in a rank of his mother's golf partners explaining why such a handsome young man didn't have any girlfriends. But, billeted for the summer in his childhood bedroom, he began to cruise the new Long Spit and met Luis, a high-spirited Puerto Rican set designer. Now the two of them were casting about for a venue for what was clearly in the offing, and they just naturally began to scheme how they could enact a fantasy each had cherished since junior high school: of having silent, volcanic sex just inches from the shuffling, routine-bound traffic of unsuspecting elders.

This first encroachment went off without a hitch. Mark was, of course, not challenged when entering, and was permitted a day guest—this demure if not perfectly white man—who the attendant couldn't have known was wearing a tortoiseshell cock ring and barely containing an outburst of the giggles. Over the next several days, they used the facilities several more times before Luis had to return to New York. They couldn't help boasting of their transgressions at Frankie's, so word quickly spread of a new kick for sexual outlaws. Soon Mark was arranging for new friends, by his closely held authorization only, to approach the cabanas from the beach side while he entered from the parking lot. He had cased the cubicles, noting which were never in use, and would direct the small coterie of the naughty to their assignations.

But quite soon he lost control of who used this opportunity; the resourceful and horny quickly realized that his connivance as maître d'hôtel was not strictly necessary. One simply had to act as though one belonged: the older members couldn't be sure what their friends' children and grandchildren looked like from year to year. And so the club took its place in the lore: a man would plop down in a booth at Angleton's, slack and happy, and confess to having been "done at the egg crate."

Once Mark was no longer briefing each user as to necessary precautions, the discreetness of the incursions quickly fell by the wayside. Members couldn't help remarking on the number of body piercings, tattoos, and buzz cuts they saw padding among the cubicles—not the grooming one would expect of Long Spit grandchildren. A few heedless sorts began to frequent the beach in front of the club building. The real gay beach was shaping up to be out at the end of Long Spit, but there were always a few too lazy for the hike. The Pequot members were thus treated to their first sightings of sun-bathing men draped over each other, sharing a beach blanket with perhaps a big black boot anchoring each corner; the first butt-floss bathing suits; the unduly prolonged mutual applying of lotions, including to body parts one could quite easily reach for oneself. The members gathered the small children around them for safety and stared covertly.

None of them seemed aware of Mark's role in this new development; only a few had chanced to see him entering with Luis, and apparently none had made the connection. He even overheard his mother talking with her friends on the phone about it, speculating as to how this distasteful nuisance had gotten started, as baffling and disturbing as when the second cockroach appears in a well-kept kitchen. He'd long been fascinated by the delicate path she walked on this subject. Without ever saying so, she made it clear that she knew he was gay, never wanted him to declare it to her, and was only concerned that he be happy. Yet she could rattle on with her friends about "that sort of person" in the harshest terms. One day he was chilled to hear her saying to Dulcie Bartlett that trying to limit the penetration of "these men" into the community was nearly impossible, that "they're like a smell, like of fish heads in your garbage; either you completely get rid of them or face the fact that it's going to be everywhere." And yet she could wonder aloud to his face why he didn't seem as much fun anymore. "We used to joke and tease each other. Is something wrong?" Was she being sly with him, obliquely reproving but not owning up to it? Or was she truly oblivious, the partitions in her mind that sturdy?

MARCIA PEPITONE had been shaken but also exhilarated by the near-collapse of the Ocean's porch. Even though it was one more case of the old place succumbing to neglect and being patched to limp through another day, it seemed a good omen that this incident was brought on by heavy use, a switch from the waning trickle of business she'd been presiding over for the last several years. She phoned Artie Kinzie a couple of days afterward.

"Yeah, you gave good tea dance, all right," he said. "Worked nice with my stuff, you know, the ship, the clambake, other stuff I'm working on. People had fun. Cool view you got up there."

"I saw you brought somebody with you," she said. "Sorry I didn't come over to say hello, but we had a disaster going on and I ended up a mess. Who was that?"

"Just a friend. Got his finger in a few pies. Did you see that big like Darth Vader gin palace tied up at the town dock?"

"Oh yeah, I did."

"That's his. Cruised out from New York." Marcia heard a sharp hiss through the phone as Artie sucked on a joint. "What kind of disaster?"

Marcia realized too late that Artie had not even known about the porch. She was a little afraid he might be put off, but couldn't resist recounting the block-stacking scuffle with Mickey. She finished by assuring him she already had a crew working on a more substantial repair.

"'s cool," he replied.

Then she ventured, "Might you go for it again? I mean, help-ing out with the DJ and sound?"

"Could happen. We'll see. Not this weekend, though. I got no ship coming. Phone's ringin' off the hook with people want-ing to do it. Been trying to find another ship. *You* could go for it, though—I can give you all the numbers. There's always DJs available."

He ended up by saying, "Good work on that, Marcia. Oh, it

could be that a guy I know, a reporter, might call you. He's just keeping an eye on how this is all going. Name's Bart. Writes for a gay paper in New York. They're thinking about doing a little weekly rag up there, just for the summer. Nice guy, little excitable. Knows I know you. Anyway, I gotta go. Take it easy—and don't spend too much on that repair." Marcia wasn't sure what that meant.

ANTHONY HAD taken on more and more shifts at Angleton's, so many that instead of providing a part-time job to earn money for starting college in the fall, the restaurant had become the center of his life for this last summer at home. He was nearly as startled as his mother by this unprecedented surrender of his free time, and mulled over what was behind it. His adolescent compulsion to be a know-it-all had turned him into a celebrated fountain of information for the newcomers, sometimes regarding matters he knew about only from eavesdropping among the tables, such as which parts of the beach were frequented by which slice of the crowd. Anthony had the aversion to tanning shared by many modern teenagers and had not taken a walk on Long Spit since he was eleven, yet he underlined with a knowing roll of the eyes his succinct description of what went on in the World War II gun emplacements out at the very end: "We won't go into that—you're at the table." He enjoyed having certifiable grown-ups listen to what he had to say, and was still getting used to the idea that they were less interested in his information than in his eyelashes.

Lattie Teachout remained quite distant with the new clientele. Though she was privately delighted at having her best season ever, she was too set in her ways to shake loose any warmth toward them, and more than happy to let Anthony play the host. So, after years of having his mother, and particularly his father, disparage his views on all subjects, he was suddenly doubly encouraged to hold forth, and it was with considerable newfound self-possession that he glided among the tables. Though he remained resolutely virginal, he was quickly learning a demeanor that verged on flirting, a playful way of hinting at the power he had discovered in his lessons with Hollis. He even managed a downright saucy retort now and then when the boys got frisky, as when one of a noisy boothful said, "Do you mind if we undress you with our eyes?" and he replied, "No, that's fine. Just fold my clothes neatly, please." He shocked himself crimson, just for a second.

Until this summer, Anthony had kept himself stuck by playing an internal game: whenever a man would catch his notice as conspicuously gay, he would say to himself, Well, if that's what it means to be gay, then I'm certainly not. This summer was the first time he had been, day after day, with so many gay men, covering such a spectrum of characters as to overwhelm his puny cast of stereotypes. He was freed to let his attention linger where it would, whether out of amusement or even, he had to admit, attraction. Wendell, the college student from New London, came in now and then; they exchanged shy hellos. Neither wanted to push beyond that into the risk zone. Yet Anthony was surprised at himself when Wendell showed up with another young man, surprised to feel a twinge of urgency: Will he be taken?

Delivering muffins and rice pudding, he would drift through patches of conversation, and then plan his route among the tables to return for more eavesdropping at selected spots. One regular, whose nickname was Eggie or some such, was capable of such staggeringly shallow observations that Anthony had to linger nearby out of snide fascination. "I've never gotten a tan on my cock," Eggie was saying one day as Anthony passed with a burger platter. "It would look too kind of animal, and it could be drying." On his return pass, Eggie had moved on: "Whenever I clip the hairs on my balls I get a few of them too short and the stubble irritates my thighs for days." A few minutes later, he detoured while delivering a Greek salad to overhear "I'm trying to train myself to chew my food more carefully. I believe it will help me fart less." Anthony stifled chuckles while Eggie's friends stared at the passing scene out the front windows, having tuned him out years before. For Anthony, Eggie's blend of the bizarre and the banal chipped away at the exotic, taboo aura surrounding being gay, and sometimes left him preoccupied for the rest of the day with some peculiar image, as when he overheard an exchange about the correlation between youth and cum-spurting range. Eggie chimed in: "I once shot cum right into a boy's eye—ruined his contacts, rotted them. . . . That one had to run straight along to the optician's." He was busing the table for another group one day when a cheerful, chubby guy observed blandly to his friends: "Honey, I don't want drugs with my sex. Sex *is* my drug. I want to *know* that boy is fucking me." Then he glanced up at Anthony, said, "Oops," and winked. It was several minutes before Anthony regained his composure.

He was used to the cheerfully empty chatter of people on vacation, but there was something bracingly bratty about these men that appealed to his rebellious teen side. He found himself rooting for the gay boys when there were tense moments. One day Eggie was prattling on ("It should come as no surprise that an antiperspirant just moves the problem. I mean, the sweat is going to get out of your body one way or another . . . and you want it to. So is it really better to have a wet spot in a different place on your shirt?"), all the while idly twirling his friend's curly hair around his finger and tracing the whorls of his ear. Suddenly a jowly man sitting with his family in the next booth said, "Hey, bud. Would you mind keeping your hands to home?"

Eggie turned with a Good grief, what now? look. "Why, now that you mention it, I would mind." The nearby tables fell silent.

The man got a steely look, as though he were about to write a speeding ticket. "I'm afraid I'm going to have to ask you to respect the ways of this community."

Eggie let out a sharp bark of a laugh and swept the attentive, mainly gay audience with a glance. "Excuse me? Which community was that?" He turned to his tablemates. "I'm like, *Hello?*" A titter ran through the place.

The man had taken on an alarming purplish color. His wife placed her hand on his arm to appeal for calm. He snarled, "You think you can just paw each other right in public. Just carry on like, like—"

Eggie shot a glance at the wife's hand. "And who's getting pawed now?" he said, recoiling in mock horror.

The man snatched his arm away, waved to Anthony for the check, and announced to his family, "Come on, we're not going to stay here for this"—he turned to Eggie—"because you disgust me."

Eggie looked wearily at him. "Honey, I don't even *notice* you." He flipped the man a snap of the fingers for emphasis, to the delight of his boothmates. Anthony politely assisted the family on their way, throwing the gay booth a complicit glance over his shoulder.

But Anthony's friends were not so pleased by his new absorption. Rain wasn't the only one giving him the message. He'd always hung out with the poets and drama club kids, so they weren't shocked; they just felt dumped. They were all headed off their separate ways come fall, and it seemed

Anthony wasn't honoring the last weeks of the circle. A couple of his friends would come into Angleton's and sit sullenly stirring their coffee, watching him. Billy Costa, who wrote sci-fi poems containing veiled ecological warnings, had passed many a school lunchroom hour with Anthony engaging in snide commentary. He had shielded Anthony from their gym teacher's taunts by becoming his partner for the wrestling unit. Billy was straight but hadn't minded the cozy quality of their tussling. Ron Alling had once been so upset after shooting a sparrow off a wire with his BB gun that he had cried telling Anthony about it. Anthony had scolded him at first, but then hugged him and comforted him. Now the code of coolness prevented these boys from reproaching Anthony for pulling away, but they knew where to find him, greet him with a slight chill, and subject him to their presence.

There was no logical reason why he needed to kick clear of these friends. They'd been each other's flying wedge through the stumble field of high school. But they'd also been part of an accommodation he'd made, settling for so little; he now saw that accommodation sliding into his wake, and them with it. It was as though, if being stuck had been his affliction, and he were in a twelve-step program to cure it, these friends would be the former associates he'd have to promise not to see.

Having one of these friends hanging heavily nearby made it harder for Anthony to maintain his onstage demeanor. Instead of arising naturally, fueled by the pleasant attentions of the clientele, his charisma needed to be generated in the face of this pouting from the sidelines. He accomplished this sunniness with at times a steely determination, but it did add a note of defiance to his voice when he would stop by the table of such a friend: "'Nother cup?" At least, he caught himself thinking one day, I hope he orders something often enough that Lattie doesn't make me move him along.

Rain, who had long—and with growing dejection—carried a torch for Anthony, was at the same time waging a chronic, all-fronts war with her born-again parents. On the most recent of the recurring occasions when she was driven to defend her moral compass at the kitchen table, she made the mistake of saying, "Listen, Mother, I have been trying to set up coming to the potluck again, as a favor to you. It's Anthony who hasn't agreed. Says he may have to work."

"It's what that place has become. They've gotten to him. That's just what they do," her mother informed her. "Recruit."

"Oh, give me a break, Mother. He's taking these shifts of his own free will. Nobody's recruiting anybody."

"Of course that's what you think, and what he thinks, too, because that's how brainwashing works. He doesn't even know it's happening. They're very tricky—flattering and cajoling, hunting for weaknesses, making it all look just as average—"

"It *is* average. That's the trouble, as far as I'm concerned," Rain moaned. "You've been watching too many of your videos. Don't you think I feel bad enough without you making him sound like an experimental rat?"

"He might as well be," her mother shot back. "I know his mom. I'm going to go see her and make sure she knows what's going on."

"Mother, don't you dare," said Rain. "This is none of your business. I can't believe I ever mentioned it to you."

"You listen to me, Kathleen," said her mother, knowing it infuriated Rain to be addressed by her real name. "This is the Lord's business."

SEVEN

OUTWARDLY, WESLEY Herndon's life continued as usual: shuttling to Washington to testify on telecommunications policy before a bunch of dozing senators; jumping the Concorde to Paris for a meeting of the *syndicat* with which he owned a tiny but fabulously valuable vineyard; ordering another round of the layoffs that, while merely sensible, the press persisted in calling "ruthless"; meeting with the governors whose support he would need for his regionalization plans. But privately, he was in turmoil.

Life decisions had been so much easier in his younger days, when a strident horniness had buzzed in the background of his every moment. He had only to add mastery of that to the list of other rigidities he had achieved, and to which he attributed his success. He had permitted himself, as a pressure relief valve, the regular company of an assortment of bouncers, bartenders,

masseurs, and personal trainers, all kept in a compartment
free of worrisome complications.

But now that he was fifty-two, his craving for release had
gone from a dependable hum to an intermittent eruption that,
once or twice a week, turned his thinking on its ear, and even
bedeviled his consideration of the Ferryman House. His mental state was enough to remind him of arguments he himself
had put forth among the armchairs of the Princeton Club as to
the unsuitability of women for top management, slaves to their
hormones and all that. On days when his libido was quiescent,
it was clear to Wesley that he had assembled precisely the correct life: a yacht of pedigree, a significant house, disassembled
and moved to a town of quiet cachet, then landscaped with
specimen plantings, furnished with important furniture, hung
with listed art. On those days, he agreed with his distinguished, silver-haired gay friends in Lyme that yes, it was a
relief to outgrow all that undignified panting and chasing
around; yes, far better to settle into the comfy embrace of dinner parties with people who were similarly advanced.

Then, when his habitual guard was down, horniness would
strike. Suddenly every hour not devoted to being around young
men was an intolerable waste of the all-too-finite number of
hours left to his sexual existence; Long Spit was fated to be the
scene of his last hurrah, and the Ferryman House must be acquired without another moment's delay. Several times, in the
grip of these seizures, he had driven the forty-five minutes to
Long Spit and idled past the sober, imposing edifice, his brain
zinging with the high-pitched certainty that there was nothing
so worthwhile in life as appraising men. Then he would cruise
the length of Front Street, spot some dazzling hottie (who
would be totally unaware of the role he was playing in a perfect
stranger's roller-coaster ride), shake his head with pleased
wonderment, and head home confirmed in his decision to call

Ray Hardman in the morning. The ensuing evening's over-heated fantasies would lead to solitary release, and by morning he would be restored to viewing a leap to Long Spit as the faintly ridiculous act of a panic-stricken dirty old man. The trouble was that the repeated pendulum swings left no residue of wisdom about which path was actually the better; it was as though his life were being steered by two different people.

Meeting Jim hadn't made it any simpler. The easy cama-raderie they enjoyed while driving around looking at houses, their lighthearted sexual play, the bonus of conversation in full sentences, revived not altogether welcome thoughts that some-thing deeper than a fling with a bouncer was not only possible, but also might offer rewards that outweighed the surrender of that autonomy he'd always guarded so stubbornly.

Jim had his own life, unlike all those feckless hunks who snapped alert only when they caught a whiff of Wesley's money. But Wesley was so unused to the myriad accommodations of rubbing one life up against another, he found himself at once drawn to and irritated by Jim's independent spirit. When squir-ing his usual escorts, he adopted a proprietorial stance, brook-ing no interference on which restaurant, which table, which wine, which paths of chat. Not only did this prevent the blight of tenderness, but indulging in high-handedness gave him a dependable frisson of arousal. With Jim, Wesley's instincts told him that this was all wrong. He permitted Jim a voice in their doings and experienced the novel pleasure of happening upon shared inclinations.

Wesley knew perfectly well that the sexual voltage was one-sided, an all-too-familiar state of affairs, given his taste in men. Yet Jim took such disarmingly zestful pleasure in showing off, and Wesley found his own lust so extraordinarily tweaked by this, that both were enjoying sex of unusual intensity, despite the slight physical remove. And when they were not engaging in this thrilling, if rather staged, activity, they enjoyed a cozy, affectionate rapport, even leading at times to falling asleep in each other's arms, something Wesley hadn't known since much younger days. In fact, Jim was so easygoing about touching, snuggling, and sex, it became less and less clear to Wesley why the customary barricades had to remain in place between the sexual realm and the rest of his waking life. What if sex, and the person you were having it with, or at least near to, were granted full admission into that less fevered domain? The notion was disturbing, radical, but Wesley was having trouble keeping it banished from his mind. Looking on the bright side, all these confusions reassured him that his lust circuitry was still well able to kick up a fuss. He could blunder along, every bit as sex-addled as a much younger man, and he linked this happy news with his discovery of Long Spit.

Betsy Haring had agreed to act as surrogate vulture and keep Jim posted on Polly Dickson's progress toward giving up her house. Wesley observed these proceedings with an amused, tolerant air, and couldn't seem to resist reminding Jim that, while Polly's house was nice for what it was, the Ferryman House was as close to a house of consequence as one could find in Long Spit. "Could be," Jim replied, "but I guess I just like the view better from the other place."

"The Ferryman House has got five bedrooms," Wesley boasted, instantly feeling silly and trying to cover it with a self-conscious leer to show he was mostly kidding.

Jim laughed. "That'll give you room to get into lots of trouble."

"Well, no, but—" Wesley checked himself.

Jim had already extended his holiday to three weeks, wreaking havoc with those Nebraska matrons who, after years of working up the nerve, now abruptly had their nips and tucks postponed. He'd booked with Helen Boothroyd for another visit over Labor Day weekend, and stood ready to zoom east any time Polly weakened. Betsy's facelift had gone from a premise for flirting to a real likelihood, and she'd introduced Jim to her friend Genevieve Pickman, a retired Broadway dancer who at the age of eighty had stopped going to the beach because she was so annoyed with her sagging thigh skin. Betsy made it clear that, if Jim were to relocate, he would find no shortage of clients on Signal Hill.

Despite his own comfortable circumstances, Jim was so un-used to wealth on the scale of Wesley's that he could just plain get a kick out of Wesley's profligacy without succumbing to the contagion of snobbism that infects so many hangers-on to the rich. His homespun urgings that Wesley be cautious about spending over three million dollars on a house "that's not even all that big" had the effect of egging Wesley on to demonstrate the importance of buying quality. At the same time, the fact that someone as impressively ensconced as Wesley could be seriously considering a move to Long Spit had the effect of egging Jim on to a much more thorough uprooting of his own life and practice. It was Wesley who first inched beyond fantasy.

The evening before, he had made one of his pilgrimages past the house. As he idled opposite the gates in reverie, an exceptionally handsome, barefoot young man padded up the lane in shorts and a sweatshirt, the Polo gym bag slung on his shoulder suggesting Wall Street to Wesley's eager imagination. While Wesley took in the play of the late, dappled light on the nicely squared-off calves, they made a right turn up the front walk of the very next house. He and those calves could be neighbors. Wesley could happily have devoted a lingering intermission to digesting this bit of fantasy fodder, but he was already late for what promised to be a soporific buffet at the home of a neighbor in Lyme, a watery-eyed, whispering old relic who had never done anything in her life but be the grand-daughter of the former ambassador to Persia. Not only had this obligation prevented Wesley from relieving his overload that evening, but the pairing of events threw things into what finally seemed an unmistakable perspective. With lust thus back in the driver's seat, his world-class-acquisitor side added to the urgency by generating speculation that the young man had actually bought the house next door, that the gay real es-tate rush was on.

"Salt Air Estates, Ray Hardman. May I help you?"

"Yes, hello. I don't know if you remember me: Wesley Hern-don. You—"

"Yes, of course, Mr. Herndon. The Ferryman house, Fog Bells, spoke to you, I believe."

"Well, actually, I'm considering a number of options. I won-der if it would be too much trouble for you to organize a look, just so I can have clearly in mind what it is we're talking about here."

"Oh, of course, nothing simpler," said Ray. "Let me make a couple of calls and get back to you." Simple this wasn't. First, he would have to locate one of the heirs by trying all the phone numbers—Palm Beach, London, Bermuda, Antibes—that he had scrawled in the margins of the family's Rolodex card over the years. Then he would hope to learn which heir could be bothered to deal with the pesky matter of Fog Bells, and only then would he come up against the family's famous tightfisted-ness and reluctance to have him involved. After a few days of threading his way through all of that, Ray managed to obtain permission to pick up a key from an attorney's office in West-erly.

Now, Wesley absently straightened the dust throw on the wing chair, adjusted the angle of its side table. He'd had his look; the house was dangerously perfect, his feet were sending down root hairs into the buttery floorboards of the upper hall, with its prospect down through mature oak limbs to the dock and cove.

Ray recognized the pregnant pause, knew not to push. "If you wouldn't mind, I've got some paperwork in the car for a meeting this afternoon. Do you want to just give me a wave when you're ready to leave? No hurry at all."

As though poked awake, Wesley said, "Oh, okay, that's fine."

SULLY'S HAD gone from being an uneasy interim watering hole used for lack of anyplace else to a fixture in the new scene. New arrivals learning the ropes would hear, "Oh, Sully's is cool, a little weird, a little boondocky, you got your old straight regulars on their stools near the TV and the boys camping all around them, but it's pretty much live and let live." Mickey Sullivan was past being shocked by the new clientele, and actually appreciated the energy level they brought to the place. With the Crab Hole nearing completion, he was a bit surprised to find himself worried that this spike in his otherwise uneventful life might be ending.

The old regulars continued to question the locals who were working on the Crab Hole, taking off from there to satisfy their curiosity about gay life in general by interrogating whichever of the gay boys happened to be inclined to act as cultural emissaries. Lou Russell, a retired fisherman, had been one of the first to overcome his reserve and distaste, and now took pride in being the worldly-wise sophisticate, explaining things to his old friends, turning to his gay guide of the moment as though to say, Am I getting it right?, then back to his friend with a shake of his head: Unbelievable, didn't I tell you? Word of mouth had spread among the blue-collar set even beyond the village and there were a few new straight faces showing up, most just wanting to have a look at the new wrinkle. Some had less harmless intentions, as became clear one night when the talk turned to glory holes.

Jeb Harkin, a local mason and tile setter, was working on the part of the Crab Hole to be known as the Gents' Lounge. "I guess you know it's basically a huge men's room, pissoirs, shitters, the whole thing, but with a full bar," he said to the knot of regulars. "But the weirdest part is, I'm tiling the stalls, you know, for the cans, off up this blind alley, and they want six-and-a-half-inch holes in the partitions at just about eye level—when you're sitting." He shook his head. "You tell me what that's all about. I mean do they want to watch each other crap or what?"

"No, it's actually kinkier than that," said a voice. The regulars all turned. Standing just along the bar were a couple of burly young men with matching #1 buzz cuts, in jeans and flannel shirts with the sleeves torn off. "Sorry to eavesdrop," said one, "but hey, if you really want to know . . ." A nervous murmur went through the regulars. "Rusty," said one of the burly men, offering his hand to Jeb. Jeb grabbed for his beer, swigged, and folded his arms around it. Rusty shrugged and nodded toward his companion. "This is Steve."

"Yeah, it's not so mysterious," said Steve. "In fact, nothing about the Crab Hole, or any place like that, is very mysterious. It's about getting your rocks off." At this, the regulars recoiled as if a skillet had spat grease. Then, as one, they tugged on their beers and leaned in for more.

"See," said Rusty, "we queers have a knack for homing in on the essence of a sex-op, stripping away all the nonessentials." He had a provocative air; a tattoo of entwined thorns encircled his massive biceps.

"The voltage without the baggage," said Steve.

"We can get away with it 'cause we're all men," Rusty went

on, "so there isn't this, like, other half of the human race forever waiting to pounce on us and say we're crass, unfeeling."

Here another gay voice piped up, "That's right. All crass, unfeeling boors looking for a no-strings moment: line forms over here." A laugh went through the gay crowd. The regulars glanced at each other, some amused, some disapproving, some both.

Lou Russell pushed forward, "W'now, I don't know about the rest of us, but you lost me back there a ways. What exactly are those holes for?"

"The glory holes?" said Rusty with a cheeky grin. He took a step forward, made a circle with his two hands in front of his crotch, and mimed thrusting through it. A sharp crackle of consternation shot through the group. "That's fuckin' disgusting." "Fuckin' pervs." "Jesus, I'm outta here . . ."

Rusty stood his ground, his cocky smile a bit uneasy. "Hey, you asked me!" he protested. The gay side of the room was now buzzing as well. "Probably drunk." "Fuckin' idiot, this is not smart." A few supporters weighed in: "Hey, the place isn't being built for them." "If they want to ask questions . . ."

"Look, here's the point," said Rusty, sensing he needed to calm things. "When it comes to getting off, a lot of guys are just totally into one thing, whatever it might be, whether it's size, or—"

Here the gay side of the room erupted. "*Whether* it's size?" "Of course it's size! What else?" Laughs all around.

"No, let me finish!" said Rusty. He turned to the now huddled regulars with a smile. "You see my point. Anyway, let's say it's size. With the glory holes, you don't have to waste an entire evening of your weekend, fancy dinner out, the whole thing, just to find out that bulge was socks in his shorts. Two seconds and you know whether he makes the grade. You don't even have to worry about what he looks like."

Here Steve spoke up. "And the maze in the back? Comes from the same thing. I mean we're all obsessed with finding somebody younger than we are, which of course is logically impossible. Sort of like a giant collapsed Ponzi scheme that just won't quit? Guaranteed frustration. So then we had to figure a way around it—the pitch-black maze—where the receding hairline, the crow's feet don't matter. Touch is all that counts; if the body is holding together okay you can still be a star. And if it isn't—you know, if the paunch is winning—you can still grab boys who normally would never let you near them."

Sometime during this exchange three men had come in and now stood near the door, surveying the scene. Two of them were big, beefy, and gave off a dense, blurry malevolence. One had on a Raiders cap and coveralls from a discount tire shop; the other, with curly hair and a few missing teeth, had on a greasy denim vest, with a buck knife on his belt. The third, in a Road Runner T-shirt, was a stringy-haired, wiry little mutt with a pinched, weasely face. The knot of regulars pulled away slightly from Rusty and Steve; a few turned to leave or pretended interest in the chicken wings commercial on the TV.

A slight, androgynous young man who had been listening from the gay side now stepped forward. Oblivious to the arrival of the three men by the door, he edged closer to Jeb Harkin and Lou Russell and spoke in a more serious tone, with surprising determination. "I'm Andy. I'm a filmmaker, so I'm interested in all sides here. What you've got to understand is that, I know a lot of this sounds gross, but what we've done is figure out how to find each other, find exactly the guy you're looking for, I mean, okay, it sounds shallow. But we didn't go through all the bullshit of coming out to turn around and play by straight rules." His audience grew restless at being lectured, but he persisted. "So, if you happen to choose to, you can be into whatever, that you'd usually be too inhibited to admit to. Say you like to be watched, maybe you like to be touched but not to touch, you know, like, don't give a shit about the other guy, but there are guys who are into that and it would be a needle in a haystack to find somebody, you know, in the dating scene, who happens to fit with your weirdness?" By now Lou and Jeb were sideways to Andy, edging away. He rattled on, "So, anyway, the gay scene gives you all these different short-cuts . . ."

Lou indicated to Andy with a cock of his head toward the back that it was time to drop this topic. The room had grown slightly quieter; an animated mouthwash commercial dominated the sound. The two groups shifted uneasily, gradually turning their backs on each other.

"Andy, how's your drink?" called a voice, and Andy retreated into the gay crowd. The three men started toward the bar; a path opened for them. They ordered and stood with their beers, saying little. The curly-haired one looked already far gone; his puffy-faced, slit-eyed gaze suggested a creature controlled not by a brain but by an on-off switch. For the next half-hour, the atmosphere in the place struggled back to a semblance of normal, though with no more chat across the cultural gap. Then Andy headed out the door alone.

Immediately the curly-haired man set his bottle down with a thud and started for the door with a slow, bow-legged walk. His friends looked at each other, drained their beers, and followed.

Andy was halfway across the parking lot when he heard the beer-thickened voice behind him: "So, you're looking for a fuck, are you?"

Andy glanced over his shoulder. "No, I don't think so." He picked up his pace. "You're not my type."

"What the fuck you mean? You ain't even seen my big dick

yet, you little cocksucker. Thought that's all you needed." The other two men were fanning out to head Andy off. He turned, at bay.

"Listen, I don't want anything to do with you. Get it?" He started back toward the bar. The man grabbed his arm and spun him around.

"Yeah, but I want somethin' to do with you, don't I. I want to plant my big old smelly dick in that girlie face of yours, you scrawny little faggot." He yanked Andy toward the bigfoot pickup truck nearby.

"Get your fucking hands off me!" Andy struggled until a blow to the side of his head sent him staggering. The weasely smaller man had come up behind him.

"Easy there, Carl!" bellowed the curly-haired man. "Don't want to mess up that pretty face. Got plans for that face. Here, let's just get him arranged." The two grappled with Andy until they had him pinioned with his back against the side of the truck. The third man was hanging back. "Goddammit, Lester, can't you see we need a hand? Pull your fuckin' weight for once. Don't you want a turn rippin' up that pretty little ass?" Lester took one of Andy's arms. Andy was still thrashing and twisting when Carl brought a knee up into his groin. He crumpled and hung gasping between the other two men. "Ah, that's better," said the ringleader. "Let him to his knees. Just the way we want him. Oh boy, I'm startin' to get excited now. How 'bout you, Carl?"

"I ain't no faggot, Dave," said Carl. "Why don't we just stomp him and clear the fuck out."

"Who you callin' a faggot, you little shit?" said Dave, swinging unsteadily at Carl with his free hand. "Don't you know these little fairy butts are fuckin' tight as a fuckin' sweet sixteen? But first . . ." He turned to Andy. "Now you hold still, hear?" He snapped Andy's head back by the hair and flashed his blade. "Don't even think about bitin' down, hear?"

Suddenly headlights played across the parking lot. The three men closed in around Andy. Dave moved the knife closer to his throat. It was a black Jeep, giant tires, with blacked-out windows and a brace of driving lights on the rollbar. Its headlights lit the four men for a split second, then turned away. Andy felt the men press in on him. The Jeep seemed to be parking when suddenly it swung around to point directly at the scene.

"I'm gettin' outta here," said Lester, and took off between the cars.

"Aw, what the fuck," muttered Dave, squinting into the headlights. "Just probby wanna join in."

Now the brace of driving lights came on as well; the doors opened. Carefully, Andy turned his head, trying to see. In the glare, he could only make out the silhouettes of two huge, rough-looking men. His terror notched up to where he began to depart from his body.

"What seems to be the problem here?" said one of them. Andy snapped alert; was that a civilized voice?

"No fuckin' problem," Dave growled. "Just havin' a little fun." He made a clumsy attempt to hide Andy.

"Does your friend there think it's fun?" said Derek. Andy saw his chance, wrenched one arm free of Carl, dropped to the ground, and rolled under the truck with Dave still hanging on to his wrist.

With Dave and Carl bent over, scrabbling under the truck, Derek and Tracy came in swinging. Despite years of meting out mock torture, Derek had never in his life aimed a blow for real. The demand of the instant was liberating: finally a use for all that excess strength. He brought a knee up into Dave's face, rocking him nearly upright. For a split second Dave wobbled, squinting in confusion as though trying to remember why this man was upset with him; then Derek slammed him in the gut and brought him down like a sack of cement. Meanwhile, Carl tried to bolt, but Tracy snagged him by the T-shirt, whirled him around, and caught him with an elbow in the belly that dropped him, slumped against the front wheel, vomiting all over himself. It was all over in a few seconds, but there was time, in the middle of it, for the village police cruiser to glide past, inspect the parking lot with its searchlight, and move on.

"You okay?" said Tracy, peering under the truck and offering Andy a hand.

"I think so," said Andy. A bruise was seeping onto his cheek-bone.

"What'll we do with them?" said Derek, his voice still vibrating with adrenaline. Dave let out a moan. Derek snarled, "You fuckin' keep quiet!" and gave him a savage kick.

"Easy," said Tracy. "Watch 'em. I think I've got just the idea." He went back to the Jeep and returned with a small black leather pouch.

"You're a genius," said Derek.

"What's that?" Andy asked.

"Tracy's travel sling."

"I may need a new one after this," said Tracy. "At least the handcuffs are machine washable."

Word now reached inside the bar, and the patrons streamed out for a look. Rusty and Steve came over to help manhandle Dave and Carl into place, and Derek and Tracy bound them with the nylon webbing, threading it through the mud-caked back wheel of Dave's truck. Andy sat by, trying to get over the shakes, two friends hovering at his side. A few minutes later, two state police cruisers pulled up. As the troopers took state-ments and snapped photos, loading the offenders into the back of a cruiser, nobody much noticed another flash going off. The bar crowd drifted into two groups, looking on, nearly silent.

"SO, DID you look for your father's suit?" Rain asked.

Phone in hand, Anthony headed for the upstairs hall closet. "Uh, no, not yet. I'll do it right now." They'd agreed on seersucker for this potluck.

"I don't mean for you to drop everything—I was just wondering. It's in four days." Over the phone, she heard the flipping of hangers.

"I don't see it. He must have come and got it when he left for Florida."

"Probably. Seersucker is *so* Boca Raton. So what shall we do instead? Pants with whales on them?" Rain sounded a bit exasperated.

"Um, I dunno—anything, I guess," said Anthony. There was a pause.

"Wow, I'm just bowled over by your enthusiasm," said Rain.

"Look, I'm into it, I know we always end up having fun. But you've got to admit, it's not the first thing either of us would choose to sign up for. So don't require that I also act excited." There was another pause.

"You know what? Let's forget it." Rain was brisk. "You're right, making fun of it was a hoot a couple of times, but—"

"No, wait, we'll do it," said Anthony.

"Nope. Executive decision. Speak to you soon, I hope." Rain hung up.

BART CONNORS couldn't have been more pleased. Long Spit's first gay-bashing provided just the hard news hook he needed to give some heft to the first issue of the *Sand Flea*, due out the next week. He'd been sitting alone at Sully's, brooding that the slim weekly's first edition was shaping up more like a suburban shopper's rag than a gay newspaper, when the first voices shouted that something was going on out in the parking lot. He'd headed out the door, feeling in the camera pocket of his cargo shorts.

"GAY-BASHING HORROR: Beginning of a Reign of Terror?" whispered the front page, over a photo of Rusty, Steve, Derek, and Tracy towering over the two sullen figures on the pavement, with the troopers crouched next to them. "Gay men have flocked to this picture-perfect New England village," Bart's story began, "lured by its white picket fences and gentle sea breezes, blind to the evil that lurks just beneath the privileged surface, the evil that always waits to remind gay men that we are hated, feared, and vulnerable." Bart missed no hot buttons. He recounted Andy's exchange in the bar and described him as a "fearless beacon of free speech." Dave Carber and Carl Dietz were the sort of "alcohol-crazed crypto-Nazis who explode in a paroxysm of retribution" whenever they heard brave words like Andy's.

At the scene, he had asked around about who had called the state police. Lou Russell volunteered, off the record, that Jim Priestly, the village constable, always did that when he came upon anything more dangerous than a yacht club mom locked out of her Land Cruiser. This gave Bart room for a blast at "the most pernicious sort of selective policing, where the marginalized in our society come at the end of the line for law enforcement protection." He ended by providing his mobile phone number, both as a hot line for tips about Lester's whereabouts and as a contact number for his proposed "Vigil Against Violence." All in all, a bravura performance of the sort that had long ago landed him out of mainstream journalism.

Other stories included one about the progress on the Crab Hole, "an ambitious, multiple-venue, sex-positive action bar, poised to rattle the cage of arrow-straight Long Spit." Leo Robbia's attorney had told Bart about Sam Jenkins's Community Decency Committee and the petition it was circulating to be presented at the pending liquor-permit hearings, so Bart headed a companion story: "Bigots in Bid to Stomp Rights," and informed readers about how "the public hearing process is being perverted to impose this fascist ideology on the village."

The piece on the first tea dance at the Ocean, "driving out the ghosts of Bing Crosby and Dinah Shore from those sagging porches," seemed in fact to have missed the actual near-collapse of the porch. Bart interviewed Marcia, who chirped innocently about "a new heyday for the old place." The story on the cruise ship's visit verged on direct promotion, listing dates of future sailings and phone numbers.

Mostly, though, the *Sand Flea*'s few pages were filled with ads, which Bart had offered at introductory rates to get things going. A quarter page simply announced SALT AIR ESTATES in stately lettering. Dot's Yankee Gulch offered "distinctive accessories, from the rustic to the refined, for people who know who they are and where they're going," and Stevie Lund plugged the Beachcomber's "racy novelties." Derek and Tracy had convinced Helen Boothroyd to put TVs and VCRs in her rooms, and to mention them in her ad for the Lilac Bush. She had protested, "I'm not sure why they need one in every room—after all, there's one in the parlor—but, okay . . ."

Sam Jenkins wouldn't let Nancy place an ad for the Gull and Rose. He'd been making life increasingly miserable for her gay guests, one night even using the dining room to host a meeting of born-again Christians he wanted to enlist for his Decency Committee. Nancy and Sam were growing more and more estranged as word of his antics spread among the visitors and she watched the early summer surge in business turn into a slump.

Soon *Sand Flea* racks appeared outside the Beachcomber, Frankie's Slice by the Sea, Yankee Gulch, Sully's, and the yo-gurt window. Lattie Teachout declined to buy an ad or, at first, even to allow a rack of papers outside Angleton's, but there were so many requests that she gave in. Bart wasn't making any money yet, but at least he was now positioned, in case the opportunity arose, to make a little trouble.

EIGHT

BART SAT in his back booth at Angleton's, happy to see people here and there perusing the *Sand Flea*. His knee jigged steadily under the table with the familiar jitters, both dreaded and addictive: how to fill next week's edition. When he'd first started coming in, Lattie had grumped to Anthony about how he hogged a booth for half the day, rattling away on his battered laptop with the "Shit Happens" bumper sticker. But Anthony detected the hair trigger cocked beneath Bart's breezy facade; he never brought the check until asked.

Anthony made his way up the aisle with the coffee carafe, fine-tuning his clientele with refills, smiles, touches on the shoulder for some favored regulars. Eggie was holding court, this morning with an especially partied-out crew. "Yeah, I'm pretty serious about foreskins," he was saying as Anthony leaned across to top up mugs. "I'd like to find one I could blow up like a balloon . . . or, no, how about one you could pull on over your head, like a snood." Anthony clucked, shook his head, returned an approving glance from one of the others with a slow flick of one eyebrow, and moved on. His flirtations had grown markedly more overt. So far there had been no down side; he put out of his mind any thoughts of what he would do if someone called his bluff.

"Can I heat this up for you, Mr. Connors?"

"Sure, why not," said Bart, letting his glance slide down along Anthony. "You know, what this place needs is a decent blintz." Anthony gave him a low-cost If you say so look. Bart's cell phone rang. "Yeah what. . . . Hey, Leo. . . . Yeah, I know; it's Thursday night, I think, the hearing. . . . No, I think they let you know right that night." Anthony ambled back down the aisle. "Yeah, I heard, what's it called? Decency Committee or some bullshit? Probably do something on it. . . . Oh yeah? . . . The old queen with the shop? . . . Yeah, like old team photos . . . That's a pisser, I'll tell you—outing was invented for that kinda ass-hole. . . . Yeah, I'll sniff around. . . . Okay, buddy." He called after Anthony, "Hey, could I get a check?"

HOLLIS PACED at the back of the shop. There had not been one customer all morning, and he knew from his continuing negotiations with Ellington Hazelett that this was the last day of Florian's holiday in Long Spit, Hollis's last fix of gazing through the telescope at what for him had come to encompass, in one buttery-skinned column of maleness, all one needed to know of mankind. His sandwich was ready in the fridge, and he was champing to be at his eyepiece; but he knew that Florian would not appear atop his dune until two o'clock, as though the burning rays were switched off by a timer at that hour. Hollis took pleasure in Florian's strict routines, more evidence that they were soulmates. But just now time had ground to a halt.

At ten of two, he flipped the sign in the window from "Open" to "Closed" and headed up the lane. He fended off melancholy; after all it was perfectly ridiculous to indulge in melodrama over an object so remote it might as well be on TV. In a fateful instant, however, this train of thought proved treacherous, leading quickly to Hmm, he doesn't have to be so remote; there don't have to be any optics between us; I could just go for a walk, look straight at him, say hello. We *have* met, after all. Normally Hollis would summarily have quashed so whimsical a notion, but his emotional recipe of the moment embraced the piquant flavor and he made a right turn toward the beach. At the same time, Bart, on his way to the shop for an exploratory interview, had seen him locking up, and was trailing behind him when he changed course. Something about Hollis's demeanor struck Bart as a bit odd, as though he were sleepwalking with his eyes open. Rather than accosting him, Bart decided to follow at a distance.

From the moment Hollis veered toward the beach, his brain unleashed a tug-of-war with his knotted stomach in the center. The calming voice saying You can turn around anytime it doesn't feel right vied with an animal hiss through clenched teeth on each breath, emanating from a wordless core that had waited too long for control to give up now that victory was near. The worried voice saying Just what exactly do you think you're going to do when you get there? was drowned out by a thrumming certainty that, having once been in the same room with Florian, having shaken his strong, veined hand, he now would be close to him again. The reflexive concerns about who might see him, what they might think, were for the moment neutralized by an eerie sense that the imperative of his mission made him as irresistible, invulnerable, invisible as the suck of the moon on the seas.

The day's breeze had just gotten up from the southwest, stirring the hot, hazy air, darkening the glassy waters of the sound, setting sailors to unfurling canvas and feeling the day's first surge of power. The first quarter-mile of sand, just beyond the Pequot Beach Club, was sparsely dotted with beachgoers, all straight, none local, who may have glanced at the tall, slightly stooped man, may have wondered why he was striding so purposefully through the sand in his khakis, sensible shirt, and old but well-polished dress shoes. He had the look of someone not only unused to walking on a beach, but unused to hurrying. And look, there came a second one, also trudging along in street clothes . . . foreign tourists, down from the casino for the afternoon?

Hollis was overtaken by a chubby, middle-aged man jogging in full Lycra, with the gait of a stock clerk hurrying to the front of the pharmacy. He was irritated that someone should think it appropriate to huff and sweat so in public.

He passed through the mixed border zone and into what had become the gay part of the beach, stretching all the way to the ruins of the World War II artillery emplacements at the end. The sight of more and more men draped over each other and sunbathing in provocative poses escalated the warning bells, the stubborn pushing on, the knotted gut. He noted the mechanical, oddly unreal way some of them moved, thrusting themselves up on the balls of their feet at each step to throw calf muscles into sharp flex, throwing their upper bodies into rock-hard spasm to pass a buddy a diet soda. The tawdry explicitness of it raised his every Yankee hackle. Three men came running in step along the water's edge, naked but holding baseball caps over their privates. They were chanting some

sort of boot camp gibberish in unison and, every time they en-
countered someone, they would stop, give a short, rhythmic
cheer, expose themselves for one beat, and then take off again.
Hollis turned away to present his back as they passed, as unavailable for their humiliations as a tortoise with its head
stowed. Then, glancing ahead, he gasped at his first sight of
Florian.

He was just ascending his dune, scrambling up the sandy
slope, long, sinewy legs kicking out sand behind. At the crest,
he stood up, adjusting his sarong and taking a first glance
about. For an instant, Hollis stopped dead, as though a leghold
trap had slammed onto his ankle. What on earth could he have
been thinking of? There was nowhere to hide. Even at a hundred yards he could see the broad, flat planes of Florian's chest
heaving with the exertion of the climb, could see the cross of
shadow demarcating the quadrants of his chiseled front. He
glanced back in the direction of his house; Bart, two hundred
feet behind, paused and gazed out to sea. Hollis could make
out his roof and, through the trees, his porch. He peered back
at the safety of it, torn, like a small child who suddenly awak-
ens from play and looks up, searching the edge of the play-
ground for Mama. But stronger forces impelled him onward.

Florian was adjusting his sarong to reveal precisely the desired hint of the twin furrows converging from his hipbones
into his groin. As he did so, he slowly turned this way and that,
assessing the choreography of certain muscle groups, barely
aware of the distant figure he was drawing toward himself as
surely as the star drew the Three Kings.

It was time for Hollis to leave the water's edge and angle
across the beach toward the ridge of dune. A defeated inner
voice was whimpering that he could also carry straight on past
and spare himself this exquisite awkwardness, but no. He
veered away from the hard-packed wet margin, immediately

filling his shoes with hot sand. He considered taking the shoes off and carrying them, but an image of his sallow, yellow-nailed feet intervened. The closer he got to his destination, the more pronounced was Florian's altitude.

Now who, Florian wondered, is this tottering toward me—a bird-watcher? A vigilante of some sort? Suddenly he placed the face and sang out, "Oh, it's you, Mr.—I'm sorry—with the slavery collection!" A few nearby heads turned. Hollis hated a scene. Still too far away to reply without hollering, he gave a tight little wave and picked up his pace.

He arrived at the base of the dune, a bit out of breath, and squinted up at Florian. "Yes, Hollis, Wynbourne, out for a walk, thought I recognized you . . ." (A pathetic lie—he'd clearly been on a beeline.) What now? This was unsatisfactory—he needed to be closer. Dignity to the winds—Hollis had surrendered to the same autopilot that guides people who are called onstage to assist magicians. He started to scramble up the steep slope, thrashing in place, sliding back, plunging his hands into the sand for balance.

"You certainly dress strangely for the beach," said Florian from on high. "Here, let me pop down to you." With that he cavorted down the dune face in a series of leaps and slides to end up, gleaming with sweat and sun oil, at Hollis's side.

"My perch," he said, with a coquettish tilt of the head toward the dune. "How have you been? Ellington tells me you are still 'deep in discussions,' whatever that means." He offered the side of his face and puckered up to kiss the air. Hollis had come this far; he might as well make the most of it. He placed both hands on Florian's upper arms and drew himself close enough for a quick peck on the jawbone.

"Oop! Aren't we friendly!" chirped Florian, touching at the spot.

"Sorry," said Hollis in confusion. "You just looked so . . ."

His hand floated aloft, vaguely in the direction of Florian's lean, muscled torso.

"Don't be sorry, honey, and don't be silly. Go ahead and touch me if you want." Florian cocked his upper body back slightly, throwing it into even more splendid relief. "I'm a total exhibitionist," he confided, "so it's perfectly fine."

Hollis was utterly spellbound; he wanted to freeze this moment, to imprint it, to brand his soul with it—this, the destination of his last forty years. He stared at the breathtaking sight, his mouth ajar, head swaying back and forth, darting glances into Florian's hazel eyes for reassurance, wondering which part of the glistening expanse to touch first. Some vestige of manners surviving the overload told him he should speak. "You have such a beautiful body. . . . I—"

"Oh, ain't it just! No, just kidding. I'm terrible. I mean . . ." Then, with mock bashfulness: "Why, thank you." He stretched his arms into the air and came to rest with his hands clasped behind his head, a naughty grin on his face.

"When I was a boy," murmured Hollis, "it was always tummies I dreamed of touching." He aimed his fingertips as though he were experimenting with a missile launcher.

"Ooh my, our lives are flashing before our eyes now," said Florian with a chuckle that vibrated every muscle down his belly. "Do go on." He batted his eyes.

"It's always been just your sort of body . . . slim and strong . . . that I've been . . ." Hollis's voice trailed off as his fingertips made contact with the velvety tummy.

"Slim and proud? You betcha!" said Florian, moving languidly under the touch. "I figure the American public spends like three and a half billion dollars a year to look like me, so there must be something okay with it."

Hollis drew his hand down the torso, tracing the orderly muscles, arranged like marimba bars under chamois.

Florian pressed at the front of his sarong. "Gracious, look out! You could get a girl excited!"

A safe distance away, Bart settled on the sand and adjusted his zoom.

———

WESLEY WAS getting nowhere with this conversation. For weeks, Walker and James, his best friends in Lyme, had been receding into a sulk of abandonment over his talk of Long Spit and the Ferryman House. He'd finally decided to take the bull by the horns, invite them for dinner, and talk it out. But it had turned into a tag-team event. Walker, an elegant retired banker, hammered away from the snob's high ground, while James sneaked in disguised as a caring friend to deliver the sour-grape bombs.

"About a month after you move," Walker was saying, "when you've walked down that tacky Front Street a couple of dozen times, and had all those ditzy airheads ignore you because you're too ancient, you'll be wondering what you could have been thinking of. It's bad enough that it's come down to you basically hiring your fun, when you should just act your age, stop trying to dress mutton up as lamb, kidding yourself that you're still in the scene. . . . Honestly. But these guys you cajole into your bed with fancy meals are just as happy if that bed is in Lyme, thank you very much. Stick around here, you better, so in a few years—I hope it's just a few—when you come to your senses and let go of it, you won't be stuck in that no-account place, which by the way will probably keep getting tackier and tackier every year those boys work on it, if P-town is anything to go by."

"I'm not paying for Jim," Wesley replied in a wounded voice.

"Oh, that one," James chimed in. "He's another thing. Look, he likes you and you two have fun, but he *is* twenty years younger than you, cute, professional. If he moves east, he is going to be high on a few people's lists. Not to be mean, but you two are not going to be riding into the sunset."

Walker persisted. "Why you would want to, at a time when, for your own mental health, you should be trying to calm down—"

"Yeah, getting a hobby," James put in, with a wry smile.

"Why you would think," Walker continued, "that it makes sense to plant yourself in a brand-new ghetto where you'll just be tormented by all these temptations."

"That don't even know you exist," added James.

"I mean, spare yourself." Walker pulled a shrimp from his paella, peeled it with a deft twirl, and popped it in his mouth. "And not just on the emotional front . . ." He licked his fingertips. "God knows we're are as fickle as they come when it comes to our haunts, but if this so-called new gay scene is any more than a flash in the pan, you'll be seeing all the old families putting all those drafty old shingle piles on the market at once, and you'll be marooned with your white elephant in a glut of mansions that'll take years to sell off."

"Jeez, give it a rest, guys." Wesley worked at keeping a smile on his face. "Can I help it if I prefer feeling alive? This town is like a mausoleum. Call me shallow. Fine. I know they don't know I exist. I'm over that. I just plain feel better around young men. The sight of one flawless lad is enough to put a whole day in the Good column."

"Good God," Walker said wearily, "and this is the man with eight thousand employees."

James took over. "What about Blaine, in Boston? Weren't you having fun with him, didn't you say? I mean, he's a little closer to your own—"

"Oh, Christ, look," Wesley said. "All right, he drives a black Porsche, but it's just camouflage. We go to an art opening, then go sit somewhere and eat some four-pound pastry till it gets dark out. This is not my future, I hope."

"So, okay," Walker said, "maybe not him, but you're a person of substance, you need to be with someone who's done something in his life besides shave his balls."

Wesley got up to clear the table. "Okay—that's Jim. But we're just going in circles."

AMBLING UP her long, curving driveway, sifting through the mail, Betsy came upon a letter from Wesley's attorneys. Through the fog of legalese, she detected that they were interested in whether the Long Spit Landmarks Preservation Commission might extend the Signal Hill Historic District to encompass the Mussel Cove neighborhood. She got on the phone to Ray.

"If I thought it was just a new ally moving to town, somebody to help me fight off the vinyl siding, I'd be all for it," she said. "But it has just a whiff of barging in about it, you know?"

"Oh, his sort always poke around for ways to lock in value," said Ray, "as though they're not already insulated enough from the ups and downs of the world."

"How serious do you think he is?"

"I'd say he had that faraway look in his eye when I showed it to him. And by the way, as we speak Polly Dickson is entertaining an offer from that other one, the plastic surgeon. And—"

"Well, well, aren't things moving along. . . ." Betsy absently pinched at the skin on her neck.

"Yes, it seems Polly was having tea at Angleton's with Bertha and overheard someone in the next booth talking about—well, actually, she wouldn't even say what they were talking about, but I played twenty questions and as near as I can tell it was foreskins."

"Ooh." Betsy's dismay was tinged with eagerness. "I'm seeing it. . . ."

"And then, they're walking back to her car and she sees, in Stevie's window, an inflatable naked man."

"That Stevie, always cutting edge."

"After I talked to her, I had to go down and see for myself. It is a hoot. I may have to get one for Herb's birthday. 'Working orifices' it says on the box. Anyway, I guess it was the last straw for Polly. Now if we can just get a contract signed before she calms down."

"Ray, honey?"

"Yeah, Bets."

"This is fun, isn't it? This old town needed stirring up."

"Yeah, I might even skim a living out of it."

ONE DAY near the beginning of August, unusually chilly, not a beach day, Wendell came into Angleton's, once again accompanied by a young man. By now Anthony was on chatting terms with a good number of the regulars, but somehow he still held a special regard for Wendell as the first man who had penetrated his working veneer with a personal word.

He waited on the two with just the slightest coldness. He knew it was absurd, but Wendell had taken on a certain importance to him and he found sharing him disagreeable. Despite all the unmistakable attention Anthony was now drawing each day, and his outward aplomb in handling it, he still regarded Wendell as his connection point to the gay world, should he ever want to connect.

After they had finished their chowder and had dawdled over

their coffee for a while, Anthony came by their booth. "I don't mean to rush you, you can stay as long as you like, but if that's going to be it, I'll just leave your check now—I'm finishing up my shift. Will that be okay?"

Wendell looked up distractedly. "No, no, that's fine." The other man looked away and down, his eyes red-rimmed. Abruptly he slid out of the booth and slung his backpack on his shoulder. "Well, I guess I should be going anyway."

Anthony put up both hands and backed away. "Sorry, I didn't mean to—"

"No," said the man, "it's all right." He glanced questioningly at the check. Wendell reached for it and gave him a brief, searching look. The man turned and walked quickly toward the door.

Anthony hovered a second in confusion. "Well, just whenever you're ready . . ." Wendell nodded without looking up.

About ten minutes later, when Anthony was ready to leave, Wendell was still sitting alone. Anthony grabbed the coffee carafe and approached him. "One last? Before I head out?"

Wendell looked up at him. His face was composed but looked close to spilling, like a brimming glass, its liquid swollen with surface tension. "Would you join me?"

Anthony rocked back on his heels. "Uh, I don't usually . . ." He indicated the carafe in his hand, as though that were the problem. "Uh, sure. Let me get a cup."

As he passed the cash register, he said to Lattie, "Um, I'm just going to hang out with that guy—he's sort of a friend—for a while." She looked at him as if to say, Why should I care?

As soon as Anthony had settled in the booth, Wendell let out a sigh and said, with false cheer, "So, you're headed off to college, huh? Pretty soon now?"

"Um, yeah." Anthony nodded too vigorously. "In about three weeks—just to Conn College, though, not far."

"Just up the road from where I live."

"Oh really?" said Anthony, even though he already knew that, had already spent many an hour daydreaming about various chance encounters that might be in the offing.

They continued with a desultory exchange about freshman courses, Wendell's stillborn dissertation, where to get pizza in New London, but it petered out quickly, leaving an awkward silence. Anthony pushed with his finger at the little pile of sugar he had spilled on the table. He stole a glance at Wendell, the first instant he had ever looked into the eyes of a man without dodging what he might find there.

"That guy who was here," he heard himself saying. "It's none of my business, but . . . was he somebody, uh, important to you?"

Wendell sighed again. "Was. Yeah." For a moment he stared blankly at his coffee, as though weighing whether to admit Anthony to this realm. Then he looked up, directly into Anthony's face. Anthony saw that his eyes were welling; deep-rooted shyness wrestled with the unmistakable certainty that he must not look away.

When Wendell spoke his voice was shaky. "Sometimes you just know . . . it can be so hard . . . but you just have to let go. . . ." He dabbed at his eyes with a napkin. "Sorry, I—"

"No, no, it's okay." Anthony felt genuinely sorry for Wendell, and surprised at himself, considering he barely knew him. Even more unexpected was an undeniable sense of cold satisfaction, an awareness that Wendell was once again available. He sat momentarily paralyzed by the tumbling together of conflicting feelings: unaccustomed sympathy, opportunity and all the risk it entailed, the first stirrings of something beyond a crush, panic at being on a threshhold, feeling pushed, an instinctive sense of Wendell's kindness, trustworthiness, and need.

When Anthony spoke, his voice had lost its usual sardonic edge, sounded almost as though he were musing to himself. "I guess I've never . . . guess I've never let myself . . . you know, care . . . about anyone really, but especially about a guy . . . like you, I mean like you are, with this guy. . . . I feel kind of funny, like I hardly know you, but I want to—comfort you." And so, after a lifetime of stifling every impulse to touch another male, Anthony permitted his hand to glide in low—in full view of Lattie, if she happened to turn around—and come to rest on Wendell's hand, and give it a gentle squeeze, and remain there, warm and limp. The action pumped a blush that included his chest, yanked his gaze floorward, but by an act of will he left his hand in place. Wendell stared at his averted eyes with a mixture of sadness and wonder. Both were so lost in the moment that neither was aware that Rain had stalked up the aisle and now stood looking down at them. She cleared her throat, flicking a cold glance at the two hands recoiling into their respective laps.

"Good, you're still here," she said. "Didn't know if I'd catch you. Just thought you'd like to know, my mom's sitting at your mom's kitchen table, talkin' God."

"What?" Anthony's tone was back to teenage-warpath.

"I tried to stop her, but she's, like, in a zone? Convinced that your brain is being reprogrammed by Satanist perverts." She glanced at Wendell. "Oh, sorry. It's her thing, not mine. Don't ask."

Anthony said, "Oh, this is my friend Wendell, my friend Rain. Sorry about this, but she's cool."

"So she's trying to get your mother to sob in front of everybody at the meeting about the new gay bar."

"But there's nothing to sob about!" Anthony protested.

Rain gave the two of them a significant look, and then laughed. "No, no, just kidding."

Anthony turned to Wendell, feeling cornered. "I'm really sorry about this, but it sounds like I have to, um, have someone killed." He started to get up.

Wendell sat up sharply, snapping out of his cloud of gloom. "Could I just—" He hesitated, glanced at Rain. "Could I give you my number?"

Anthony stammered, "Oh, uh, sure," blushing from the waist up as he stuffed the scrap of paper in his pocket. "I'll call you. Sorry I have to go like this." He left in awkward haste, with Rain trailing behind. It wasn't so much that every second counted; but rather that rushing would help avoid a messy exchange with her.

"Hope it works out okay," Wendell called after him.

On Anthony's way past, Eggie was glancing in the mirrored end of the booth, primping. "With this hair," he said, "I should be able to park in handicapped spaces."

NINE

RACE MEEHAN, Rain's mother, sat beneath the fluorescent ring in Maria Giannini's kitchen, steadily stirring her third cup of coffee and plunging ahead, despite little encouragement, into the extensive back alleyways of her beliefs. "Now, some say homosexuality is nothing more than a lifestyle choice, but that never made much sense to me because so many people get into so much trouble over it, or end up dead of it, nobody with half a brain would ever choose it. And of course, the scientists don't have any idea where it comes from. You got your arguments on all sides there, take your pick." Anthony's mother couldn't bear confrontation, nor would she ever willingly join in a conversation on any subject even remotely as racy as this, especially with someone who was barely an acquaintance, never mind a friend. She hunted for things that needed another pass from the damp dishrag. "So," Grace droned on, "only way I can see it is to me it's like a virus, like for the common cold. It's always there, always around. Some get it, some don't. But you can do a few things to improve your chances of not getting it—like cut down your exposure to it, for instance, same as like the flu. And that's where your Anthony needs to be careful."

"Oh, he's a good boy," said Maria, absently straightening a stack of recipe clippings, glancing about as though for the exit. "He's never been one to run with a bad crowd."

"Oh, sure, but this is different." Grace waggled her finger. "This crowd is bad in a very different, very sneaky way. As a matter of fact, they are generally very clean, often have good manners, and many of them are actually quite accomplished, all of which makes them sometimes hard to spot for what they are, which is sick, perverted, and dangerous." She sat up extra straight. "They want nothing less than to violate your Anthony's sacred body."

Maria recoiled. "Now hold on. You mean when he's at work?"

"No, no, of course not." Grace shook her head at the ignorance. "They'll make him want to follow them"—she gestured like a snake—"wherever they lead. Now if he could just give his heart to Jesus—"

Maria replied heatedly: "Now, you know I don't want you talking about that in this house. This is a Catholic house and we are just fine with that."

Grace backed off, though her body language continued to register tremors of fervor. They heard footfalls on the back stairs. Anthony and Rain burst into the kitchen.

"Oh, what a nice surprise!" said Maria to Rain, glad of the diversion. "We haven't seen you over here in so long. Your mother and I were just catching up. What can I offer you?"

Rain looked ready to pounce. "Very nice to see you, Mrs. Giannini," she said, eyeing her mother. "Is my mother being a pain?"

"I may have a conversation if I want to," said Grace. "Hello, Anthony, you look thin. Are you all right?"

"Yes, Mrs. Meehan," said Anthony. "Why wouldn't I be?" He had long since reserved the right to an edge with Grace Meehan.

"Well, you're working under a lot of stress."

"Pardon me, but I'm working at Angleton's. Maybe you know it, on Front Street. Yeah, I guess those burger platters get heavy sometimes."

"Anthony, don't be a snip," said Maria.

"He's under a lot of strain." Grace reached out to give Anthony a comforting touch; he dodged.

"Mrs. Meehan," he said testily, "I don't know why, but you have cooked up some weird way of looking at my life. I am fine, okay? I don't need you going around getting my mother all upset about nothing. I can take care of myself."

Grace sighed as though to say, Dear me, why does it always have to be this hard to get through? "Listen Anthony, I respect you as a young person, full of dreams, full of questions—"

"Oh, please, Mother, I'm going to puke," said Rain. "Can't you see when your preaching isn't welcome?"

"This is more important than whether my feelings are hurt, or even whether I hurt Anthony's or Maria's feelings, for that matter. This is about a soul being tampered with. This is about evil people preying on an innocent, leading him astray—"

Anthony slammed his fist onto the table. Grace stopped cold. There was a moment of shocked silence; he had never done anything like that before; his brain spun with how to speak now, when so much was at stake. Why should he let her push him into this moment? "Listen, if you weren't my best friend's mother, you would never have weaseled your way into this kitchen."

"Anthony!" Maria protested. He waved her silent, never taking his eyes off Grace.

"This is between you and me," he went on. "I don't need your sermons. You're way out of line telling me how to run my life. I don't have to explain myself to you. I'm not in any danger. Nobody's leading me astray—"

"But don't you see? You'd be the last to know." Grace spread her hands wide. "This is exactly how they turn you into their own perverted kind, by—"

"Mother!" Rain burst out. "Will you please—"

"Ssh! This is *my* thing!" Anthony said to her, with a sudden steeliness. When he spoke next, his voice was quiet. His eyes played between Grace and his mother. "They didn't have to turn me into anything." A silence. "I was already there." His mother stared at him, dumbstruck, not willing to take in what she'd just heard.

"Now, this is the tragedy of it," Grace nattered on, "that he could say that. He doesn't even know that he is under their spell. It's like when a hypnotist makes someone commit murder and they don't even know why they're doing it." Anthony stared at the floor, not hearing her; Maria stared at him. "As a matter of fact," Grace plowed ahead, "with the AIDS going around, it's exactly like that." She plumped her hair as though merely listening to the words. "Someone's going to kill him, and before all is said and done, before he dies, he's probably going to kill somebody else. Oh, Maria, I hope it's not too late. . . ."

"Mother! Stop it!" Rain exploded. "Just shut up!"

Grace quieted, her face a mix of studied meekness and defiance. She went to give Maria a hug. Maria backed away. Grace said, "Oh, of course, you're too upset."

"Just leave her alone!" Rain reached for her mother's arm.

"Don't you talk to me that way!" said Grace.

"I'm sorry, I think you had better go now. I'm sorry," said Maria, still gazing warily at Anthony.

Rain propelled her mother out the back door, quarrelsome murmurs passing between them.

When they had gone, Anthony and his mother shifted awkwardly about the kitchen, unable to meet eyes. Anthony said, "It's not like she says. . . ."

Maria looked suddenly very tired; she sighed. "What *is* it like, then?" She sat down at the table, pointed at the chair beside her. For several long moments they sat, each staring ahead.

Finally, Anthony spoke, as though musing aloud, "I've wondered for a long time . . . sort of known, but . . . never done anything about it. . . ."

"Oh, my darling, you're just a boy." She tried to run her fingers through his hair; he flinched away. "You're all confused, just growing up. . . ." She brightened. "You've got Rain, a girlfriend—"

"Mom, she knows about me. She's still my friend, my best friend, but not a girlfriend. That just doesn't work for me. . . . I've tried. . . ."

"Someone will come along, you'll see."

Anthony replied with irritation, as though merely parrying her argument, "I think someone has, maybe." Then he realized what he had said. After a moment's silence, he added, as much to himself, "I'll be careful."

RAY HARDMAN got a call from Sibley Briggs, who reigned over the gold-plated real estate market of Fishers Island, just across the water from Long Spit. Sibley had made a small fortune recycling the same forty mansions over and over through the contentious tentacles of some of America's grandest families. A Macon gentleman who would not pop out for a quart of milk without a blazer and ascot, he had endeared himself to the various Du Ponts and their ilk by the sheer passion of his regard for the island. A couple of the right marriages, to women pleased to have a courtly companion without all the sex fuss, had secured his place in the island's fossilized social order.

"What in hell's going on over there?" Sibley's gentle accent, more pronounced than when he'd arrived on the island sixteen years before, always made him sound as though he were smiling. "I've got two of the bluest-blooded old queens on the Eastern Seaboard telling me to look into establishing a position for them over there. These two—Alec and Preston, maybe you know 'em, Eastern Point?—sold the land for the golf course to the country club back in fifty-nine, for golly's sake. We weren't expecting another peep out of them till the reading of the will, and now they're saying Fishers is too boring."

Ray crooked the cordless phone under his chin so he could go about his morning. A Sibley monologue was not subject to interruption.

"Seems they'd been over there on their boat, the *LouLou*—silly name, idn't it?—for a dinner party with some of their ancient friends, remember the Stacks?—she's Wellesley—and ended up wandering into this place Sully's on their way back to the boat, used to be straight, I guess now sort of mixed. Anyway, who did they run into but Wesley Herndon, who they hadn't seen since the party the year before where they suddenly had to send all the gay boys home because Preston's straight son showed up unexpectedly from Boston. Anyway, Wesley was going on about how Long Spit is going to be the next happening place, replace P-town, easier to get to, make South Beach look sick, sprinkled with washboard tummies but still the real New England, and on and on, and how this young friend of his, some sort of surgeon, is buying right on the beach, and made it sound like some kind of feeding frenzy gettin' up and we're already behind the curve but maybe there's still time, and golly! said you had been very helpful, well, my, my . . ."

"Always happy to help," said Ray, phone in one hand, plant mister in the other.

"So what's Wesley up to?"

"Oh, mostly snooping around, is all, at the moment."

"Well, if Alec and Preston *do* do anything over there, there will be some other lemmings from around here taking notice, I can assure you. Maybe you and I can dine out on this a bit."

"Here I am," said Ray.

THE NEXT Thursday, the sixteenth of August, the second issue of the *Sand Flea* hit the stands, with a front-page picture of Hollis Wynbourne standing in the dunes, stroking Florian's tummy, over the headline "Look Who's Trying to Keep Us Out of Long Spit." The photo caption read: "Local gay rights opponent shows true colors with an unidentified African-American vacationer."

"There is nothing quite so intolerable," the story began, "as when gay people find ourselves up against our own kind in our struggle for equal rights. Hollis Wynbourne, a lifelong resident of this town, very much of the old-money elite, has taken it upon himself to stand in our way by becoming a charter member of the blatantly homophobic Community Decency Committee, organized for the sole purpose of preventing gay people from exercising our right to function in the marketplace with the same freedoms as every other citizen. And who is this gay-baiting oppressor, in reality? A look at the picture above says it all. He is, in fact, one of us, but so lost to cowardice and self-hatred that he's become an ugly tool of the hate-mongerers, an impediment to us all. Whatever sympathy you may have for someone wrestling in the closet, surely such a struggle gives no one the right to hold back the rest of us.

"One only has to look at incidents like the vicious gay-bashing that left blood on the parking lot of Sully's Bar only last week to see the level of hatred and bigotry we are up against in this 'quiet, peaceful' village, and to understand therefore the need for a gathering place we can call our own." The story went on to portray the Crab Hole as a sort of community center for gay men and to urge attendance at the impending hearing.

The buzz was instantaneous. Lattie Teachout was on the phone the minute the bundle of papers was dropped into the rack in Angleton's entryway, and before long large station wagons began gliding up to the racks outside Stevie Lund's shop and Frankie's Slice. The occupants would leave the engine running, totter across to the rack, and then sneak a look—one mustn't stare—at these new places that had sprung up since their last venture into the business district. Edith Tiddle tucked a copy into the basket on the front of her walker. Arnold Prendergast parked his Jaguar for twenty minutes while he ran a couple of other trumped-up errands before furtively stashing a copy in the game pouch of his shooting jacket. When he returned to his car, there was a "Hunky Boys for Private Parties" flyer tucked under his windshield wiper.

Ray picked up a copy with his morning bagel and phoned Betsy immediately. As soon as they hung up, she strode down the hill to pick up a copy, and stood outside Yankee Gulch reading it, shaking with rage. Dot Bradley came out to say hello.

"Did you see this yet?" Betsy asked. "Garbage!"

Dot peered at the picture. "Well, I'll be—we knew he was a bit that way . . . but he's the last person I would ever have thought would be doing that right out in public."

"He was ambushed," Betsy fumed. "Somebody's getting a piece of my mind."

She spied the sign hanging a few doors down Front Street: "The Sand Flea. The Little Paper with Bite." She stormed into the single-room office over the shell and honey shop to find a solitary young man listlessly peddling ad space on the phone. He saw trouble in her glare.

"Pardon me, young man." Betsy's voice was a sheathed talon. "Where might I find this Bart Connors?" She pointed to the byline. "The one responsible for this trash."

"Um, he, like, stepped out? Maybe try Angleton's?"

Betsy strode past Lattie without saying hello and found Bart in his booth.

"Is this your work?" She brandished the paper, voice level, eyes blazing.

"Who wants to know?" said Bart, reaching for his coffee.

"Listen, maybe this is how you scrap it out down in New York, but it's not how we settle our differences in this town. You—"

"Hey, step back, lady," said Bart, pulling himself to attention with some annoyance.

"Shh!" Betsy stabbed a finger toward him. "You have taken the liberty of shattering a very private man's dignity. He is going to have to go on living here long after you've cashed in your chips and moved on to trash somebody else in some other little town."

"Hang on here! He didn't have to sign up for that committee, all right? He didn't have to walk out to that beach in the broad daylight, know what I'm sayin'? But it's a free country.

He chose to do both those things, and from where I'm sitting, it looks like he's—"

"You stalked him! You ambushed him! You can't just—"

Bart turned up his volume. "From where I'm sitting, it looks like he's trying to have it both ways, and we don't have time anymore for that kind of bullshit—excuse the expression. We put up with it for long enough. We got enough people standing in our way without adding in this kind of two-faced coward from our own side." He swept the air dismissively. "These fence-sitters, still stuck like it was the fifties, the big drama, hating themselves, sabotaging the rest of us. He needs to wake up. Things are different now." The entire restaurant was rapt; a tink of fork on plate rang out.

Betsy was imperious. "Was any attempt made to warn him of the position he was getting himself into? To give him a chance to see your side of it?"

Bart said to the ceiling, "Do I need this aggravation?" To Betsy, "Look, I can see you don't have any understanding of what this tactic is about."

"I can see," Betsy hissed, "that *you* don't have any idea—and what's worse, don't care—how this can *ruin* someone." She turned and walked out, followed by dozens of pairs of eyes. As soon as she was out the door, the pent-up buzz filled the restaurant.

Within five hours of hitting the racks, the entire printing had been snatched up. Another of Artie's cruise ships was to arrive the next evening, so Bart phoned the printer and ordered another thousand copies. The next day, the *Westerly Star-Reporter* got into the act with an editorial that started off by accusing the *Sand Flea* of racism and sensationalism for hyping the issue because Florian was black, then went on to say: "We have no problem with gay people enjoying our beautiful towns, but they have brought with them another element that does not fit in. There is a tradition here of mutual respect, privacy, and discretion, that has been breached by the arrival of a certain sort of urban, take-no-prisoners mentality, as manifested by this publication."

The outing of Hollis Wynbourne brought the rare lively topic to Friday's round of dinner parties on Signal Hill. In general, the reaction was against outsiders meddling in the affairs of the village rather than anything to do with acceptance of gay people. The frustration townspeople had felt as their village was overrun now came spilling out. The Stahls, the Hollisters, and the Van Gelders sat on Leverett Stahl's broad porch. "Perhaps if we're patient," Leverett said, "they'll all just keep taking shots at each other until no one is left standing."

"Well, yes, but . . . Oh, I don't know," said Dorothy Van Gelder. "After all, poor Hollis . . . and what about his family?"

"Poor Hollis, my foot," said Leverett. "He's had a free ride long enough. And as far as his family is concerned—well, after the way he's run down that property . . ." Murmurs of agreement all around. "Let's face it, he's had one foot in the closet and the other on a banana peel for years."

HOLLIS LAY on his bed, on top of the covers, fully clothed, staring at nothing. Every few moments he took an enormous breath—as though trying to stretch away the knot in his chest—and let out a great sigh, with an undertone of groan. Oh, to undo that hour . . . Nothing had even happened. Every time he replayed it in his mind, a fresh cloud of butterflies would take flight inside him. The memory was oddly partitioned from his mind's main stage, as though he knew of it only through hearsay; he understood the frightening dislocation that sufferers from multiple personality disorder must experience. When, that fateful day, he had ventured to move on from his mesmerized stroking of Florian's tummy and flanks to touching the tantalizing bulge at the front of the sarong, he had gotten a playful swat. "Oh my no!" Florian scolded him with a laugh. "Mustn't move on to *serious* naughtiness. Heavens forfend! We're just a couple of *wholesome* boys out in the country." This had rocked Hollis back to his senses, left him mortified, left him feeling, of all things, marooned in the very presence he had dreamt of these last three weeks. Florian— feeling a mischievous urge to punish him a bit—had left him dangling a long moment, and was not cottoning on to the full measure of this disaster for Hollis. Neither yet knew Bart was in the picture. Then Hollis had mumbled, "Must be going," and beat an ignominious retreat, forced to slink the entire length of the beach under Florian's heartless gaze, or so he imagined. In fact, Florian had almost immediately been distracted by the sight of a spare but gifted man displaying his interest from a nearby hollow in the dunes.

Hollis had spotted the picture this morning on his way to the shop, picked up a copy (he had an urge to pick up the whole stack, to scour the village for stacks), and, face hot and breath shallow, had turned back for home, not even wanting to be seen reading it there in front of Stevie's. To his dismay, Dot had emerged from the Yankee Gulch to call after his departing back, with all best intentions, "I don't get all the fuss. If the boys and girls do it all the time, why not the boys and boys? Bet you there are things a lawyer could do." He'd sat on the back porch, rereading the sanctimonious prose until it had become a taunting refrain, and then he had taken to his bed.

Part of Hollis wanted to be found dead several days later, but part of him was kindling a giddy sense of no longer having anything to lose.

TEN

FOR SUPPORTERS of the Crab Hole liquor license, the timing of the Pequot Beach Club raid could not have been worse: five days before the Liquor Control Board hearing. Use of the club's changing stalls for sex, briefly the privileged frolic of Mark Blais and his friends, had become a commonplace of Long Spit gay lore, passed on to each new arrival. Daytime use remained too chancy for the average law-abiding guy, but late at night, when Sully's was looking like closing and libidos were growing insistent, the "egg crate" was more and more the venue of choice.

Apart from a few romantic moon-gazers, the club's members had never used the facilities at night. And, since there was really nothing to steal or damage, and the village had not needed to fortify itself against the homeless, no one had ever bothered to secure the premises. The door from the parking lot was locked, but if you went through the break in the lattice-work under the building you could reach the cubicles, most of which were left unpadlocked, without having to walk all the way around by way of the beach.

One of Artie Kinzie's cruises was in town; for this one, he had worked out a tie-in with a male video company called Newcomers, so this was being promoted as the Heat Wave Talent Search Weekend. He had wheedled the shipowner into attaching a neon rainbow flag to either side of her funnel whenever she was chartered for one of his cruises, so she was looking quite festive out among the anchored yachts, all her lights ablaze, her tenders steadily ferrying passengers back and forth. The Ocean had enjoyed its best tea dance yet—Marcia was now doing them Thursdays through Sundays, with guest DJs—and all evening Sully's and Frankie's Slice had been solid with trolling men. The portion of the beach club's parking lot near the break in the lattice had become a cruising ground in its own right, as Tish Jensen noticed when she pulled into her reserved space at midnight.

She'd gone from an afternoon here at the beach straight to a dinner party, and had then driven all the way home to Mis-quamicut only to find she'd left her Palm Pilot rolled up in a sandy towel in her changing room. Her headlights played over the dozen or so oddly spaced men lounging on the low wall be-tween the blacktop and the sand; they were not managing to look very plausible, having chosen such a barren setting for a late cigarette. Nonetheless, several of them greeted her with comments on the lovely evening as she headed for the gate.

Feeling her way toward her cubicle, the passageways lit only by stray shafts from the parking lot and the moon, she had the strange feeling that she wasn't alone in the building. Indeed, she seemed to be traveling in a pocket of silence created by her approach, as when, in the woods, you approach a wet spot full of peepers. Did the building always creak in the breeze and you just never noticed it during the day? She tried to put it out of her mind; after all, she only needed to be here one more minute. Fifty feet from her door, she was fumbling for the key to her padlock when a sharp "Oh! Yes!" shattered the twitchy silence, followed by the sound of a heavy body crumpling against a partition not ten feet away. Tish panicked, turned, and ran back the way she'd come, her clogs clacking along the decking. With the whites of her eyes showing she bolted outside, past the loitering men, jumped into her car, and called 911.

Jim Priestly, the village constable, was dozing in his cruiser next to the convenience store out at the bypass. With pension in sight, he was growing steadily more timid. He had never faced any real danger in thirty-eight years, and now the day never passed that he didn't worry about how the odds must be piling up against him. The troopers had started razzing him for calling them in on every little thing.

"Down to the beach club? Be right there." He slid his neck pillow under the seat. "Christ, what now . . ."

Back at the club, one of the trollers from the parking lot hurried inside to let everybody know what the running clogs had meant. Now the rustle of denim, the jingle of belt buckles and chains, the clunk of boots and chirp of zippers sounded here and there along the passageways.

Most slipped out along the beach, but some were too absorbed in their activities to hear or care what was going on until the pulsing blue strobes on Jim's cruiser began to play off the plywood. Jim took one look at the numbers and, though his prejudices reassured him that these men were harmless, called for backup. Not only were they not trying to run away, but more and more kept arriving, wandering down from Frankie's to see what the lights were all about, guys used to hanging out in New York or Boston, watching the police do their thing. A few of the perpetrators who hadn't gotten the message even came blinking through the hole in the lattice, seeing nothing alarming in a police cruiser surrounded by a few dozen guys standing around joking with each other—figuring somebody had probably caught a pickpocket going through the pants crumpled around his ankles.

Jim cursed to himself; the troopers would have a field day with this one. He sat in his cruiser with the windows up, pretending to fill out a report form. Tish Jensen came toward him, clutching at her cowl neck, glancing nervously at the men. She'd been hunkered down in her car with the doors locked and her thumb on the panic button of her alarm, but now she too was disarmed by the spectators' casual air, and she was starting to feel a little silly as they greeted her: "D'you lose something in there?" "Need a jump?"

Sam Jenkins, dozing in his TV room in front of a right-wing talk show, was jolted awake when Jim's call for backup triggered his scanner. Something about the intrusion of Jim Priestly's voice into Sam's conspiracy-laced reveries propelled him to his pickup truck to go have a look.

Word came up from the beach club parking lot to Bart's table at Frankie's, and he headed down to see what was up. By the time the two state cruisers came silently along Front Street with their blue lights twittering, thirty or forty men were gathered around Jim's car, chatting. Tish had let Jim into the beach club, where he was shining his flashlight uselessly down the empty passageways. Back outside, the men were helpful, explaining to the troopers where they could find Jim. A couple of the men pursued the conversation with the troopers, especially with the beefy, baby-faced one, rather more avidly than was appropriate under the circumstances, but this seemed to pass unnoticed. The troopers conducted themselves by the book; only a brief exchange of smiles between them hinted that they were more interested in tracking down Jim than any trespassers.

Jim was peeved, holding the light while Tish finally retrieved her Palm Pilot from her cubicle. Not only could this damn thing unleash a blizzard of paperwork, but he was in for it when the troopers arrived. "Hell, it's just open to the air, not like they even had to break in. Not much we could get 'em on."

"Well, I know," said Tish, "but it *is* private property, and it was very, very frightening."

"But how are you going to prove anything, don't you know, is what I'm saying."

"Freeze!" a voice barked. Two flashlights lit up Jim's face, followed by a gust of laughter as the two troopers came up to them.

"Well, goddammit," muttered Jim with a rueful laugh.

"Holdin' 'em at bay okay, are you?" said the big one.

"Yeah, they'll kill you for your uniform, soon as look at you," said the other, a smaller man with a black regulation mustache. Manly laughs.

"This was not funny," said Tish. "I am a woman alone."

"You're absolutely right, ma'am, we meant no disrespect," said the first trooper, gazing around. "Not the safest place for you, this late. Taking a moonlight swim, were ya?"

"I was getting something from my cabana," said Tish frostily, "not that I should have to explain myself to you."

Back outside, the three officers held a muffled conference. Sam Jenkins walked up to them. "What seems to be the problem here?"

The smaller of the troopers turned partly toward him. "Everything's under control here. You can just move along now."

"What were they getting up to in there?" Sam persisted.

"Oh, hi, Jim." Jim nodded without looking at him. Sam had tried to have him fired for failing to enforce the village's loitering ban in front of Frankie's Slice.

"You just let us worry about that," said the other trooper. "Ma'am? Could we ask you a few more questions over here, please?"

Sam hung nearby, ear cocked.

"Now, could you actually identify anybody you saw in there?" The smaller trooper had the clipboard.

"Well no, I—"

"Did you even really see anybody?"

"No, but I heard somebody." Tish's arms were folded tight.

"Did anyone say anything to you?" She shook her head. "And what made you think it was a trespasser? Couldn't it have been a member?"

"Oh for heaven's sake, club members never use it at night."

"You were."

"What in the hell is going on?" Sam burst in. "Why in hell don't you believe her? Why in hell are you badgering her? She's just trying to report a crime. This is the damnedest thing I've ever seen." The audience was paying attention now.

The big trooper stepped forward. "I'm going to have to ask you to step back, sir. If there even was a crime here, it sure wasn't any of your business."

"If you want to know the truth," said Tish, "it sounded to me like somebody having sex."

"That's just what I thought!" cried Sam. "These perverts—"

"Okay, buddy, clear off." The big trooper crowded Sam away, still sputtering.

Suddenly a voice spoke from among the onlookers. "I use the club at night. With a friend." Jim and Tish and the troopers turned to see Mark Blais step forward. "Hi, Tish," he said.

"You know this man?" asked the trooper.

"Yes, well, only from the club," she said.

"And you're a member?" the trooper asked Mark.

"Lifelong," said Mark.

"And you were on the club premises tonight?"

"Let's say I was." Mark pulled out his key ring and held up one of the keys. "My friend and I use the room sometimes . . . for changing. My family joined in 1953."

"Okay," said Tish, "he has every right to be there, but now— I think I was hearing a number of people there, not just him and his friend."

The trooper with the clipboard responded: "Look, here's how we'd like to handle this, ma'am. We'll make a report and take your particulars and that, but there's not a lot we can do with what you've given us. But there'll be a record, and if it happens again, maybe we'll get a little more to go on. The constable here should be able to handle that part of it, right, Jim?" He smirked for an instant. They all settled down to the filling out of forms.

Bart Connors sidled up to Sam. "I'm a reporter," he said. "What's this all about?"

"A reporter!" Sam snorted. "I'll tell you what. This town is overrun with, with . . ." He glanced around at the men watching, some amused, some stony-faced, and lowered his voice. "Let's just say they're dangerous, and now we find out the cops are afraid to do anything about 'em."

Mark was still hanging around. The trooper with the mustache stuck his head out of the cruiser. "We won't be needing any more from you, sir. Thanks." Mark nodded.

Bart approached him next. "Bart Connors." He extended his hand. "I write for the *Sand Flea.*"

Mark looked at him. "Are you the one who outed Hollis Wynbourne?"

"Well, you might say he outed himself," Bart said with some annoyance.

"I haven't got anything to say to you," said Mark, turning to walk away.

"Were you really in there tonight?" Bart said to his back.

"Doesn't much matter, does it?"

WORD OF the raid spread instantly through the village, whipped up to frothy peaks by the operatic imaginations of the gossip network. There had, by some accounts, been a beating, though it was not clear whether the beating had been carried out by the police or as part of a sexual encounter before they arrived. Sam had become a vigilante posse in some tellings, with shocking epithets in supply for a party of eight. Mark Blais, who normally turned his share of heads anyway as he went about the village, was variously described as coming through the hole in the lattice still buttoning his fly or pulling his tank top on over his head, even though a few patrons of Frankie's were interested enough in him to recall with certainty that he was eating pizza right up until the police arrived.

The beach club membership was slow to find out—Tish lived well outside town and was less plugged in to the club old-timer circuit than Mark Blais was, and Mark certainly wasn't going to be spreading this one. It was only when the stacks of *Sand Fleas* appeared two days later, and the Buicks from up the hill paused for their copies, that the whole village began to buzz.

"PURITAN DRAGNET. Police in Coordinated Raid on Law-abiding Citizens," ran the headline. Bart had managed to take a shot of the three police cars, cropped so the scattering of onlookers appeared to be a crowd, facing away from the camera so its mood was unreadable. "Enraged gay citizens face down cops in tense encounter," the caption panted. Bart described Mark as "voluntarily surrendering his privacy in order to expose this raid for the staged fraud that it was, leaving the police no alternative but to retreat in confusion," and concluded, "Even now, they are planning the next trumped-up harassment stunt. This should be a wake-up call to those gay people who think our rights are going to be protected for us by the dragoons of the law enforcement ranks." He included a full-page ad encouraging attendance at the Liquor Control Board hearing: "Remember, vigilance is the price of freedom," and so on. Leverett Stahl tossed his copy in the trash and turned to his wife with a sour look. "They demand to be allowed to solicit sodomy in public. If that isn't a special right, I don't know what is." His wife gave a perturbed whimper at the word "sodomy" having spattered her walls.

Several of the beach club members resigned immediately, irretrievably squeamish at the thought of the crusted bodily fluids that might now be lying in wait for them on the seat planks and door handles of their cubicles. The cadre of matrons in charge got a number of hysterical calls from members demanding something be done; shortly a membership mailing went out with several paragraphs of useless recommendations: report all strangers, don't leave possessions in the changing rooms, blah, blah. Mark Blais's mother got a number of calls from friends ostensibly wanting to comfort her, but actually just wanting to sample the chagrin in her voice so they could cluck about it on their next calls.

Nightlife in the cubicles trailed off for the moment. Jim Priestly swung through the parking lot several times a night, but at regular intervals which the boys quickly noted, so cruising along the wall continued unabated.

Those of the village's upper stratum looked nervously over

their shoulders, clinging to a vague notion that, while such a thing could indeed befall that tacky club, it posed no threat to higher altitudes. But, undeniably, this incident, on the heels of the ugliness in Sully's parking lot, had shoved their genteel enclave worryingly toward the tawdry outside world.

Sam Jenkins made the rounds of the more receptive precincts—the bait shop, Malley's Auto Parts—telling anyone who would listen about how "the cops sat there and made complete fools of themselves, doing nothing. There's this woman, scared half out of her wits, you got trespassing at the very least and who knows what all else, but they don't even go near that, and here are all these queers standing around laughing at them because they *know* who calls the shots. I'll tell you, it was a lesson to me." Sam and his wife teetered closer to divorce. He held another meeting of his committee in their dining room, this time with a strident infusion of new Christian talent, so that Nancy felt she must go out on the porch and apologize to the two quiet men—an accountant and an IRS auditor—who had just arrived for their honeymoon.

By the day of the Liquor Board hearing, the stew had simmered to a rich mélange. Normally, such hearings were attended only by the applicant, whichever aggrieved neighbors wanted to pout, and their respective lawyers. But, catching the buzz leading up to this meeting, the town hall staff decided to move it out of their conference room and into the Congregational church hall, which happened to be directly opposite the Ocean Hotel (now known by the boys as the Bun Box).

It was a hazy, warm evening, colors bright in the late light, when the forces began to mass. The venerable patriarchs—here and there showing evidence of the salty Yankee gene pool in a jawline or fierce eyebrow—squired, not to say herded, their mates toward the steps with sidelong glances at the men. Three members of Sam's Decency Committee milled about self-consciously with signs—"No to Vice"; "Think of the Children"; "Save Our Town"—while a fourth shoved a petition at everyone coming up the walk.

"Honey, I don't think so," said Eggie, deflecting the woman's hand. The protestor, registering that he was the enemy, let out a low growl. "Oh, you say that to all the boys." Eggie threw her a slight, taunting flounce and rolled his eyes conspiratorially at his companions.

Some of the more politic men were wearing their Dockers and golf shirts; others came straight from the beach, greased up and lugging giant gym bags; and others were still damp and stringy-haired from the four-to-seven tea dance across the street. There, at the Ocean, boys were now appearing in the upstairs windows, some with towels wrapped around them, just showering before dinner, some settling in, elbows on the windowsill, to watch the scene.

Close to the eight o'clock start, a van of Christians pulled up with more signs: "Drive Out Satan"; "Go Back to Sodom"; "Do You Know Where Your Child Is?"; "Forgive Them, Father, for They Know Not What They Do." They joined the Decency Committee group, and one with a bullhorn immediately began hectoring the newly arrived. "We must be vigilant, drawing *firm lines* around our community, and *manning* those lines, to keep out this contagion. . . ."

This was greeted with jeers and hoots from the windows across the street. "Ooh, yes! *Man* those lines!" "Check 'em out!"

The Christians began to sing "Onward, Christian Soldiers," whereupon a roomful of men aimed their boom box out the window and put on a bootlegged techno-rave CD. Artie Kinzie and Leo Robbia looked up on the way in and shook their heads. "Depend on the boys to fuck you up," said Leo.

"Yeah," Artie grumbled. "They should open a fucking consulting firm."

Inside, the seating, with some ill-at-ease trial and error, was coagulating into like-minded clumps, who regarded each other with mixtures of distaste and curiosity varying according to their upbringing and the temperature of their views.

"Wow, just like New England," said one of Eggie's sidekicks, gazing around the austere hall, trimmed in white and varnish.

"Darling, it *is* New England," Eggie sighed. "You've heard of Salem?"

The seven Liquor Board members shuffled in one by one, without fanfare, looking around with dismay at the charged scene, pausing to greet acquaintances. The board members were volunteers hailing from all over a jurisdiction that encompassed Westerly and its surrounding villages. None of them were of the Signal Hill families, who preferred to make their influence felt from further behind the scenes; but rather, the sort of solid retired citizens possessing a busybody streak. They gradually took their places behind the long folding table.

Walter Brundage gaveled the meeting to order, retreating from all the eyes turning toward him by conferring a moment with Bill Zinn, the retired Dodge dealer to his left.

"Okay, then," he finally mumbled, and then, speaking up, "The matter of Application 2803. It's been posted and published for the requisite period as per regulation." He looked to the front row, where Leo and Artie and Leo's attorney were sitting. "Are you all set?"

The attorney, a big man, half stood. "Yes, sir, we believe the submission is complete, all the requirements have been met," his voice adequately polite, a whiff of insolence. "There should be nothing to discuss. . . ." The board members were all leafing through their copies of the paperwork.

"There's plenty to discuss," a voice rang out. All turned to see Sam, red-faced, getting to his feet.

"Sit down, Sam," said Walter. "We've all got your committee's letter in front of us. You'll get your chance."

Walter plodded through the parliamentary rite of having the papers included in the minutes, dithering as though to put off the unpleasant scene he anticipated. Then he murmured, "Now then, public comment." He nodded to Sam. "Mr. Jenkins?"

"Yes." Sam got to his feet again. "I just think we can't go on treating this like business as usual. I mean, this may be the first time we've had a chance to talk about it, but the town's already all but taken over." The locals squirmed, arms folded; a low hiss set in. "It might already be too late, but at least we've reached a point here tonight where we can say, 'No more.'" He glanced down at the card in his hand. "I wonder how many people here have taken the trouble to find out exactly what this place, this 'Crab Hole,' is going to be like." He spoke the name as if it were the vilest obscenity. "I have. You wanna know?" He cast a truculent look around. "A pitch-black maze, for going in and having sex?" A tremor went through the room. "Holes cut in the partitions between the toilets, for sex? I'm sorry if this offends anybody, but that's just why we have to talk about this, it *is* offensive."

"I'll tell you what's offensive." Heads turned toward the new voice. It was Andy, the filmmaker, getting to his feet. The side of his face was still a smear of bruise. Walter put up a finger toward Sam and nodded to let Andy speak. "It's offensive when people hijack this kind of a process, twist it into a tool for hassling people they don't like. That's what's offensive. That's not what this country—"

"No way!" Sam bellowed. "No way. That's not what's going on here. You all have made your lifestyle choice, and we just want to make ours, and it doesn't include trash on Front Street." A rumbling undercurrent grew.

Andy's voice took an edge of moral certainty. "Every time a town tries to keep us out, it sends a message to everybody, to your kids, that discrimination is okay"—he pointed to his face—"that what happened to me is okay."

"Yes, but *you* have to remember," came a woman's voice, "you have to remember, this town has been under siege this summer. This is just one way, legal and peaceful, of fighting back." It was the woman who'd been pushing the petitions. "I can love an individual homosexual, I can pray for him. I don't necessarily hate him. But we've got a hive of vice wanting to establish itself right here in the middle of the village, just waiting to send *killer bees* into the community." The room was stirring now. "What happened over in Sully's parking lot the other night is just the beginning. I'm not threatening, or saying it's right or fine, but it's what you get when you force this kind of unwanted change on the people of a community." Her every pause now released a swell of scoffs, amens, chatter, grumbles, at volumes approaching a decent sports bar. "And what happened," she shrilled over it, "what happened the other night at the Pequot is proof enough, if you still needed any, of what kind of *sick perverts* we're dealing with here." A heavier wave of outcry broke out.

Andy protested, "No, it just shows what happens when you deprive any group within the community of a place of its own to gather." He stabbed the air: "It's a basic human need and right."

"Gather! Gimme a break! That's not my word for it!" someone shouted, unleashing a roar from both sides, with a new ugliness—taunts, finger-pointing, purple faces. For what seemed an ominously long time, Walter banged his gavel to no avail. Finally he pointed to Helen Boothroyd.

She stood demurely waiting for the room to quiet down, and then spoke timidly. "I never would have thought I would stand up in this kind of meeting, but it's a worry the way this is going. I'm seeing a side of my town . . . well, it has me concerned. I've learned something over these last couple of months, or re-learned I should say. I guess you'd put it, It takes all kinds to make a world. These men are not bad people, or at any rate some of them might be, like any group, I guess, but I've had no problems with them coming to stay, right in my home, and I've even made friends with some." She looked back at Derek and Tracy, who were sitting one row back, pulling for her. "And I can tell you that's another thing I never expected at this point in my life. Now, I won't probably ever go to this place they want to open, and goodness knows you don't have to, either. I guess I just thought in this part of the world we believed in let-ting people be. That's all I have to say."

Mark Blais stood up. "Mr. Chairman, what happened at the beach club was just a big misunderstanding. I'm a lifelong member and had every right to be there—with a guest. There were no arrests, it was all settled that night—"

"That's only because the police in this town are completely *cowed* by what's going on around here!" Sam was up again, set-ting off another roar.

For the next few minutes, a succession of increasingly stri-dent views were lobbed from both sides and the level of agita-tion in the hall racheted steadily upward. Finally, Walter wielded his gavel again and recognized Artie.

He stood. "Yeah. Art Kinzie, business associate of the appli-cant." He nodded to Helen. "Thank you for your sentiments of a few minutes ago." His voice suddenly grew hard. "But, you know, what gets me about the opposition here is the hypocrisy of it. I mean, every shop on Front Street has already had the best season ever, all right? And it's not even over. The Ocean is back from the dead, restaurants are packed . . . and then we try to open our own place so we can be outta your face and what do we get? A committee trying to drop-kick us out of town, but get this, headed up by a guy who's making money off us. And then this petition, letter, whatever, signed by this guy who's so twisted he can't stand us, and why? just 'cause he can't handle that he's one of us. I mean, he's got this issue, so now we should all disappear? Hey. We're here, we're everywhere, all right? The sun still came up this morning. Get over it."

There was a flicker of applause, a few decorous cheers from the boys. Sam, shaking his head and looking down in disgust, complained loudly, "Everybody knows my wife's the one lettin' 'em in, wasn't my idea." Some of the locals scanned the rows of folding chairs, looking for Hollis, not seeing him.

Walter pointed with his gavel, recognizing Anthony. The locals clucked and whispered: hadn't seen him in years, since the earring, since he'd become a young man.

He was nervous, but his tenor voice was determined. "I can't let this pass, talking like this about Mr. Wynbourne. I guess you know that's who they're talking about. He's been treated really badly lately, by gay people . . . gay people who play on somebody else being gay, for all the bad they can put him through out of it. Well there shouldn't be anything bad about it." He glared around. "We should be allowed to be happy about it . . . proud." The room had fallen silent. "Mr. Wynbourne has his way of being gay and the Crab Hole isn't it, and he has the right to say so. It doesn't have to be such a black-and-white thing. I mean, if he was straight and somebody wanted to open a strip joint on Front Street, nobody would think it was weird for him to oppose it, so why is this any different? And I mean, if you need a reason why he doesn't like the sort of people who want to get this place open, just look at the way they treat people, what they've done to him."

His voice dropped. "I've been taking voice lessons from Mr. Wynbourne for almost two years and he has always treated me with total respect. We each have our ways of being, like I said, and he has been a perfect gentleman." He paused for a moment, then sat down. A spell was on the room.

Suddenly Walter looked over the heads with a start. "Ah, Mr. Wynbourne, you are here." Hollis was stepping from behind those standing at the back of the hall. "Do you have anything you want to say?"

"Yes, I do, Mr. Chairman." Hollis walked a few steps up the center aisle, finding Anthony's eyes for an instant. "Thank you for speaking up for me . . . but I have to speak up for myself." Hollis spoke slowly, in his trained, steely voice. "I almost can't find words for how outraged I am, being forced into this mess—by both sides. I know for years I've been the butt of jokes in this village. I've put up with that, believing I was at least safe, because this place is what it is, safe from anything worse. I've never harmed anyone. . . ." He looked down in the silence, then swept the room with a fierce glare. "I have nothing to hide, nothing I should need to be ashamed of. But I think those of you really from this town, who've known me, even if you've had a laugh now and then, at my expense, I think you'd agree that there's a lot about my life, and your life, that is nobody else's damn business, and I'm not here to explain myself." There was a murmur of agreement. "I can't stand the drivel I hear from these born-agains, telling me what I can and can't do or even think about. But it just so happens I agree with you on one thing. A sex club on Front Street is not what this town needs." Another wave of murmuring, now from all camps. Hollis put up a hand. "Perhaps I wouldn't have taken a public stand on this on my own, it's not my nature, and I'm mad as hell that you"—he turned to Sam—"bullied me into joining your committee. But now that I've done it, I'm not backing down. Because what angers me most is to be attacked, just for speaking up, to be called a fascist, called a coward, of all things—to have my privacy destroyed, by people who then turn around and call me one of them. Well I'm not one with any of that. A person who could do that . . . whatever we may have in common counts for *nothing* compared to the ways we're different."

Bart could stand no more. "Mr. Chairman," he stood up. "He talks about what this town does or doesn't need, but he was trying to have sex outdoors on a public beach, for God's sake. He can't have it both ways. This kind of hypocrisy has got to—"

"Order! Order!" The chairman gaveled down the growing roar. "You will let Mr. Wynbourne finish." It took a moment for a tense quiet to be restored.

"I have nothing more to say," said Hollis. He shot a black look at Bart, turned, and left the room.

"Ladies and gentlemen," said Walter, "we're to where we seem to be going in circles. I think we've heard the basic sides of it by now. So what we're going to do is, this hearing is going to adjourn to a closed-door deliberation for one hour—we'll go downstairs—and then we'll take our vote and announce our decision at, let's see, nine-thirty." He struck the gavel once again.

The crowd was immediately up and buzzing in a dangerous way, unstable, in high need of discharge, hands placed on hot-heads' shoulders. The board shuffled down into the rector's silent, fluorescent-lit office. As they settled around the wood-look conference table, they made much of pulling out each other's chairs, offering each other cups from the water coolers, needing solidarity to fortify them.

"In all my years of doing this, I've never seen people so worked up at a hearing," said Walter.

"Yeah," said Eunice Shively, the retired dietician, "and it's not just the gay thing. I think a lot of folks are okay with that, I think I am. But it's more this sort of big-city hardball attitude, like trapping Hollis . . . just never mind who you have to drive over to get where you're going."

"I'll tell you, it makes me want to dig in my heels a little bit," said Bill Zinn. "I don't like them thinking we'll just roll over for them." He paused a moment. "So to speak."

A couple of others weighed in, tiptoeing around their distaste, hunting for acceptable avenues of disapproval. Many of their meetings went through a stage like this, where board members unloaded their real response before putting on the other hat, but this time it had a different quality. As they spoke, they stared distractedly into their piles of documents, their faces slightly scrunched as though there were an unpleasant odor in the room.

Walter shifted gears. "Well, 'course we don't any of us much like what's going to be going on there, but that's not what this commission sits to decide. It looks to me as if we got no legal grounds to refuse this . . . no objections from abuttors, just this letter from Sam's committee, which I didn't think had anything in it we needed to pay any attention to. Course they still got to get the C.O. and police and fire sign-offs, and that, so they could still run into a snag. But seems though all we can really do is let it go through and see."

Outside the meeting hall, a television truck had arrived from the Westerly station. The reporter, a brittle anorexic, scanned the crowd. Edgy encounters were taking place here and there, some heating to confrontations, others resulting in bummed cigarettes, none as yet leading to a mass stand-off. "Okay," the anorexic said to her producer, "find me a drag queen." The closest they came at first was Eggie, who was not exactly framing the issues for the camera.

"Are you one of the people who wants to bring this bar to this town?" the reporter asked.

"Honey, I'm as straight as a knitting needle," Eggie replied. "You can just keep those fairies away from me." He glanced at his entourage for encouragement. "I'm serious, very butch. I'll tell you something, honey, I once even played football—literally once. And, honey?" Eggie waggled a finger at her hair. "A little brassy, that rinse? I could sort that out for you." The producer was nodding across the street toward the Ocean. Two bikini-topped iron pumpers in matching tennis skirts, opentoed stilettos, and starched chambermaid hats were emerging from the Ocean with feather dusters. "Perfect," said the reporter, and they left Eggie feigning bewilderment.

The feather dusters were not available for comment, but they nonetheless locked in their slot on the eleven o'clock news, flitting among the cars that were idling by to see what all the fuss was about, dusting windshields and headlights, posing as hood ornaments, bantering with the occupants, whose faces registered the gamut from amusement to terror, sometimes within the same car. The gay crowd encouraged the amused and taunted the terrified. Even the Christians paused in their chanting to watch, momentarily disarmed by the unapologetic camping. Artie and Leo stared glumly.

Artie exhaled smoke. "At least the fuckin' board members are in the basement."

Anthony walked among the people outside, nodding with a stiff smile to those townspeople he knew, noting but not quite prepared to acknowledge the comradely looks he was getting from the gay contingent, although he did throw a brief smile at Eggie, who had saluted him with a wink from a few yards off. Even that very morning, Anthony had not been sure whether he would go to the hearing, much less speak. Rain had snorted at the idea: "You're turning into such a little civics dweeb." He certainly had not decided to come out to the whole town, but had been dimly aware that, under the circumstances, anything he stood up to say would amount to that. Now he was in the opening minutes of waiting for the sky to fall. Rain's mother gave him a lingering look of infinite pity. Her sign said, "Love the Sinner, Hate the Sin."

The door of the hall opened and the board secretary announced that the hearing was reconvening.

ELEVEN

WALTER BRUNDAGE gaveled and waited for quiet.

"Now, of course, this is just the first step in the permit process. You've still got your referrals and sign-offs to get before the permit is actually issued, but, for our part of it, there isn't really a problem, so we're going to go ahead and what we call grant the permit, contingent, as I say, on those other things . . ."

His last words were drowned out. The audience was on its feet, some hugging, some leaning forward against the pew backs, booing, jeering, cheering, ranting, fingers and fists punching the air. Rattled by the tumult, the board members busied themselves stubbornly with their papers, glancing at possible escape routes. The crowd gradually began spilling back outside, but now with no bumming of cigarettes between the camps. Someone shouted up to the onlookers in the windows of the Ocean. Word shot through the old hotel and within minutes the clientele was turning out to join the raucous, vibrating throng—in equal parts contention and celebration—that was beginning to taffy itself into motion down the hill toward Front Street.

Sam was on the church hall phone to Bob Fresno, a member of his committee who hadn't shown up. "Well, now I hope you believe me. You all sat home on your asses and now we got a real problem here. . . . Nah, they didn't give a shit about a few signatures, and that fuckin' letter was a waste of two hundred eighty bucks. What we need is your ass down here. Seems like there's hundreds of these fags coming out of the woodwork, so get on the phone . . . that's right, get some people down here."

Bart strolled around outside on his cell phone, eyes darting eagerly about, chatting with a friend in New York who was a stringer for a wire service. "Already over? No way, this is just lighting the fuse. The guys are totally into it, you know, any excuse for a parade. . . . Yeah, hundreds. . . . Well, see who's interested. . . . Okay, we'll talk."

Anthony jogged home to make sure his mother wasn't going out, and then called Rain to tell her what he had done. "Yeah, I think there's going to be like a riot down on Front Street, a lot of people heading down there, your mother leading the pack. . . . Really, like what is their problem? . . . And tell Libby too, and Jack. I'll hang out in front of Frankie's and wait for you. . . . Because that's where I want to be tonight. You join *me*." A reflex going back years: call the circle. He was dimly aware, though, that these were no longer the people he wanted most to share such a moment with. But if not them, who?

On Front Street, traffic had ground to a halt: the cars full of moms picking up their kids from the yacht club after their evening dinghy race; the beach club members who'd stayed to watch the sunset; a few loads of new arrivals just in for their long weekends—all were halted in the clogged street, their cars merrily jostled and rocked by the crowd and dusted by the chambermaids, all bobbing along to the music pumping from Frankie's outdoor speakers.

The opposing forces occupied the length of the small waterfront park, their backs to the harbor and the remains of the sunset. Sam Jenkins wore a dogged face; he was deeply, primally unhinged by the thought that these men had driven them nearly into the sea. "We're losin' it, the whole goddamn shootin' match, right here before our eyes!" A few of the devout tried to get chants of the "Two! Four! Six! Eight! Stop the sinners at our gate!" variety going, but these would fizzle after a few fitfully accompanied solos. Mostly the protestors engaged in noisy commiseration, stoking one another's outrage. Numbers on both sides were swelling as word spread, as some abandoned their cars, as the usual summer-night strollers took sides. There was a sense in the air of pushing ahead with something that could blow.

Anthony leaned on a geranium barrel in front of Frankie's. Four or five guys had already come right up to him and called him cool for speaking up; quite a few others had nodded, waved, winked, some realizing that he was the kid who'd brought their clam strips at Angleton's, who'd briefed them on which part of the beach they should head for. This felt like stardom. Across the way he could see Rain's mother, reveling in this opportunity to project anguish, waving her "Love the Sinner, Hate the Sin" sign as though, if only people would pause to learn from her, this whole mess could be resolved.

Stevie Lund decided to keep her shop open, reckoning a lot of the boys would welcome an interlude of shopping with their parading; rainbow caps and suspenders were flying out the

door. Dot Bradley stood in the doorway of Yankee Gulch, a bemused smile on her face, never wanting to miss anything, selling a few collars and leashes. Angleton's was doing a brisk
take-out trade in the current fad, fries and vinegar. There was
a distinct air about the locals—worried, alert, excited. This
was the first time in anyone's memory that the village had been
bumped around by such flexing of public emotion. Long Spit
was dedicated to orderly escapism; unrufflable routines were
its stock in trade. But now, however much some of the local
folks might have been trying to sweep the gay invasion under
the rug, it could no longer be ignored: the place was under oc-
cupation.

Anthony spotted Wendell approaching. A jolt of electricity
shot through him; this was the first time he'd seen Wendell in
just shorts and a T-shirt. Life seemed to be picking up speed.

"Wow, this is wild, huh?" Wendell said, clapping him on one
shoulder with appealing awkwardness. "I heard about it on the
radio coming home from the video store."

"Yeah, amazing." Anthony smiled, plunging his hands into
his pockets. They glanced about for a few seconds, jumpy with
delicious unease. "Did you hear about the meeting?" He stood
very straight, rocking on his heels, his eyes shining. It was dis-
orienting, looking at Wendell through eyes that were right out
on his face; no more peering furtively, as though through mailing tubes, from a vantage point deep inside.

"No, I just got here. I haven't talked to anybody."

"I told them," Anthony said, and then, blushing, "I mean I
let 'em have it." He held Wendell's eyes with a look of such
pride and vulnerability that Wendell opened his arms and Anthony rushed to embrace him. "What are you talking about?"
Wendell chuckled into his neck, sniffing fresh laundry.

"That is a child!" came a shriek. "That is a flower of our garden!" It was Rain's mother, striding toward them. Anthony and Wendell turned, their arms still across each other's shoulders. "Like vampires! Swooping down on our young!"

"I did the swooping, all right?" Anthony shot back, leaving his arm where it was. "You wanna just *butt out*?" He muttered to Wendell, "Jesus, why are we, like, such a magnet?"

"I could have him arrested," she screeched, "if he so much as touches you!" She brandished her sign as though to swat Wendell. Anthony turned to him and planted a kiss on his panicked, retreating mouth. A flash went off. They turned to see Bart giving them a thumbs-up—Perfect, guys.

A moment later, Rain and two other friends, Jack and Libby, maneuvered through to join them. Anthony felt a paroxysm of awkwardness.

"I see Grace is on duty," said Rain.

Anthony realized they had not seen the kiss. "Oh, yeah," he affirmed with a sardonic nod, then added vaguely, "Um, I'd like you to meet—this is Wendell. Wendell, my friends Rain, Libby, and Jack, from high school." There were polite murmurs. Having thus slighted everyone, he ended the silence: "Well, shall we walk?" and beckoned Wendell to his side, in the lead.

The crowd needed to keep moving—parade and evening stroll rolled into one—so there was a vague flow snaking, bobbing, past the end of the arcade and toward the Crab Hole. Sam's side was vaguely under way too, mostly out of an instinct to hound the boys, who now had the chambermaids marching in the lead with American and rainbow flags from Stevie's, their feather dusters poking from their tennis skirts like scabbards. The boys were mainly just enjoying themselves; this was about as lively as a good party night on Commercial Street, and they weren't particularly alarmed by a few hecklers. It might have remained just a bipolar parade if not for the arrival at the head of the traffic jam of several bigfoot pickup trucks, out for an evening's cruise.

These grumbling totems to testosterone lodged themselves in the gridlock, their tires alone taller than a puny normal car. One had purple lights underneath, illuminating the giant red shock absorbers; another, spattered end to end with mud, had a front bumper studded with surfcasting rod sockets like a brace of fangs. They sat *ruckruck*ing their straight pipes, sending a carborundum grinder of skinhead guitar out over the other sounds, the drivers hollering encouragement to Sam's side and, from the other side, hearing the catcalls of the boys protesting the music. Jim Priestly flapped and whistled uselessly, attempting to keep the traffic moving. He'd been so hoping he wouldn't need to call in help again, but this was starting to look like something to stay ahead of.

Hollis sat on his porch with a tumbler of gin, smoking his first cigarette in weeks, listening to the roar from the bottom of the lane, peppered with toots and cries, underthudded with bass guitar and drums. He had watched the sun set behind a wall of cloud, black armorplate, now advancing stealthily over the fading dusk. Was that heat lightning?

It was odd to feel so disconnected from something he had helped set off, especially after years of purposely disconnecting himself for protection. He'd finally stepped out of the shadows, and here was the town just jouncing along on its own, heedless. He was free, but a bit chilly; the closet cozy, beckoning. Ellington Hazelett was due the next day for the signing: the Schomburg Center was acquiring Hollis's collection. In a couple of weeks his house would be virtually empty, after twenty years as a vessel for these thousands of bleak artifacts, a collection run amok, the impulse behind it long lost, and likely suspect, anyway. He would need to think about what to do with these rooms after he took down the drop lights, disposed of the dozens of card tables, étagères, steel bookcases, clothing racks, print bins . . . Too many things were happening at once.

Anthony and Wendell strode along toward the Crab Hole, holding hands; Rain and the other two friends straggled along behind, Rain looking stony, lost. Anthony was exquisitely uncomfortable passing in front of Angleton's holding Wendell's hand, but Rain's mother had absolutely ordered him to let go of it, so he really had no choice. She huffed alongside them at ten yards off, scowling, shining the beacon of her sign on them. Up ahead there was a patch of turned-up volume gathering around the Crab Hole, a dark shape with only its sign lit. Anthony spurred them on slightly, tightening his grip on Wendell's hand for a second. He was naggingly aware of turning aside Rain and the others, but there was simply no doubt that something more important was going on here.

The Crab Hole sign, with the phallic crab plunging into its pink, puckered hole, marked the point where the sparring tributaries converged—or noisily failed to, being suddenly brought up short, disturbingly close to one another, the comfortably distant taunting now spiked with eye contact. Adrenaline dumped into the milling throng; voices took on animal qualities, some resonating oddly, as though emanating from a cave, others cracking and bleating, unused to being raised. Here and there postures were struck—standoffs—cocking hammers, mostly between young, blue-collar brawlers and gay men of the *Soldier of Fortune* ilk. Shrill spats flared between Christians certain they hollered from the high ground and men whose tongues had been sharpened at Upper East Side dinner parties. Into this walked Anthony and Wendell.

Their arrival precipitated a lull in the roar immediately around them. While the sight of two men holding hands in public had not exactly become a commonplace this summer, most folks had seen it enough, or at least heard enough about it, to get over the shock. Still, it was startling in this setting. There was nothing defiant about it—Anthony was simply new to this; it was just a mildly affectionate gesture, caught in the headlights. It sent an odd thrill through both sides: *Local youth, lost!* or *Local youth scores!*

"That you, Guido?!" bellowed one of the truckers, who had dismounted from his steed and was leaning on the shoulder-high running board. "What the . . . *fuck?*"

No one had called Anthony "Guido" since eighth grade. The trucker was Chet Sickler, the school bully who had shared his school bus stop, whom he had sweet-talked with dirty jokes into not beating him up, and who now had grown into a malignant oaf with hands permanently the color of truck tires. "Guido! . . . I don't fuckin' believe this!" He started to hitch himself toward them, a step at a time, thumbs in his belt, his face twisted with the effort of grasping how disgusted he was.

Wendell let go of Anthony's hand and urged him sideways toward a knot of muscle-bound men. Groupings started to take shape, wary, shoulders squared.

"These scum got to you, did they?" Sickler's voice was gravelly. "I wanna puke. . . ." He took a step that forced two men in his path to move aside.

Things began to happen quickly. The atmosphere ratcheted taut. There was a convulsive surge of movement, like iron filings aligning to a force field: hotheads, spoilers, watchers, revelers glancing sideways, the heated and hoarse, the ones who pull fighters apart, the ones making determinedly for an exit. Jim Priestly was on the handheld radio. A knot closed around Anthony and Wendell, another around Sickler and his sidekicks—knots of buffers and reinforcements. The short volleys of taunts gave way to a roar; some of the loudest voices were pleading for calm. A momentary tussle—a swap of shoulder shoves—set off a spasm in the crowd, like a twitch on the hide of a beast, then another, another, coming faster, each with an uptick in volume.

Wendell had placed himself partly in front of Anthony, on an impulse to shield without insulting. Anthony and Chet Sickler regarded each other from their respective knots, now just a couple of yards apart. For several seconds they stared, a still center in the tumult, each in his way astonished to be in the presence of such an alien.

"I could fuckin' see it," croaked Sickler. "I could fuckin' see you playin' stinky finger, you fuckin' little . . . Jesus . . ." He shook his head.

A hoarse "Shut the fuck up, asshole!" triggered a fresh burst of cries, of shoving to get at Sickler; circles tightened. "One a you doggy-fuckers wanna try me?" Sickler had gone over a biochemical line into the zone that had earned him a number of stays in the county jail. He sized up the fighting weight on his side and growled at Anthony, "Looks like we need to put you outta your misery." Jerking his glance side to side to firm up his support, he suddenly lunged forward. Instantly, the jeers ceased, gave way to furious stomping, charging feet, grunts, thuds, straining snarls, barks. In seconds the knot around Anthony and Wendell fell back; the two reared backward; but before Anthony could figure which way to bolt, a familiar voice screeched, "Oh no you don't!," and suddenly Chet Sickler was fending off an onslaught of blows from Mrs. Meehan's sign. "I will not see this child harmed by *anyone*!" she howled, flailing wildly. Sickler toppled backward into a heaving, shouting scrum, as much stampede as brawl. In the confusion, Anthony and Wendell ducked back away into the crowd; Anthony glanced back to see Rain anxiously scanning for him. Wendell yanked him onward. Just then there was an uproar—with cries of "Fire!"—from around the far side of the Crab Hole. Anthony and Wendell continued their retreat from the shoving snarl, fear trumping curiosity.

Somebody had thrown a match into the scrap pile in the crook of the building, and a ragged edge of flame was chewing across the dry grass of the construction site toward the freshly painted clapboards. A line of men with giant hiking boots stamped at the flames. For the second time in a week, the blue lights of the trooper cruisers came ricocheting into the village, this time with sirens going. A couple of minutes later came the first fire truck, and the first pickups of the fire volunteers, bouncing across the grass of the park. The sultry night stirred with a sudden breeze from the north.

THE SAILORS anchored behind Long Spit felt it first, the boats swinging to the new direction, halyards beginning to slap on masts. A first distant rumble, an evening thunder squall; Wesley put the cushions below, poured another glass of Pouilly-Fuissé, and gazed peacefully from the shelter of the companionway. Very soon the rigging began to whistle; then came the first crackle-edged explosions, the *scraaak* of sheets of big drops on the deck. He looked across the bay, flattened to pelted velvet, and enjoyed the remove from whatever fuss had set off all those red, white, and blue strobes in the village.

THE FIRST drops didn't dampen the flaring crowd, by now in full cry, with curses and punches hurled, panicked scurrying, colliding, tripping and trampling, human shielding, prying, spikes of outrage. Then the state police bullhorns pierced the roar: "Clear the area at once! Repeat! All to clear the area!" As this penetrated to the brawlers' ears, the downpour moved in with a vengeance.

Anthony strode alongside Wendell under the arcade; they had made cover just ahead of the rain that now blurred the inching cars. Anthony was feeling as though he had taken a very strong hallucinogen. He had never felt in such danger in his life as right then facing Chet Sickler, but he had also never felt under the protection—flimsy though it might have been—of another man before. Now that it appeared he was not, after all, going to be beaten and left for dead, he felt a strange elation welling up.

But, emerging from the press, from the demands of survival, Anthony also felt the thrumming unease resurface, not altogether unpleasant, but gripping. Had he really kissed Wendell, in front of everyone? Could he really reach over if he wanted to (if he *wanted* to?!) and give that sandy-haired nape a squeeze? His mind darted away, serving up images of Rain searching the crowd for him. He and Wendell chatted as they walked, their pace slackening, the question in the air taking hold. Angleton's was out.

"We can make a run for my truck," said Wendell. "It's about half a block up from Frankie's." Anthony nodded.

They slammed the doors and sat in the fogged cab, catching their breath, laughing at being soaked. Wendell gave Anthony a hearty pound and squeeze on the leg, then retreated into wiping his glasses. "So, what's the plan?" he said.

"I don't know," said Anthony. "I live just a few blocks."

"Oh." Wendell's voice fell. "Sure."

Anthony sneaked a direct look. He'd never seen Wendell without his glasses on. His eyelashes were clumped into damp spikes by the downpour. Anthony was transfixed, still couldn't get used to being permitted to regard a male this way. Wendell returned the look. Anthony looked away. Wendell started the engine.

Anthony essayed a conversational tone. "Umm, you been okay with, you know, breaking up with that guy?"

"Not now," said Wendell, and backed up the lane away from Front Street.

When they glided to a halt in front of Anthony's house, there was a long silence, engine running. They both stared ahead; Anthony drummed on his leg in time with the windshield wipers.

Finally, Wendell said, "I'm so glad I ran into you. . . . This has been amazing. . . ." Anthony nodded. "Anthony," he started again, and then, aside, "I love your name . . . so dignified . . . Anthony?" Anthony glanced at him and quickly away. Wendell continued, "There's something I want to ask you, but I'm so afraid it'll ruin everything, that you'll freak out."

After a second's pause, Anthony turned in his seat and met Wendell's gaze. "Whatever the question," he said, "the answer is yes."

The two burst into smiles and threw their arms around each other, eyes welling. For the first time, hands explored openly. Anthony felt his shirttail being eased out. Wendell murmured into his neck, "Are you even legal?"

Anthony murmured back, "I don't know, what do I have to be?"

"Beats me. Never thought I'd need to know."

After a minute they pulled back a bit and sat, glancing about shyly, stroking each other's shoulders and arms. Wendell let out a huge breath and said, "So . . . what are we going to do about this?"

Anthony put on a snide voice. "I don't know, but, whatever it is, let's not do it in front of my mother's house." They both laughed, and Wendell put the truck in gear.

TWELVE

ESLEY WIPED down the rain-washed cockpit, drawing the chamois over the varnished teak coamings, recalling with mild curiosity the shoreside clamor of the night before. He savored the fresh morning; there was in this simple ritual a vestige of the elemental pleasure he had first taken in living aboard, the mug of coffee steaming on the bridge deck, the languid perusal of the morning harbor doings. Somehow over the years his boats had gotten bigger and bigger, and what had once been a glance at the breeze in the treetops and the impulse to dash across the bay had become the scheduling of crew months in advance, with their flights to Nantucket pickups locked in, reservations for choice high-visibility berths bribed from the avaricious harbormasters of urgent stops like Newport, Cuttyhunk, and Edgartown, arrangements for refits and upgrades on boatyard waiting lists, and on and on. That moment of arrival in harbor, when heads turned, was supreme, no doubt, but it had all become a bit too much. This morning, though, he would undertake a quiet, solitary celebration.

In his pocket was the key to the Ferryman House, Fog Bells—how he loved the name. His minions had handled the paper shuffling; reserved to him was the pleasure of conducting *White Wings IV* to her new home. Alas, he had simply not been able to scare up a bouncer or personal trainer to accompany him, an annoyingly common snag. And Jim Hornswich couldn't join him, either, because he, too, had a big day in store: closing on Polly Dickson's house. They had agreed to meet at Wesley's later for a celebratory drink.

So, for this brief voyage to the innermost cove of the harbor, Wesley would be single-handed; but for once, it felt just right. Perhaps for him to come alone to his new domain, nestled as it was in this fresh hotbed, showed the gods an appealingly hopeful spirit. Perhaps here the man awaited who could somehow fly under his radar, straight to his heart. In a few minutes, he would push the button on the polished anchor windlass and get under way. But first, obeying the same sort of hankering for hankering that had led his family to wash the breakfast dishes before opening the Christmas presents, he would have a look at the paper.

The harbor's doughnuts–ice–and–*New York Times* boat had for years been a beat-up flat-bottomed skiff operated by a couple who looked as though they might be spending their nights in its bilges. But this summer that operation had disappeared, as had so many of the village's wartier scrabblers, to be replaced by a perky replica of the *African Queen,* piloted uncertainly by a dazzling cutie Artie Kinzie had spotted working in the Mystic Seaport parking lot and lured away with promises of big tips. The boat's offerings now included croissants, bagels, fat-free muffins, and, from noon onward, a raw bar. Customers in the know could always request the free garnish of condoms. Assessing the boy's boat-handling skills, Wesley ordered him to stand clear and place the newspaper in the net he extended on its long handle.

The story caught his eye immediately: page one, below the fold, one of those slow-news-day features the *Times* had started running so as not to appear so above-it-all: "Sleepy Town Wakes to Find It's Hot." Wesley glanced at the picture, a crowd scene with two handsome young guys kissing in the foreground, a glowering Christian waggling a "Love the Sinner, Hate the Sin" sign in the background. "Toe to toe in the picture-perfect seaside village of Long Spit," ran the caption, "where not everyone is happy that it's become a trendy gay resort." The story began, "A Rhode Island town, long known only to a few fine old families and a straggle of beachgoers, has just been claimed by a most exuberant—and controversial—summer set. Thursday evening an impromptu march by jubilant gay men, celebrating the liquor board go-ahead for the village of Long Spit's first gay bar, abruptly turned ugly as an odd-bedfellows coalition of local elements turned out to make their displeasure known." Wesley made himself very comfortable. The account went on to describe the way the evening developed, with Jim Priestly quoted, "Weren't for that cloudburst, it's anybody's guess what might have happened." The piece jumped to the back of another section, Wesley in hot pursuit, as it delved into the background of the confrontation, the rebirth of the Ocean, the booming shops and B&Bs, the hemorrhaging of the beach club membership after the raid. His rapt look changed to a smile as he read, "The town's gold-plated Signal Hill enclave boasts the finest collection of Shingle Style summer homes along the entire Eastern Seaboard, yet the village had remained largely unknown to outsiders, its finest properties passed along within families for generations. That's changing now, for a combination of reasons, chief among them dismay at the new arrivals. Something of a sedate feeding frenzy has been set off as wealthy gay men vie for the mansions of the disaffected."

Wesley permitted himself a smug chortle. Nothing could have made his day so. With the pick of all those nattering, shingled contraptions, he'd nailed the one house that was different—substantial, better—and now the village was certified, happening. He was suffused with the warm glow of the prescient acquisitor. The story rambled on about how the hurricane of '38 had stripped clean the sand spit, "pristine to this day apart from the remains of World War II artillery emplacements, where now the only sentries are men looking for casual sex." Wesley felt his life opening before him, a glittering path. The rest of the paper could wait. He wanted to see his new trophy right now. A manicured finger went to the control panel and, deep within the varnished joinery, the yacht's diesel growled to life.

"AT LEAST this time I unbarricaded the front door," Hollis said, emerging from the house to greet Ellington and Florian as they came up the walk. "Please come in, and welcome. And Florian, I'm so glad to see you again." Actually Hollis was unnerved by seeing Florian for the first time since the fateful day on the beach, but was in his heartiest postrecital mode, not easily knocked off balance. As they exchanged greetings, Ellington glided up the steps wearing his amber-tinted glasses and a black silk kimono with a single persimmon-and-gold serpent lounging across the shoulders. Florian, in his usual spotless jeans and white sweatshirt, flashed Hollis a brief, breathtaking smile. He indicated Ellington with a sidelong glance, "He does not travel any longer without his personal assistant." Florian and Hollis engaged in a brief muddle of pressed hands, air kisses, and a tentative near-hug. Hollis thought him even more beautiful than he remembered, the face even more finely chiseled, the cheekbones perhaps slightly more prominent, the soft hazel eyes bigger, more heartbreaking.

"Well, come in, come in," Hollis was brisk, snapping himself to. "I've hardly done a thing with the collection. It's been a bit disrupted around here, as you may have heard."

Ellington waved his concerns away. "Our archivists actually prefer to do the packing themselves. Saves them time on the other end. Yes, we have heard—found a copy of that little homosexual shopper's rag in our room at Mrs. Boothroyd's."

"Hated the picture," said Florian.

"Well, of course, despicable, a total invasion," said Hollis.

"Oh, I just mean the tum—big old blomped-out thing, terrible angle." Florian patted his lean midriff. "I mean, it's not every day I get to *appear*— And: 'unidentified African-American'? Excuse me? My people came straight from Paris. The *idea*."

Hollis had cleared room to open the interior shutters in the dining room, flooding the room with natural light for the first time in years. "May I offer you something? Tea?"

Ellington was already engrossed in the nearby tables of artifacts, holding up a slave child's doll made of cotton scraps and feed sacks.

"Tea would be lovely," said Florian. He came up behind Hollis and put his hands on his shoulders. "I hope you haven't been too—put through it, by all this. You did nothing, but nothing, wrong." He gave him a pat. "Don't you worry about some raggy queen declaring how we all must live." Here Florian gave Hollis a motherly, if slightly seductive look. "You are a decent man. Hold your head high." He gave Hollis a lift under the chin with a bent finger. Hollis flushed, startled at these touches, cast back to his lessons with Anthony, in this very room, seeming so long ago.

"Yes, well, thank you," Hollis stammered. He cleared his throat. "Let me put the water on."

A few moments later, Ellington trailed him into the kitchen. "If you wouldn't mind," he said, "I'll have this." He produced from the sleeve of his kimono a small pouch. "It's blended for me, seems to clarify me. No one else can stand it. *He* says it smells like cat spray." He paused a moment, seemed to study the biscuits. "Pity. He could use it."

"He could?" Hollis replied. "He certainly seems to me very . . . clarified."

Ellington waved this away. "More and more tired . . . He's started the afternoon naps."

Hollis was speechless, staring out at the algae-choked wet spot that had been a goldfish pond. From the pause, Ellington was certain this was news. "Yes, he's talking about cutting back, maybe retiring . . . not my way, but"—he arched his eyebrows, staring off—"each to his own." Then, shaking his head, he said briskly, "May I feel free to wander? I may not see these things out of the crates again for who knows how long."

"Oh, by all means." Hollis pulled himself together. "I'll bring this through in a minute."

When he returned to the dining room, Hollis found Florian idly trying to fold one of the shutters into its recess in the woodwork. "Oh, yes," he said, putting down the tea tray, "I'll have to sort all that out. I'm like a salamander coming out from under its rock, but I guess I always felt the sunlight would damage everything. Don't know what I'm going to do with all these rooms."

"Honey, they are going to *resume* being rooms," said Florian.

"Ain' *nothing* more fun than helping that along." With a coy glance he succeeded in latching the shutter in its hiding place.

Ellington drifted back to the table. "Mr. Wynbourne, this is truly an important acquisition for the Schomburg. I am so pleased."

"Yes, well, it feels like the right time," said Hollis. "I'd sort of lost track of what it was all about. Very lucky you came into the shop that day, both of you."

"Indeed," said Ellington, reaching for a well-used lizard portfolio. "Shall we get down to business?"

ANGLETON'S WAS crackling; Lattie sat behind the cash register, looking on with mixed concern and thrill. The picture of Anthony and Wendell had gone on the wire services and been picked up, not only by the *Times,* but by all the area papers plus the *Boston Globe* and papers as far away as Portland and Miami. Every booth had a paper going, home fries getting cold, readers' expressions ranging from delight to disgust, discussions warming to steadily higher decibels, most of the locals stony. At ten A.M. Anthony arrived for his shift.

He spotted the stack of Westerly papers displayed in front of the cash register, and stopped dead, staring at the picture. He glanced up at Lattie, who regarded him as though he were an exploding cigar. It took only a few seconds for the first yips and cheers from the boys—and urgent murmurs from the locals—to swell to a roar. Anthony flashed a big, blushing grin, threw his arms out in mock bravado, and gave a stiff, boyish bow, whereupon the entire gay contingent rose to give him a standing ovation. Lattie made change for an older local couple, exchanging small head shakes of amazement. Working his way back to the wait station, Anthony greeted his fans on all sides.

But as he attached his name tag to start work, he had an oddly distant air about him.

Outside, Front Street was a hive as well. Dot Bradley greeted passersby with an expansive smile. She was going to ride this thing to glory. Men commanded the street with a bit more strut and swagger, a bit more display of affection. The TV news truck had caught everything the night before, had led at eleven with the chambermaids, the flames. This morning, the crew was out sampling opinion on the street, and some Radical Faeries were providing precisely the required sensation, hovering behind the mumbling locals, upstaging them with punk camping. The *Globe* had mentioned that the Crab Hole's grand opening would be the next weekend. The phones had been ringing all morning at the Ocean; and at Sea Breeze Properties, Lonnie was swamped with calls for every available condo unit and was passing people on to the last remaining B&B rooms—even a couple of motels in Westerly—for the occasion, which would just be the warm-up for the next weekend, Labor Day.

The monthly luncheon meeting of the matrons of the Beach Club at Hattie Wiggins's house was abuzz with talk of the riot, the beach club raid, the club's prospects. All through the macaroni salad, heads bobbed in agreement that something was going very wrong in the village, though of course gay people are just fine, many of them, it's just the few, Well, it's always the few who give a bad name, But, anyway, why did everything have to be done in such an ugly way, couldn't folks work things out anymore? And have you seen the way they behave on the beach? Each to his own, so to speak, but still, with kids around . . . Yes, you have to think about the children. I frankly don't feel that comfortable sharing the beach with them, I'll tell you I worry what I'll suddenly be faced with. You can be minding your own business and suddenly one'll reach over and touch the other—you know, there. I mean, they're on every TV show now, it seems, so the idea isn't exactly shocking, but . . . Well, in my day we didn't have time to worry about whether we were . . . gay, maybe the economy is doing *too* well. Maybe it's wrong to say, but, you know, a lot of them are very good-looking. Oh I know, isn't it a waste? And such a shame about Marie Blais's son, Mark. I remember him as a drum major in the high school band. Who'd've thought he would turn out like this? Well, they say it's in your genes. *I* certainly don't know which gene it is that makes a grown man want to put on a tutu, but anyway . . .

Over tea, Hattie started off the business part with the membership report. The mailing they had sent out after the raid, suggesting various security precautions, had backfired badly. A number of families who hadn't used their memberships in years but had kept sending the check along, hoping some grandchild might appear the next summer to use the changing room, had now been reminded of the club in a most unfortunate way, had concluded it wasn't making it anymore, and had resigned. "At the very least, we're not going to be able to do the painting we put in for," Hattie finished, "and I don't know what-all else. I'll tell you, some of the letters were kind of mean, too. Made me cross, like it was our fault what's going on in town or like we'd come down with something."

Lizzie Hopewell crunched a ginger snap thoughtfully. "There's a real question of whether we can manage, in terms of property taxes, upkeep, and whatnot, with so many dropping off the rolls."

"Yes," chimed in Edith Morse. "And not to mention that, if we want to stop the losses, we're going to have to look at re-vamping the whole building for better security. Close it up on the sea side. I don't know, it'd make it a whole different kind of place than what it was."

Nods and murmurs around the room. Alice Carson said what was on a few people's minds: "You have to ask, at some point, does it make any sense to try to make it all over, or should we just look at it, face it, just a victim of the changing times? I mean we all of us don't have that many more years left of wanting to use the beach. We say we're keeping it going for the kids, but *my* granddaughter, anyway, just wants to go to the mall anymore."

Hattie spoke up. "Well, here's one idea that I didn't even take too seriously when I first heard it, but maybe we should. Of course we all know the snack bar has been a sad affair, with having to close it and now it's becoming such an eyesore. The committee back then, to my way of thinking, didn't really think it through, just close it down and decide later. Water over the dam, but anyway, a couple of days ago I got a call from Ray Hardman, Salt Air Estates? Asking whether there'd be any interest in selling it. Of course, I said I didn't think so, and that was the end of it, but you know, now I'm thinking, it's not doing us any good just sitting there, and it might give us the capital to stay going, make some changes . . . might give us a chance to hang on."

"Did he say what would go in there if we sold?" someone asked.

"Well, not really," said Hattie. "But at least there couldn't be any drinking, what with the seashore regulations, the state."

"At least we wouldn't have to go through *that* again," said Lizzie, nodding toward the newspaper. General agreement.

"Isn't he a—bachelor?" Lizzie spoke carefully.

"Well, maybe so," said Hattie, "but at least he's local."

"It's just—it feels like letting the, not exactly the enemy, but, more like the fox, too close to the henhouse."

"Well, maybe if they had their own place to be, you know, down by the beach at night, they'd leave us alone," said Edith.

"I'm sorry," said Lizzie with a snort, "but if only it were just the beach they were looking for at night." She nodded at the fidgeting circle with a significant look.

"Well, I'm sorry too," said Hattie, "but tell me a better way out." She set down her cake fork with an imperious *tink*. "You're acting as if we have a choice. Everything's different now. The fox's money may be the only way we can keep the hens safe."

"If we're going to think this way, why not put up a For Sale sign and try to make a killing on it?" challenged Lizzie.

"It's a little of 'Better the devil you know,'" said Hattie.

———

ANTHONY WORKED his shift as though in a dream. The burger sent back for being too rare, the chowder not hot enough, didn't begin to register. Cataclysmic events—the picture on the wire service, the ovation on his arrival—couldn't quite command his attention. Even last evening's declaration before the whole town, which had already put that occasion in a category of one in his life to date, was bulldozed off his mental screen by candlelit images: Wendell's gentle hand tracing his collarbones, the first flick of tongues on lips.

They had driven the twenty minutes back to Wendell's apartment in near silence, both of them vibrating with excitement. When they arrived, though, the charged unease they'd both experienced at times with each other suddenly lifted. They were no longer reaching across a threshold to each other, but were finally both past it, ready. Wendell had been the perfect lover for a novice—patient, quiet, letting Anthony's wonderstruck perusal control the pace of things, offering his friendly body as a banquet for Anthony's touch and taste, and in turn exploring and murmuring over Anthony's body until it sang. "I want to touch you everywhere at once," Anthony whispered. It was as though, for all those pent-up years, he had cat-alogued every urge to touch, to know the feel of another man's finely ribbed flank, of the impossibly soft skin on the inside of the forearm, and was now determined to order from every page of that catalogue in a single night. The crescendo had been measured, savoring, drawing on bottomless reserves to build to writhing, ecstatic release. And then, the best part of all: damp, still embrace, a perfect fit, the slow climbdown from thudding hearts to quiet, profound breathing, lapsing to bliss-stunned sleep. Wendell had been the good citizen, prodding the spent boy awake for the dazed drive home at four A.M.

This morning—his mother's call somehow busting through his armor of sleep—he'd been ambushed from the first wak-ing instant by the realization: Everything from now on will be reckoned as coming *after* last night. After a quick shower (Is this the same body?) and a piece of toast accompanied by a perfunctory exchange with his mother—"Just out with a friend; don't pry"—he headed to work, jogging past the news-paper in its plastic bag at the end of the driveway. And now he appeared to Angleton's patrons as that same cute young man who'd been dispensing advice all summer, the one who was clearly gay. Only now it was true.

FOR THE hundredth time, Wesley consulted the sketch chart of the cove, rechecking the leading marks: the end of an old stone jetty on the far side to be brought directly below the cupola on Betsy Haring's house up on the knoll. Satisfied, he swung *White Wings'* bow onto the course for threading the ledges at the entrance. The line lay disquietingly close to the mussel-crusted outcrop on the starboard hand, but the Ferry-mans' attorney had assured Ray it had seen many generations of the family's craft safely in and out of the cove. Only after passing through the narrows, when the depth sounder stopped its warning beeps and started reading twelve and fourteen feet, could Wesley finally allow himself a look at his prize.

He realized, in that first glimpse from the water, that this was the vantage point the architects had given top billing. As much as he'd been captivated by the street facade, so formal, almost forbidding, he was even more enchanted by the private world he now beheld—exclusive yet expansive: the gallery along the side facing the water, letting onto the low-walled patio, the terraced gardens stepping serenely down to the granite bulkhead, benches of stone and timber placed here and there, partly hidden beneath arbors or behind scrims of foliage, as summery and romantic as anything he'd ever seen. An upper-story verandah surmounted the entire length of the gallery, offering an intimate yet commanding preserve. His mind danced with images of gym-buffed hunks dotting the property, leafing through their health magazines, not a thought in their heads but how best to relocate as the sun traversed the gardens. But wait—wasn't the idea to find someone he could respect? He scolded himself with a grin.

He brought *White Wings IV* alongside the massive float, noting the shipworthy bollards; these old families knew how to do things right. He secured her as though a hurricane were imminent, fiddling lovingly with the fall of each dockline so that, when he glanced back at her, she would be the picture of yachtsmanlike perfection, peaceful but ready. As he flaked the tail of the last line into a formal flat spiral, he heard a toot and looked up along the side of the house to see Ray Hardman's Range Rover, with Ray, Jim Hornswich, and Betsy Haring spilling out of the doors.

Jim waved and called to him, "We could see your mast coming in, through the trees!"

"Hey! I'll let you in by the garden!" Wesley shouted, striding up the dock. "I haven't even figured out the keys yet. If I let you in the gate, will the police arrive?"

"No, no," Ray called back, "don't worry, I had them leave everything disarmed for you this morning."

Wesley threw open the bronze-bound cedar gate and they all churned, clucking and fluttering, through to the garden, Wesley helplessly beaming like a catering hall host. He hugged Jim and congratulated him on his closing. Jim was modest. "Yeah, it's pretty cool. I've got a lot of work to do before all my stuff arrives—floors, you know, trim . . . but it's going to be great. Nothing like this of course, but—"

"Nonsense, you found a very special house," Wesley gushed, for the moment clearly out of his mind with delight. "Let me see if I can figure out which key fits these back doors." Ray took the keys from him, unlocked the French doors, and stood aside with a sweeping gesture of welcome.

The large, cool room had been cleared of the odd pieces of furniture left by the last of the Ferrymans. Four pairs of doors onto the gallery filled the room with soft, dappled light from the garden. In the center of the room, on a kitchen stool, stood an ice bucket with a bottle of champagne and four glasses. Wesley looked at Ray, who made a shy gesture. "It was nothing."

Wesley read the card: "Wishing you all happiness here. Tell your friends. Ray." He looked up. "I shall, I shall. I *have,* don't worry." He gave Ray a hug and a peck on the cheek.

"I am *so thrilled* you-all are coming to town"—Betsy nodded to each—"and not just for personal reasons." Winking, she put a finger to each temple and stretched back the skin around her eyes.

"Oh, so you're booked?" said Ray. "Guess I better get on the waiting list."

"That's right," said Jim. "Oops, did I violate doctor-patient confidentiality?"

Betsy laughed. "Not to worry. I'm going to be your poster girl up on the hill."

Wesley eased the cork out. Jim said, "Oh come on, not going to let it fly?"

"You know me," Wesley replied, "not the let-fly type." Jim had what seemed to Wesley a stubborn propensity for landing on little reminders of how different they were. Their rather odd sexual M.O. had felt like a good fit at first, but Jim had taken to commenting on the proceedings at the most inopportune times, shattering Wesley's highly evolved fantasies. Maybe Jim was just babbling his discomfort, but he wasn't, any longer, satisfying the boy-toy part of the casting requirement. They were in the throes of seeing whether a friendship could be salvaged.

They held their glasses aloft. Wesley said, "To—the invasion." All clinked and repeated the words.

"Take no prisoners," said Ray.

"But show mercy on the womenfolk?" said Betsy.

"Yeah, yeah, whatever." Ray chuckled.

They drifted back outside and sat on the low stone wall by the patio.

Ray told them about the bid he and Sibley Briggs had made to buy the beach club snack bar. "Ever since a couple of his clients started sniffing around over here, Sibley's just been sitting over there on Fishers going crazy because he didn't have a piece of this. It'd be perfect for him. He could just buzz over in his Whaler and walk ashore. No need to drive lit. Anyway, the beach bags are holding their monthly meeting today, so there could be a message on my machine when I get back to the office."

"What kind of thing you thinking about?" asked Jim.

"Oh, snacks and juice bar all day, tea dance, sundowners, perfect location for sunsets. No booze for the moment, but I'm working on that."

"You'd go up against the Ocean for the tea dance business?"

Ray smiled mischievously. "I've got a feeling they won't be doing tea dance for much longer."

"Why on earth not?" asked Wesley.

"Let's just say I'm not at liberty to tell you . . . but it's not bad news."

"Well, they always close around Labor Day, anyway," said Betsy, "and there's a lot more good weather after that." She shook her head. "That old pile has been such a headache. As a preservationist, I can tell you, what a sad story. Years back, Milam Sandermeyer, the owner, applied for landmark status. And you'd think it would be a natural, I mean the place *is* a landmark, it's even on the nautical charts. Normally, I'd have been helping him along, with all the red tape?" The champagne was smoothing her voice more and more into Charleston. "But I've learned the hard way, we in the preservation dodge can paint ourselves into a corner sometimes, you get the wrong owner. We all knew he wasn't ever going to spend the money to even keep it up to code, never mind bring it back to perfection. Looked like it would just rot there, losing more business every year, gettin' to be more and more of an eyesore. And a lot of the fogies that live around it—Lev Stahl, Arnie Prendergast, and them—have never liked having it moldering there, you know, they hate having anything remotely like a business operating on the Hill, so they piped up—for once we agreed on something, and that gave me cover for turning it down."

"And now it's jammed to the walls," said Jim.

"Yep, you never know," Betsy said. "I worry it's going to topple over just from all the bodies upstairs. Golly, haven't I been running on? The bubbly . . ." She looked at Ray. "And am I 'at liberty' to mention what's up with Sibley's clients?"

"Sure, why not. Or I will." He explained that Alec and Preston, the elderly couple on Fishers Island, were about to close on the Van Gelder house, a Shingle Style behemoth in one of the choicest positions on Signal Hill, a house that had suffered many indignities over the years.

"I am just thrilled!" crowed Betsy. "That house has been my cross to bear, one thing after another, and you know, those guys have already been asking me can they tear out that godawful glassed-in porch, restore the original railings, blow up the concrete retaining wall and put in stone. I swear, it's like all these houses are getting thrown a pink life ring." She put her hand to her mouth. "Oops, was that all right to say?"

"Perfectly, darling," said Ray. "Oh, they've got the deep pockets, all right. And they're already talking it up to the other house queens over there, and in Stonington, and Easthampton. They're not interested in being lonely pioneers."

THIRTEEN

ARTIE KINZIE had not taken a day off all summer—not that he was complaining, mind you. Things were building nicely and after this next big push, they'd be positioned for the next year with the whole winter for construction. He was on the phone with Simon Whetstone in Switzerland: "Yeah, they say they can string the whole building with fuse wire in three days. . . . Permit's in hand, police notified, yup. They were nervous about it, you know, a party in a wired building, but I said, Hey, every bridge and tunnel in Switzerland's been wired to blow for decades. . . . Yeah, that's right, think about that next time you throw a roach out the car window. So, about a half-hour to place the charges. Oh, you'll definitely be on the map. . . . Lots of interest, *Times* Style section coming, already did background with them. . . . Yeah, two ships sold out from South Street, bigger ones than before, and two others from Providence and Boston. The line usually takes geezers to Florida, but they're in between trips. . . . Yeah, they're delighted. . . . Oh don't worry, the whole crew is gay on both of them. Got a slice of the gate going to AIDS groups in the city, Boston, and Providence, too, so a triple boost there."

Simon had seen the potential immediately when he visited the Ocean during the first tea dance. Even as he rumbled back toward New York aboard his yacht, the hotelier was setting in motion the first exploratory enquiries. He had been looking for a seaside opportunity in New England to complement the South Beach triumph: something in a smallish, two- or three-hundred-room operation, quietly posh on the outside, harmonious, salty, but radically hedonistic within. Milam Sandermeyer had been happy to grant a first refusal option while Simon's people hurried around putting the money together. Milam had been expecting the old pile to become more and more of an albatross, especially after Marcia told him about the porch nearly collapsing, so any way out was an unexpected plus.

At first, Whetstone had been skeptical about Artie's Wrecking Ball idea; he usually liked to keep a low profile until a project was much further along. But Artie had argued persistently that Long Spit was a unique case, having taken off out of nowhere in just one season, and that the Wrecking Ball was therefore the perfect, maybe the only way to elevate the place onto the crucial roster of annual circuit parties that would bring thousands of gay men from all over the world. "So far we've got one season under our belt, could be seen as a flash in the pan. Got to jump on this while the newness is peaking, get it installed in the big picture. A spectacular like this, 'First Annual' written all over it, would nail it."

Meanwhile, Artie was just as persistently selling the idea to the cadre of promoters and circuit mavens who presided over the world circuit calendar, showing them the video from the helicopter, going out on a limb: "I'll personally guarantee you twenty-five hundred boys for this, and once it's inaugurated, once they see this place, it'll lock in automatically. It's the first time any place has taken off this way, everybody's talking about that already, I've sent shiploads, everybody else just needs an excuse to go there, see what the fuss is all about, what better excuse than this spectacle. Picture it, a few thousand boys, out of their minds from whatever, just been dancing all night, they file off the dance floor and head outside, you got your rosy glow in the east, they're holding hands, excited, toasted, maybe a few tears, you know, he's the one, they're all standing behind the barricades, maybe the right music, maybe the *2001* music, the sun's coming up, and ka-*BOOM!* The whole frigging hotel is history—imploded—a pile of scrap." Here Artie got a Mickey Rooney–ish little-guy-with-a-dream look in his eye. ". . . column of smoke mixing with the cheers for the new dawning, I'm getting myself emotional here . . . and then the next year, they'll all want to come back to see how the new hotel came out. By then, you're in."

His graphics people had come up with a webpage, print ad, and flyer design that used superimposed maps, homing in on Long Spit from, first, the world, then the U.S., then the Northeast corridor; last was a town map, overlaid with a dreamlike figure of a naked man so that the spit itself could be seen as his semi-erect penis. "Perfect!" Artie said. "You could miss it unless you're queer."

The clincher was lining up B. J. Gelson, the impresario (he preferred "events planner") who was a behind-the-scenes legend, his company, Unexplained Events, fresh from back-to-back smashes doing Desmond Tutu at St. John the Divine and the Dalai Lama at Madison Square Garden. Once Gelson was on board, Garnett Black's syndicated gossip column and website, "Circuit Buzz," quickly followed with his official stamp of approval, closely watched by pilgrims from Sydney to Paris to Oslo. The project now began to take on its own momentum, as all the heavy hitters angled to make sure nothing with their names on it would fail. Their teams swung into action, people who knew how to pull things together fast, veterans of pop music tours, video crews, and political campaigns. The best DJs vied for billing; full-page ads appeared in big-city gay party papers across the country, jump-starting a ticket hot line and website, lit up from the first day. The four ships alone would bring almost a thousand men, every room in town was snatched up, a clearing house was set up, blocks of rooms grabbed at the giant Indian casinos nearby, a luxury coach fleet chartered, with videos and hot serving staff. Apart from an ad in the *Sand Flea*, Artie did no promotion in Long Spit. Despite the boost in the town's visibility from all the riot coverage, another riot might be bad for business. So at first it was mainly the visiting men who found out about the party, and those few locals who had gotten in the habit of picking up the *Sand Flea*. Rita Benoit, the secretary at the town clerk's office who handled the blasting permit, was able to keep quiet about it for several days.

So the town went unsuspectingly about its quiet business, with now and then a twitch or a spat to remind everyone there'd been no official truce. One evening a thief broke into a car parked behind the yogurt shop because he saw a shopping bag on the floor behind the front seat. When he found the bag full of gay porno videos, he started smashing the car windows with a pipe, and got arrested for disturbing the peace. The newspaper decorously referred to the tapes as "X-rated materials." There was some talk of busting the car owner, a friend of Derek and Tracy's from Boston, for bringing the "materials" across state lines, but cooler heads in the D.A.'s office prevailed. Jack, the car owner, told Derek that he never got the videos back. "No great tragedy, they were old, I'd lent them to a friend . . . The boys had Beatle haircuts. As long as someone is enjoying them, ummhh . . . especially someone in the police department."

The gossip mill at Frankie's and Sully's passed along a tidbit about a man named Paulo something, who somebody said was from one of the old Portuguese fishing families in Westerly, who was walking out Long Spit beach one afternoon and came upon two men sharing a blanket with a twelve-year-old boy. He glared, shook his head in disgust and went on by, but apparently started stewing and was back a minute later in a rage. Just as he began to rant—"Look at him! Jesus! He's just a child!"—and the men were still trying to ignore him, and surrounding people were beginning to pay attention, a fourteen-year-old girl appeared out of the water and screeched, "Dad!? Who is this creep and why are you letting him so close to Evan?"

One particularly unfortunate incident involved Louise Bettencourt, one of the grandest of the village dames. Known as "Wheezie" ever since her asthmatic childhood in Lausanne, she had summered in Long Spit for sixty years in a thirty-two-room "chalet" hidden within a copse of cedars atop Signal Hill. She and her much younger husband, Gerard—she had once been considered racy—walked to the end of Long Spit every Sunday morning for a picnic lunch; they were a familiar sight carrying their antique French striped beach umbrella. They had gradually become inured to the barely-veiled carnality this summer had brought to the cubist ruins. But on this Sunday, as they approached their regular spot, they heard the insistent thunk of techno. They rounded the last vine-engulfed pillbox to find a solitary young man, entirely naked but for a black baseball cap and sunglasses, dancing full steam to a boom box on the concrete next to him. Having, perhaps, miscalculated and taken his last tab of Ecstasy a bit too close to dawn, he was thoroughly enjoying his party of one, with his considerable endowment at least partly stirred up by all the flapping and flinging around.

Wheezy was thunderstruck and puffed up to full outrage, normally enough to scatter any unacceptable debris in her path. But he simply pivoted toward her, twirled his hands playfully—moderately glad to be joined on the dance floor—made his mouth into a come-hither nozzle and stared through her to some higher truth beyond. On surrounding perches, other boys looked on, clucking but riveted. Wheezy would not cede her territory without making a stand. She ordered Gerard to begin erecting the umbrella about twenty feet from the sweating dervish, while she stood looking imperiously out to sea. The dancer paused for a swig from his water bottle and knelt to dig in his pack for something; it looked as if the standoff might be defused. He stretched out on his back, his head propped on a hiking boot, looking as though he might nod off. But then his still-incipient erection caught his attention, as though it were an attractive bauble in a flea market, and he began stroking himself as idly as one might apply sunblock to a forearm. Gerard strove to arrange their kit to divert Wheezy's attention, but she was locked in a cycle of glancing back at the outrage, then glowering at the horizon with fresh fury, as though ladling hot sauce into the stew with each glance. One by one, the boys on the surrounding ruins, staring, tut-tutting, gingerly pulled on their Speedos.

Suddenly she advanced on him and planted herself, pointing at him, but refusing to look at him. "I'm sorry to tell you, but you must not do this." The accent never failed to materialize at times like this.

The young man paused in his activity and looked at her as

though there might be a language barrier. After considering her objection for a moment, he let out a peevish "Whatever," and sulkily pulled a towel over himself, pretending to doze.

After a couple of minutes, Wheezy said, "Kind sir? . . . And the music?" She waggled her finger and shook her head. The man gave the off switch a petulant swat. In the sudden quiet, there was a smattering of applause from the sparse gallery.

HELEN BOOTHROYD was all set to break ground for an addition that would add eight more rooms for the next season. Designed by a young architect from Hartford who'd become a Lilac Bush regular, it was to feature private sunporches and Jacuzzis, and had space for a small basement gym and sauna, whenever Helen felt ready. (She had drawn the line at mirrors over the beds.) She had hired new help—replacing her chambermaid, who'd been objecting to the bed-hopping, with an appealing couple of young men, illegal Haitian immigrants—and so had much more time to devote to her role as beloved grandmother of her clientele. Meanwhile, up the street at the Gull and Rose, Nancy Jenkins had kicked Sam out and filed for divorce. He'd moved into the Fish Hook efficiencies on the outskirts of town.

One after another, Signal Hill's old guard—the Weatherhills, the Stamps, the Wendlandts—made oblique, muted approaches to Ray Hardman. As they bemoaned the town's transformation, he would nod solemnly and let out a long commiserative sigh, while mentally matching their house with one of his eager buyers. He and Sibley expedited the closing on the snack bar, and Ray called in some favors to get a crew going on a quick cleanup. In a matter of days, they had hauled away Dumpsters full of rotted plywood and years of guano, and had made a good start on a stylish, rather Japanese-looking assemblage of cedar terraces and gazebos, centered around a simple, open-air pavilion that would house the juice bar. A vaguely Polynesian sign appeared, announcing the Sand Box. Stairways at each corner of the pavilion led to a roof terrace, the Upper Reaches, cleverly tucked within the roofline to offer "moonlit intimacy," as the ad in the *Sand Flea* promised.

The men who had attacked Andy Meltzer in Sully's parking lot had their trial date fixed for November. Andy was slated to be making a film in Mexico at that time, so had some handling of matters to do. Derek and Tracy would come down from Boston to testify. Sully had a new light in the parking lot of the bar, one of those free lights the power company will come and install that made the lot look like a private investigator's photograph. He was baffled when some of the boys complained.

Betsy, with the best of intentions, arranged for Wesley to meet Hollis. She thought it made perfect sense: they were both gay, single, a bit older, shared an interest in antiques, lived in fine houses. She could be forgiven for being a bit obtuse about the impetus behind men's connections. Wesley genuinely liked her—she had certainly made him feel welcome in town—so he felt obliged to accept an introduction. He agreed to meet Betsy in front of Hollis's shop, where she could introduce them without any fuss, but they found a sign saying "Open by Appointment Only." Wesley hoped he was off the hook, but Betsy persisted.

"I know what," she said. "I believe Hollis is a life member of the yacht club. You could meet him there for a drink. Something about—his grandfather was a founding member . . . or great-grandfather. Anyway, you're a sailor, this'll be perfect. I don't get inside the place more than once a year, when they raise money for the town dock or whatever, but it's rather nice, and I think they'd treat you a little differently than they do me. I'll call him and set it up. It's not exactly his style, he'll probably kick and scream, but it'll be good for him. And then I'll just stay right out of it."

The Long Spit Yacht Club was a smallish, rather formal building, white-painted cedar shingles with dark green shutters, window boxes full of geraniums tended by the Auxiliary. It sat on a dense clump of pilings in the harbor, accessible only by boat or by a small footbridge from the shore, its porches facing the harbor and the sunsets, its back to the village. Branching in several directions were floating docks, for members' dinghys and for the junior sailing program that had so far soldiered on through this peculiar summer as though it were merely unusually rainy, the children picked up from their sailing lessons a bit more promptly than in past years, rather than being left to dawdle along Front Street for a yogurt or a slice of pizza.

Hollis doddered regretfully across the bridge. He'd always believed that Betsy shared his aversion to change, so he didn't appreciate her bulldozing him into what felt like a blind date, but word had come back through Dot about how Betsy had gone to bat for him on the dinner party circuit: he owed her. He paused, with a diffident stoop, at the reception desk. The young woman looked up, a deeply tanned, black-haired, blue-eyed product of Yankee eugenics. "I'll just be having a drink up in the bar," Hollis said, barely meeting her glance.

"That's fine, and the name?"

"Hollis Wynbourne."

A cloud crossed her face. "Wynbourne, that's W, i . . . ?" She opened a register of members. Hollis pointed, shyly but a bit impatiently, at the wall above the foyer fireplace. She followed his finger. "Ah, I see. I'm sorry, sir," she said, as she spotted the name "Asa Wynbourne" beneath one of the glowering founders' portraits.

"And I'm expecting someone to join me as a guest," he said.

"No problem, and again, I'm sorry," she said. He nodded and trudged up the stairs.

Wesley showed up directly. Hollis had taken a stool at the bar. There were just a few other men having late-afternoon drinks.

They shook hands and introduced themselves, sizing each other up. For their separate reasons, neither was any longer accustomed to meeting another middle-aged man on purely social ground, and neither knew what Betsy might have reported to the other. Wesley donned his executive demeanor, and Hollis his postrecital, although, after taking note of the room and the weather, they confirmed, with a bounce of the eyebrows, each other's approval of the bartender.

"Betsy tells me you've just acquired the Ferryman House," said Hollis, to end the first lull.

"Yes, indeed—very pleased. Do you know the house?"

"Well, only as a child, you know, trespassing to fish off the dock. They were not mixers, the Ferrymans." Hollis was darting glances at the others at the bar, trying to peel away the years from their faces to recall which tormentors of his childhood they might be, and warily searching for disapproval in their return glances.

The two persevered, speaking in oblique code about what had befallen the town. Wesley found himself telling Hollis about having been at a board meeting for a giant conglomerate and running into a famous gay movie producer. "Just making conversation, told him about the housing stock, and other stock"—he leered—"and he said he'd already heard about it over in the Hamptons and was getting about ready to come over for a look." Wesley was surprised at himself. Why should he care to impress this slightly odd, rumpled man? And if he did care, why say *this,* of all things? It certainly didn't seem to be working.

Hollis's stiff manner was becoming even more remote. "Yes, well . . . a lot for a small town to absorb in such a hurry. It isn't what I knew, anymore. Changes for me as well," he said, probing.

"Yes, I should imagine," said Wesley, opaque. "Okay, though?"

Hollis paused a moment, glanced around again. "Well, now the dust has settled a bit, yes. Actually something very good, yes." He nodded with a tight smile, as though he'd thought better of going on. They sat for a minute in silence.

"Betsy and I met at your shop yesterday, she was going to introduce us in person," said Wesley. "It looks interesting. I must come back when you're open."

"Well, more or less a hobby now, really," Hollis seemed distracted. "I may let it go. A lot to do around the house these days." Then he caught Wesley's eye for the first time. "I have a young man coming to live—to stay—with me."

"Lucky you!" said Wesley with envious cheer.

"Well, I suppose," said Hollis, looking down. "It's not exactly what you might be thinking. But he is an extraordinary young man, I would say a beautiful man . . . a black man . . . Not well." Now it was Hollis's turn to wonder why on earth he was telling this to a total stranger. He was surprised to feel his pride nicked by something slightly condescending in Wesley's tone, and had an obscure urge to trump his worldliness.

"Better watch out," Wesley tried to sound lightly naughty, but immediately regretted the whiffs this left in the air.

One of the men from the other end of the bar approached them now, putting on a crinkly, reliably effective smile. "Hollis?" Hollis nodded at him quizzically. "Thought it was you." The man smiled and put out his hand. "Chip McLellan. I used to come to your family's house for cookouts in the summers growing up."

"Ah," said Hollis noncomittally. "And still living here?" *What does he know?*

"Well just for a month, you know, my share of the house each summer. Live in Simsbury."

"Right. This is Wesley . . . Hern—?"

"Herndon," Wesley put in, a trace peeved. They shook hands.

Only then did Hollis put out his hand. "Wesley is new in town. I'm just showing him one of the sights. Thought he might be interested. Unlike me, he's actually a sailor."

"Really?" said Chip to Wesley. "That's great. This is a real sailors' club. Nothing fancy—well, you can see. But we've got a great junior program, for your kids?"

Wesley ignored the question with a mild smile. "I guess I'm pretty well set up right out the back door, where I ended up here," he said. "Over in Mussel Cove. Mooring, dock, float—the whole picture."

"You have a boat, then?" asked Chip.

"Yeah," said Wesley, crisp but clearly wanting to be drawn.

"Would I know the boat?"

"Quite possible. I've been sailing around here for years, but on this boat for just the last couple seasons. A Hinckley . . . 51? *White Wings IV?*"

Chip's face opened as the balance shifted. Once again Wesley's purchase had the desired effect. "Oh, sure, definitely know the boat. A favorite." He paused to take this in, then went on: "Well, best of luck to you on that. It's a great town. You and your—family?—are going to love it."

Again Wesley skipped the question. "Thank you. That's very kind."

There was a silence. All swigged. Finally Chip blurted, "So. Sounds like Wall Street . . . None of my business."

"No, I work up in Hartford." Wesley's voice had taken on a conclusive breeziness. He turned slightly toward Hollis and glanced into his face with a split-second hint of kinship.

"Are you single, then?" Chip popped a beer nut into his mouth.

Wesley cocked his head slightly at him, as though confused by this impertinence. "A great pleasure to meet you," he said, rising off his stool and looking around as though for the men's room. "I'll look forward to seeing you out on the sound." A quick brick wall of a smile.

Chip straightened at the dismissal, rubbing his hands. "Well, me, too. Listen, didn't want to butt in, but—"

"Nonsense, pleasure," said Hollis. Chip returned carefully to his group.

SAM JENKINS pulled on his lineman's overalls, the same ones he had once worn to inspect the hydraulics of nuclear submarines, before he retired. He cinched up his black, steel-toed boots. If he was going to do this, he wanted no mistake about who *he* was.

Ever since the Liquor Board hearing, Sam had felt a perverse but growing need to see the inside of the Crab Hole. He'd mentioned it once at Runcie's Bait Shop: "Yeah, it's like wanting to go down to the courthouse and see the murderer who's on trial." But the dock geezers had snorted, "Never. Never go near the place," so he'd not mentioned it again. For good measure, he would go late, after the townspeople had gone to bed.

There was still a lively scene outside when he approached;

men leaning on the parked cars. Listen to that whoop, just like a woman. Jim Priestly had deputized a couple of extra local lads for the evening, who were shifting from foot to foot near the entrance, one of them drawing more saucy looks than he might have wished. Christ, that's Jed, the janitor at the Elks. Sam ducked behind a knot of boys and slouched inside.

"That's five dollars cover, gets you your first drink," said the black-clad boy, one of Leo's New York staffers. Sam slammed down a twenty. Shouldn't fuckin' have to pay, I'm certainly not here to enjoy myself.

"Just give this to the bartender." The boy handed him a chit. "Fifteen and that's twenty." He handed him the change and a condom. Jesus Christ, what the . . . ?

He thrust it back. "I sure as hell won't be needin' that," he growled.

"Whatever. Long's you're careful," said the boy.

The first room was crowded and dim, with an oval bar in the center. Sam fought his way toward it. Goddammit, people don't keep clear when they go by you—Keep your hand . . . ! When he finally squeezed in, the bar dancer was just beginning a tip lap, stepping gingerly among the glasses and bottles in his black steel-toed boots, boys reaching up to stick bills in his leather thong and kissing him on the kneecap. While most at the bar paid little attention as the gigantically muscular young man minced past languidly, blowing kisses, thrusting his pelvis, jumping his pecs, twanging his thong, Sam couldn't take his eyes off him. Son of a . . . He's just sure I want to look at him. The dancer suddenly threw him a from-under, sidelong look. Sam snapped his stare away as though trying to dislodge a fly from the end of his nose, and set off bulling his way toward the next room.

Here was a pay-for-pool table to one side, most of the room

taken up with a dance floor flanked by large carpeted steps, like bleachers, generously studded with sentinels and draped with cuddlers. Christ, it's like bein' punched in the stomach every beat . . . feel the wind comin' off the front of that speaker. The strobes shattered the jouncing heads and twitching limbs; white T-shirts flashed under the ultraviolet. Sam had been gawking for a minute or two before he realized he was being considered a dance partner by a heavyset man, late forties, also in overalls, beaming at him as though they had achieved an amazing simpatico moment. Great, now I've got a fuckin' fairy biker after me. Sam labored the length of the dance floor, fending off the crowd with a raised hand as though warning that he was covered with wet paint. In the middle of the floor he made out a bumping, snaking chain of entranced boys, six Zs, arms in the air.

A sign in deco lettering over the entrance to the next room anounced "Gents." Holy— I heard about it, didn't think they'd do it. . . . Holy shit. The entire room was tiled in seafoam green with tiny cobalt-shaded lights dangling over the bar and over the ranks of urinals that ran along both walls. Christ, and there are a coupla couples of women over there. . . . What in the—? . . . He drifted among the tall tables, feeling as though he were in a bad dream.

"I'm, like, what is it with them?" It was Eggie, just behind him. "I mean, grow up. They're like horny beagles, just so obsessed." He and his court were regarding some punkish youths engaging in a group paw nearby. "The most deviant thing about them isn't that they're homos, it's that they're nymphos."

Gym-buffed waiters circulated in ripped cutoff shorts and black boots, hoisting aloft trays of free Opening Night Jell-O shots. One paused to serve Eggie's circle. "Isn't he adorable?" said one, staring after him.

"Oh I don't know, too bulky." Eggie pouted. "I'd go to the gym if I thought I could strengthen my nails. Tried it for a while, just seemed to be building up my armpits." Sam had turned, was looking at them as though they were roadkill.

"These lights make everybody look like they have on death masks," Eggie observed.

Another man, willowy, dangerous, joined them. Air kisses, shoulder squeezes: "Yes, here with sordid friends," he said.

One of the sidekicks said, "Eggie has gone pure, Puritan, native. Sex is wrong."

"Oh, please," said the new arrival, casting a bitchy glare around the room. "This is so—dainty. Look, every one of these boys is here because he wants to fuck, so why do they just stand around holding a drink and *conversing*? Hello?! They should be checkin' to see who's got what." He gave the man next to him a squeeze in the crotch.

Sam sought refuge beyond the far end of the bar, where the room rounded a corner out of sight, but when he got there, he was able to see the TV monitor, whose screen had been hidden when he entered—the management's one concession to community sensibilities. NO . . . FUCKIN' . . . WAY. One man was buried to the hilt in another, up to attack speed, chanting in sporadic grunts, "Yeah—you like that—don'tcha—you like that—big—tool—don'tcha . . ." Two and three deep at the bar, men chatted calmly, not even glancing up at the jiggling buttocks and slapping balls. Sam fled around the corner, past a row of stalls with kneeling pads in front of the toilets. He felt a rising panic, came upon what looked like a loading dock with a series of truck bodies backed up to it, each of a different darkness. The last one was pitch-black, with shipping crates partly blocking the entrance. Leaning against one crate was a wiry young man, hips cocked, stripped to the waist; just beyond him a shaved-headed giant in a studded harness lurked at the edge of the darkness. What the fuck is that now, bait-and-switch, I guess, Christ awmighty. Sam felt a sudden upwelling of panic and loathing and plowed the entire length of the establishment as though he'd just escaped from kidnappers, didn't stop until he hit the street, the bouncer's words in his ears: "Did you want me to stamp your hand?" and then Deputy Jed: "Hey, Mr. Jenkins, didn't expect to see *you* here."

FOURTEEN

T'S PROBABLY nothing, but my balls have been hurting."

"Wh—!" Wendell chuckled, nonplussed. They were a couple of minutes into a late phone chat. "I swear, youth today."

"Hey, I'm sorry, but who else can I ask?" Anthony sounded a bit piqued, but only at not knowing it all. "I mean, any new body thing, new ache or pain, you know, you start thinking . . ."

"You're probably just not maintaining a steady interval between wanks," Wendell advised. "You get to where you've got too much momentum up, the cum production night shift coming in, and then, if you, you know, skip a shot, it's like—pressure."

"So you're saying whatever you do, don't skip?" The clear tenor took on a nasal quality when Anthony was trying to be cool.

"Yeah, do you have alarm settings on your watch?"

They limped on to other topics: Anthony's impending move to the Conn College dorms; the Crab Hole opening. Anthony asked, "You want to go to this Wrecking Ball thing next weekend? Saw an ad in the *Sand Flea*."

"Absolutely."

"Lattie's freaking that I'm leaving. Now she'll have to come out from behind the cash register, face the queers."

"It'll be good for her."

"She's afraid once the season's over the local trade won't come back."

"Could be true."

"She offered me to be manager."

"Good for you. I'm proud of you. But don't do it."

"Don't worry. . . ."

A silence, held, attained pregnancy.

"Does . . . does fucking—feel good?" Anthony's voice now boyish.

Wendell coughed a laugh. "Anthony . . . Jesus . . ."

"Sorry, but I guess I feel like I've got to make up for lost time." The hot blush came through the phone. "I mean, I've been posing for years as if I was doing all kinds of weird stuff, where you touch things—lick things, ooof—things I never want to think about ever again. To you maybe, this is like garden variety stuff, but to me, it's been so off-limits . . . but ultimate too . . . I guess."

Wendell trembled on the other end. "Are you sure no one can hear you?"

"My mother's watching one of her shows. I'm up here on my bed."

"Yes, it feels good." There was another silence, each gathering himself, after the lightning, before the thunder.

"Is this phone sex?" Anthony had regained his adenoidal twinkle.

"Must be," said Wendell.

"Cool." A pause.

"What's that I'm hearing?" asked Wendell. "Like a fast-food jingle?" They both listened a moment. Then there was a click and silence.

"Oops," said Anthony.

His mother never mentioned anything, that day or the next. In fact, he wasn't really sure she'd been on the line—but who else, after all?—or how much she'd heard, until Rain called him to say, "My mother threw another scene—at your mother —at the Pick 'n Pay yesterday."

"No."

"Yes. Grace in space. No one is safe. She says she found your mother broken down in the cat litter aisle, sobbing over you."

"Fuck. I'm afraid I know what this is about."

"Well, don't worry. Grace alerted her to what to be watching for, your basic morbid decay, that kind of thing, leading, of course, to insanity. Just so *you* know, too, where you're headed."

"Wow. Well, guess I better get my affairs in order. Thanks."

"Oh, don't thank me." It was only in the last words that a sullen distance came into Rain's voice. Since the night of the riot, she had been torn between wanting to cut Anthony off for disappearing with Wendell, and wanting to show him she was just fine with his outward turn. His minor celebrity risked making her feel like a groupie; she needed reassurance that she was still firmly in his inner circle. Anthony, for his part, felt only the occasional pang at not calling her every day as usual.

"Hey, soon, all right?" he said. "Maybe come in after my shift? Got so much to tell you."

"Yeah, I'll have to see."

ON THE Friday evening of Labor Day weekend, Artie had two ships coming out from New York. Finally having the Crab Hole open was helping. Leo was promoting it heavily in the New York party rags, and word of mouth was spreading fast. Artie also put together a gambling package for the first time: the boys could take the Indians' high-speed ferry out from New York, stay at one of the casino's hotels, and take a free shuttle bus to Long Spit. He wasn't sure the boys would bite at either the gambling or getting on a bus, but the casino was easy to work with, agreeing to put the lip-syncher Mince Pie on the bus as hostess. This, in turn, gave Mince Pie a chance to promote her Saturday night show at the Crab Hole. The package clicked, and Artie upped his commitments for the next weekend's Wrecking Ball. Over at the Sand Box, Ray and Sibley pushed the construction crew hard. They knew the place wouldn't be finished, but they were determined to be able to hold a sort of pre-opening for tea dance on the Saturday. They blizzarded the village with flyers of a cartoon porno building crew: "We've had our tools out, pounding away. We're only semi-erect, but it'll still be fun. Come anyway."

Saturday around lunchtime, Dot Bradley was in the window at Yankee Gulch, fussing over a display of chaps. She'd been carrying a selection for a few weeks now, and finally felt ready to do a window. She told herself it was a business decision, but it still made her nervous. Not only were they going in the window but also they were of a rather arresting sort: black leather, buttless, crotchless, from a company on East Ninth Street and Avenue C. And she'd gotten it into her head that she wasn't going to put them on the mannequin over jeans. She'd gotten the leather bikini briefs pulled on and the chaps cinched up, and was cranking the mannequin's arms and hands into a modest drape over the lap. Passing men were tapping, egging her on, acting scandalized; she waved back in mock confusion. One pointed to the bullwhip hanging nearby on a wooden peg and shouted: "Go for it, Dot!" She was gamely adjusting this prop when a woman's voice from behind her, inside the shop, said, "Doesn't look like that comes very naturally."

Dot turned to see a stocky woman, with short salt-and-pepper hair, wearing cargo shorts, a safari vest, and aviator sunglasses, flicking through the panchos with a pewter-tipped walking stick.

"No, window dressing is not my thing," said Dot. "I should hire one of those guys to do it." She nodded outside.

The woman snorted, then said, "I'm Gret. Heard you were head of the Merchants Association."

"That's right," said Dot, climbing down from the window and offering her hand.

"Town looks like it's cookin'."

"You got that right," Dot agreed. "I'm just trying to stay ahead of the curve; it's been quite a ride."

"Pandering, yeah. We all do it. Think it'll last?"

"Well, I don't know," said Dot, "but I'm here whether it does or not. Been here through a lot of slow years. Here, let me give you some of the association's handouts."

They talked on about the changes. Gret asked about the three vacant storefronts along the arcade. "Oh, yeah," said Dot, "the card shop, the used-book shop—well, he just decided it was time to retire—and the other was a kind of women's specialty shop."

"Not a lotta women around, that's for sure," said Gret, with a steeliness Dot noted.

"Well, no," she said. "Tina's was more for the— Townspeople don't come down along here so much anymore. I heard there was a company—Bodybody?—looking at one of those spaces."

Gret took her sunglasses off. "Lookin' to do a restaurant somewhere. What do you think?"

Dot chose to ignore something in the air. "Oh, absolutely. There's nothing but Angleton's, the same old coffee shop, been there forever, and of course, Frankie's, but that's just pizza and stuff. The boys tease me that there's no decent place to eat."

They got onto zoning, parking, choices of cuisine, then reached a lull. Gret broke it.

"So you on your own here?"

"In the shop? That's right."

"And in life? A hubby?" The last word a trace mocking.

"No, no, been there." Dot laughed uneasily.

Gret let her gaze linger a second. "Hey . . . nice talkin'." She headed for the door. "This place is ripe. Time to kick some fairy butt."

———

"AND WE haven't even started on the hatboxes yet," said Florian, a moving heap of coats coming up Hollis's front walk.

A couple of weeks earlier, Hollis had gotten up the nerve to call him in New York: "If you ever need a place to come and just, relax, you're welcome anytime." A week after that, Florian called to ask if he could "bring a few things up." Now they were unloading his rented van, Florian in cutoff sweatpants and flip-flops.

Hollis was in shock at having this beauty steadily in sight, the sinewy arm emerging from the bundle. After the years of settling for veiled worship of Anthony—the muffled ache, furtive touches—he was overwhelmed by this jaunty show-off, whose breezy sexiness was not meant to lead anywhere, not intended to be cruel, yet insisted on Hollis's full attention. At the same time, because Hollis had been sheltered here in the hermitage, he hadn't learned to adopt the brisk, armored empathy now so often bestowed by the uninfected; he couldn't help seeing Florian, if not as a tragedy that had already happened, at least as an incipient invalid. He hurried down the front steps. "Here, let me help you with that."

"Honey, I'm just fine. Don't you worry about me, nothin' I can't heft." He flexed the arm playfully. "I left you plenty to carry. There's all the skillets, if you're so mighty." Reaching the van, Hollis glanced across the lane and caught Hilda Merson retreating behind her curtains. She had noted the removal of every heirloom over the years.

Hollis had always used the same back bedroom upstairs, with its modest view now mainly blocked by an oak that had grown during his lifetime. He stuck there, partly out of habit and Yankee modesty, but also out of a muddle of barely conscious instincts: to expiate looting the family manse, to overlay his peculiar obsessions with a monastic veneer. Whatever the reasons, the result was that he could now offer Florian, as though it were nothing, the master bedroom, with its windows on three sides, commanding Ledge Knoll's entire prospect, from the beach stretching away to the dawn horizon, south to Block Island on a good day, and west to the wicked tip of Long Spit and beyond. He was even able to offer the sleigh bed, which had somehow escaped the auction block, and was now in fact, the only piece of furniture in the room. Florian's presumptuousness was so far outside the Wynbourne family bounds, Hollis could only chuckle, cowed, and meekly play his assigned part. He had tugged the dust throw off the bed with a shy flourish. Florian accepted the room graciously, but as his due: "Even Princess Never-Enough should be happy here." Now the bed was disappearing under piles of clothes. As Florian descended to the van for each new load, he gestured at choice moldings, hinted at the color palette he had in mind for the front hall, wondered aloud whether the wiring was up to the lighting changes he would require.

On his second trip upstairs, Florian ventured back to glance into Hollis's room.

They met up a minute later in the front hall, Florian glistening with sweat from lugging. "Listen, honey, I'm not here to turn you into a nurse. Lot of fight left in the boy." He mimed a second of dancing. "Gonna pull my weight. I just figured, get started on my retirement while I can still enjoy it. And we gonna start on that dining room ceiling, scatter those bats, this afternoon, yes?" He started back outside. "What do you say, tromp l'oeil clouds? Cherubim? Gulls?" A wink over his shoulder: "Then maybe we'll go find a mall—isn't that what you do out here?—and get you some *jeans*."

Hollis didn't know what to do with himself, hung around the front door with a dopey smile, backed awkwardly out of Florian's way on his next trip up the walk. He was so unused to being lighthearted, to allowing himself to be ribbed and jostled, that strong instincts were drawing him inward, at the same time that he was pleasantly agitated by Florian's playful insistence that he respond every minute. He wanted badly to believe that Florian had arrived out of at least some sort of feelings for him, but knew better and was trying to get used to settling for the mere stunning presence.

"Gonna lead me to the airport to drop this van off?" Florian was piling the last odds and ends by the curb. "Then we'll come home, and I'm for a long bath."

RAY PICKED up Sibley at the town dock. "Hope that Range Rider or whatchacallit has a vanity mirror." Sibley poked at a stubborn cowlick. Wearing his most casual attire—blue blazer, khakis, and an ascot—he had zoomed over from Fishers Island in his Boston Whaler.

"I didn't say it was a costume party," Ray chided.

"But no socks!" Sibley protested, pointing to his Cole-Haans. "This is excitin'!"

At the Sand Box, the Grand Opening Tea Dance was kindling. Sibley took up the welcome post at the top of the wide raw-lumber stairs leading to the complex of multilevel boardwalks, decks, terraces, and the open pavilion, all still dusted with pressure-treated sawdust and smelling of fresh cedar shingles. Bowing slightly from the waist, he clasped the hand of each arrival, gave the same enchanted, garden-club-president smile whether it was a posse in Mylar beelining for the dance floor, or a pack of sand-caked, oil-basted boys fresh from the beach.

Ray scurried around in the din of the dance music, checking on things, gratified to see patrons taking to the various perches he'd sketched into the plans. The day had been hot and hazy, but now the late-afternoon sun shone out of a clearer sky, couldn't have been luckier, although lowering away too early, summer's end. The music was alarming—could it break windows on houses he might want to be selling? He wove through the gyrating bodies. Good, they seem to have found something to get high on. He had a waiver of the State Seashore alcohol ban in the works, but these things took time. He approached the DJ, trying to project approval.

"They seem to be liking it!" he screamed. Holding a headset to one ear, the DJ nodded tolerantly, as though that were the last thing he was concerned with.

"What do you call this!?" Ray howled over the gut-shattering bass, eardrum-frying synthesizer snarls, and cymbal bursts that made him involuntarily wince in tempo.

"Oh, it's just, like, progressive house, you know." The DJ could have been a steamfitter, talking to a visiting politician. "I'll get into some deep house, some remixes, feel it out, you know, probably no industrial, here, like, the great outdoors . . ." He gestured with a waxy arm at their surroundings. Ray nodded sagely and gave him a thumbs-up.

He made his way back toward the entrance. Despite being a nervous detail man, he found himself catching the excitement of the occasion. Boys were streaming in from all directions, from the village, from the beach, from the two ships and the yachts at anchor; the Long Island Men and Buoys sailing club had organized a Labor Day Jamboree with clubs from the Hudson River, Newport, and Boston. For a moment, it didn't matter that summer was fading, that this hurry-up opening was just to lock in trade for the next season. They'd made something, and it was working. Mel Cleveland had his biggest clambake of the season starting in two hours, then Mince Pie was performing at the Crab Hole; then Sully's, a warm night in front of Frankie's late—this was reaching critical mass. He fancied he saw the whole thing working in the sunburned faces on all sides. His chest tightened with an entrepreneurial thrill.

"This is heaven!" Sibley exclaimed when Ray emerged from the throng to check on him. "I can't believe it's just a plop in the boat from Fishers." He placed his tiny, plump, manicured hand in the mitt of a giant. "Welcome, how y'all this evenin'?" He glanced back at Ray. "Not one of 'em squeezin' by me without a pat! Why didn't I think of this years ago?"

Ray greeted Jim Hornswich, to Sibley's extravagant dismay.

"Great!" said Jim, with a sweep of his arm. "This is my idea of a *perfect* thing to have in a place like this."

"What, because you can see your new house from here?" Ray replied. "Get cruisin', honey." He swatted him on the butt.

Jim got a ginseng seltzer and took up a position along one of the railings, gazing at his house a half-mile distant, so right, nestled on the hillside among the beach roses, one of those places on earth that set you dreaming . . . He savored the sense of being an insider, a pioneer—a prowler, with big-time cards up his sleeve. Then he spotted a lanky, sun-browned young man, his denim shirt unbuttoned, leaning against the railing farther on, also gazing away to the east. Jim sidled over, feeling, for once, bold.

"Nice angle on the town from here," he said.

Mark flicked him a dark-eyed glance that left him weak in the knees. "Yeah—I've been right here a thousand times, in another life."

Jim's smile tightened: Oh brother, New Age? He was cautious. "You having some kind of a déjà vu?"

"No, I grew up here, and right where we're standing used to be the snack bar where I'd come for ice cream sandwiches from the beach club there . . . take one back to my gran."

"Oh, so I *have* seen you around," said Jim. "I thought so." His nerve was faltering. They stood a moment, looking at the beach club, paint peeling, smudges of roofing tar and mildew, railings askew, defeated. Mark moved to the music in a minimal, taut way, with a serious expression. Jim had to speak or move away.

"I've been here off and on all summer," he said.

"Yeah? Me, too," said Mark. "Just about to head back, though, up to UVM. First time I've ever been sad to leave here."

"I know what you mean," said Jim. "I've actually just moved here." He couldn't resist.

"Oh, yeah? Where?" Mark turned to face him, his shirttails falling away from his brown body, further derailing Jim.

"Well, right there." He pointed, feeling ridiculous. "You

caught me starin' at it, a little outta control houseproud. But, hey, I just closed a week and a half ago."

"I can't believe it!" Mark flashed him a true smile. "Polly Dickson's! She used to yell at me for cutting through her rose patch. That's amazing!" His reserve vanished. "What's that place like inside? I only ever went trick-or-treating there, and she would never let us past the front door."

"Well, you'll just have to come see," Jim said, near liftoff.

"Hey, who knows." Mark glanced aside. They talked about Polly, kid pranks, grown-up pranks, the beach club raid, Mark's mother and her friends, Mark's friend Luis from New York.

"Oh, I see," said Jim.

"No, we're just, you know . . . Well, he *is* pretty hot." They both laughed nervously. "But nothing serious," Mark concluded. Jim was just recovering when Wesley approached, attempting to saunter.

"Pointing out the sights?" His smile had a covetous glint.

"No need, this is a local boy," said Jim, a quiz-show host. "But, where did you say you were heading, back to school?"

"UVM," said Mark, extending his hand. "Mark."

"Wesley and I closed on the same day," said Jim.

"Oh, yeah?" Mark said, leaving a beat before asking, "Where'd you end up?"

"Mussel Cove." Wesley tried to sound offhand.

"What was it? Ferryboat?" prompted Jim.

"Ferryman," said Wesley.

"Knew it was something to do with fairies," said Jim. Mark absently gathered his shirt around him.

"Wow, good for you," he said without much enthusiasm. "I grew up on Tanner Street, around the back of Signal Hill."

"No, don't know that one yet." Wesley looked terribly interested as he felt the gate being closed. Accoutrements could cut either way.

For a moment, the music took over. The dancers were throwing long shadows across the decks, and the whole fanciful structure threw a craggy shadow several hundred feet along the beach. There had always been a divide between Signal Hill and the jumble of the front, but from this vantage point, amid the racket, the hill had an even more remote quality, a sulking stillness, like an old tortoise who's pulled his head in. In the last hour, many pairs of eyes, drawn by the distant thudding, had glared from those privileged windows to see what new affront the invaders had devised.

Wesley spotted Hollis and Florian coming up the steps. "Well, I'm going to mosey around. Talk to you later."

Hollis was in a muddle. This was the first time since his long-ago conservatory days that he had ventured out into the world with another man, to say nothing of this man, whose allure had caused him such public humiliation. So here he was, no more free to touch that tummy than ever, though now for different reasons, and yet perceived by all who saw them as the companion in a startling mismatch. He was agitated at the thought of who might know him, repelled by Sibley's fawning greeting, thrown when Florian playfully linked arms with him, proud of all the attention they drew, though he well knew it wasn't focused on him, and all these conflicting emotions canceled each other out on his face, leaving him with a wary half-smile.

"My!" said Florian, as they edged into the crowd. He was sweeping the scene with a purring, what-have-we-here look, while Hollis trailed behind, eyes held straight ahead, except for a few nervous darts. Good grief, of all people . . .

"Hello, nice to see you!" said Wesley.

"Yes, well, had to have a look," said Hollis with a cringing smile, demonstrating a cursory glance around. "Anything new in the village, you know . . ." Florian was still scanning, at a slight remove. "This is my friend Florian." Florian immediately surrendered a few seconds of full attention, a low-cost but dependably dazzling smile. "Pleasure to meet you," he said in a voice like a late-night love-song DJ, then resumed his scanning.

Hollis and Wesley struggled to chat, Wesley feeling, as at the yacht club, obscurely compelled to appear the more worldly, to impress this stiff, uneasy man—difficult, though, now that he unaccountably had this exotic creature on his arm. Hollis, beneath his doddering, abstracted manner, wanted to bolt. Being in public, period, was already uneasy-making, never mind with anyone, even his mother, on his arm, never mind a man, and seriously never mind this shade of man. He had taken the naughty taboo of his years as a recluse and was literally wearing it on his sleeve. He was shocked at himself that this shameful but undeniable tension was what had surfaced. Paying little attention to Wesley, he relinquished tight little nods to a few acquaintances. Derek and Tracy passed, giving him frisky, knowing smiles. His chorus of worries about each passing person—How much does he know about who I am?—was in their case abruptly drowned out by the lewdness of their looks. The raciness of the fantasy they conveyed hummed in discord with his deep unease at his private life even being considered.

Florian had locked onto several passing radars, but nothing held long until he spotted a demure collegiate type at the corner of the juice bar and exchanged several lingering glances. After he had satisfied himself that attention was being paid, he patted Hollis on the arm. "I'm going to do a stroll. Can I get you anything *if* I come back? Just kidding."

"No, no that's fine," said Hollis, with a twinge of possessiveness and sudden panic at being left alone with Wesley.

As Florian sidled away, he heard Wesley ask, "So, is he . . . ?"

Hollis was curt. "Just a friend." Florian smiled to himself.

Approaching the collegiate man, Florian could see the gentle green eyes, the long lashes fetchingly magnified by the glasses. He took up a position next to him at the bar, looking down with an inward smile that said, Your move. The music thumped; seconds passed. He gave a brief, lazy glance with a nod—Yes, you, honey—then slightly jutted his chin in tempo, touched his lip with the tip of his tongue.

Wendell shifted in a little spasm of voltage at the attention, covered it with his own slight dance-floor face for a second, then, after another pause: "I'm waiting for my boyfriend to get off work."

Florian turned toward him with an instant, pleased-to-meet-you smile. "Uh-oh. Do we have time?" Then he slapped himself, laughing. "Listen to you, girl! Got to *clean* it up in the country!"

Just then, as they were laughing and Florian was touching Wendell's forearm, Anthony approached, with a look that said, I'm sure there's some explanation. Wendell gave him a strong, relieved hug and kiss, and a quick look of pride. Reassured, Anthony struggled happily to free an arm. "Hi, Anthony."

"Florian." He took Anthony's hand with evident approval. "This town doesn't quit. . . . Well, I should let you two lovebirds alone; my date will be wondering where I've fallen."

"Who's that?" Anthony inquired, ever Angleton's gossip reporter.

"Master Hollis Wynbourne is his name," said Florian sternly. "Right over there."

Anthony was dumbstruck. He hadn't seen Hollis since the day of the hearing; the voice lessons had trailed off with the summer. His face reflected the figuring out. "So you're—" Florian nodded. "In the paper?" Anthony persisted.

"That's me. What was it? 'Unidentified African-American'? And the picture"—he rolled his eyes—"don't get me started." He gave his tummy a quick strum. "Well, come on, then, let's go say hello. Do you know him well?" Anthony raised his eyebrows and chuckled.

As they walked over to Hollis, Anthony leaned toward Wendell. "So, do you—? This guy is"—Wendell nodded—"and the other, Hollis? I told you?" Wendell nodded again.

Hollis was alone, sheltering by a post, obscurely unable to set out across the floor toward the exit, yet not quite wanting to leave. Florian had gotten him into this situation and then deserted. He had grounds for feeling marooned, although, without Florian at his side, he was less anxious about the passing crowd, to be sure. He just felt a little pointless. There was no earthly reason to be here except to be at Florian's side. He started at the sight of Anthony, Wendell, and Florian coming toward him, and felt color creeping up his neck.

Anthony came to face him, hesitated for a moment of internal debate, shedding years of distance, and embraced him. After several seconds of awkward thumps on the back, each pulled away to clasped-arms' length, each saw the other's eyes welling, looked aside, embraced again.

"Small town," Florian clucked. He turned to Wendell. "I think we have time now."

FIFTEEN

THE OCEAN Hotel loomed heavily, the clapboards drooping more skinlike over her sagging bones than they had a few months earlier, as though the summer's hundreds of one-night stands had vibrated her into a slump. The rows of identical windows, formerly eyes trained ahead like a congregation's, now dangled beach towels and boys leaning on their elbows, as hooked into the street as an apartment building in Istanbul.

The hotel had never been elegant and snooty, but rather like an auntie whose clothes betray insufficient modesty, whose very striving to earn her family's respect keeps it out of reach. The acres of narrow yellow clapboard had always given the place an industriously detailed, eager-to-please quality, but now, haplessly transformed into the "Bun Box," the hotel resembled that same auntie caught smooching with her tango instructor and trying to hold her head high amid the whispering.

Word of the hotel's impending fate had seeped out on Signal Hill, passed on by those few surreptitious readers of the *Sand Flea* who'd seen the ad for the Wrecking Ball. Many among the old families had a vague feeling they ought to be indignant, but couldn't quite muster it. The building's recent tumble was just the culmination of years of slide, during which it went from grudgingly tolerated landmark to mutteringly decried eyesore. And too, there was a growing mood of passive resignation among the old guard. That Betsy Haring doesn't seem to care, so why should we? Come to think of it, she hasn't put up much of a ruckus about any of this onslaught—too busy trying to keep me from building a new garage. Maybe we need to see about getting somebody else to run that Landmarks thing . . . next year, maybe let's look at that.

The fact was, Betsy did care, and she was thrilled.

On Simon Whetstone's orders, Marcia Pepitone had kept a low profile, managing the last weeks of the hotel's existence as normally as possible, maintaining a discreet silence with her friends. That is, until her own curiosity drove her to ask Artie for a peek at the new hotel.

He FedExed her the "New Ocean" prospectus and, with that in hand, Marcia's resolve quickly faltered; it was too juicy to sit on. She decided she could control herself if she could give just one other comrade a glimpse, and so called Betsy for coffee. Opening the booklet, Betsy beheld a two-page spread in which the architect's rendering had been photoshopped into an aerial shot taken during the highest summer, gardens blazing and lawns emerald on all sides, the sea scattered with sails, Long Spit a beckoning finger in the distance. The accompanying text described "an exuberant confection, opulent but not grandiose, lovingly concocted of the crisp, summery vocabulary of the best local 'cottages.' Its premium rooms will command a rank of open timberwork gables marching on a diagonal upward along the seafront roof, each containing a private spa under a pergola, the whole effect a feathery play of light and shadow resembling a flight of giant seabirds." The architect, a Lebanese, currently the darling of the Hamptons set, "had learned well," the text purred, "how to impart a spirit of dignity and substance, yet also of fun—imagine the architectural equivalent of a Duesenberg boat-tailed phaeton." For years, Betsy had thought of the Ocean property, perhaps the most splendid overlooked opportunity on the Eastern Seaboard, as a sitting duck, waiting, naked of landmark protection, to be noticed and then defiled by some philistine purveyor of condos. Now Simon Whetstone had been sent by heaven, the best outcome she could have hoped for.

Besides that, she had two more permit applications on her desk, from newly arrived men wanting to strip the jalousies from their porches, the vinyl from their shingles. And best of all, once the season wound down, she had her facelift appointment with Jim—he called it "a couple of safety pins in the slipcover"—followed by two weeks in Quebec City while the bruises paled. The gluey old chowder of her life in Long Spit was being sprinkled with cayenne; gone were all thoughts of giving it up for Tuscany.

WESLEY WAS happily immersed in settling at Fog Bells, making excuses at work to spend every possible hour at home supervising the placement of hutches and highboys, selection of window treatments, installation of specimen trees. The encounter with Chip McLellan at the Yacht Club had reminded him that the village hadn't yet become the fantasy zone he hoped for; he would need to soldier through more such while he waited for the demographic to shift his way. He was used to it; his endless rounds of corporate board meetings had always entailed some deflecting of tedious heterosexual assumptions. Looking back on his Lyme days, he had to admit that at least the fossils there knew better than to blunder ahead in so unworldly a fashion.

As far as the gay side of his new life was concerned, it was taking some getting used to, this business of situating oneself smack in the middle of one's cruising ground. He had grown accustomed to his trolling being a naughty, and therefore rigorously sequestered activity, conducted far from his nest, and incognito. In those days, only the rare muscle-bound lunk had learned of his lofty stature in the world at large; now all such a lunk had to do was trail him home.

And the details of open-air cruising didn't come easily either. For a start, loitering went against deeply ingrained instincts. He tried a number of times just sitting on a bench in the waterfront park, but apart from being unable, in such an egalitarian space, to project a carefree indifference to the passage of time, he was also ruffled at having his bench invaded, once by several small children with ice cream cones, and another time by an elderly man with a productive cough. Seeking adequate remove, he briefly considered sitting on the grass, then resorted to bringing a folding chair so he wouldn't get stains on his khakis. This wasn't looking very alluring, and he hadn't even begun to experiment with reading materials. Barron's lasted just one day—wrong message. He realized that even *The New York Times,* in the lap of someone his age, might well deter his quarry. This would take more research. But still, the passing scenery was exhilarating enough that he remained upbeat.

THE OCEAN Hotel's preparations for the end weren't meant to start so early, but Simon Whetstone's project team kept adding to the task list. So, even during Labor Day weekend, with the place booked to capacity, guests had to maneuver past workers carefully removing the paneling from around the reception desk, the mantel from the main dining room, and several other signature woodworking flourishes of the old structure, numbering each fragment for eventual reassembly in designated nostalgia niches of the new building.

At noon—checkout time—on the Tuesday, the Ocean closed its doors, as it had on the day after Labor Day every year since the holiday's inception in 1894. But this was the last time.

By three o'clock the place was swarming with workers. The Eastern States Demolition trucks appeared and, over the next few days, their crews began boring the timber framework with huge augers for the eventual placement of the charges, and drilling, poking, and fishing hundreds of yards of fuse wire throughout the termite-, worm-, and rot-riddled structure. "Damn building's to where it's just standin' out of habit," muttered one worker, as he ensnared the basement support pillars in the malignant cat's cradle.

Huge moving trucks arrived one after another; hundreds of steel beds, washstands, mirrors, braided rag rugs, rocking chairs and yellowed watercolor seascapes were carted off to a county assisted-living complex nearing completion in Maine; the restaurant, bar, and kitchen fixtures headed for auction in Providence. Sound and lighting trucks arrived from B. J. Gelson's company, Unexplained Events, and crews began erecting spidery lighting trusses in the enormous main dining room and snaking miles of cable over the grounds to towers along the perimeter and to the soundproofed diesel generating truck in one corner.

Meanwhile, elsewhere on Signal Hill, those of the cottages still used in the old-fashioned way were vacated on that same

Tuesday, their occupants setting off back to Pittsburgh, Philadelphia, Shaker Heights, as family retainers began the draining of the plumbing, the hauling out of the numbered storm covers for the windows, the deer powder on the rhododendrons, dust throws on the sunroom wicker, velvet sacks for the silver: the putting of each manor to bed. Fewer lights came on with each dusk. Always in the past, those departing families had permitted themselves a brief twinge of melancholy at the end of another season at the shore, but then had bucked their chins up at the certainty of the endless, changeless summers to come. This time though, more than one family left town wondering whether it still made sense to do the same thing every year. Apart from the muffled late-night thump from Front Street, the invasion hadn't really affected Long Spit's upper reaches all that much—not yet, anyway. But after so many years of a dependable diorama of a lost age, there was something unsettling about this rowdy reincarnation, something that, for a number of the old families, broke the spell of routine.

Artie Kinzie spent the week tweaking and double-checking arrangements. Leo Robbia was balking at headlining Mince Pie at the Crab Hole for the Friday night opening event, even though the lip-syncher's followers had packed the place over Labor Day. Artie worried that without her as the celebrity hostess on the shuttle bus, his ferry-casino package could be in trouble.

"Hey, she's not my thing," Leo said. "Last week, my guys are like, What the fuck? You got girlie-boys flouncin' around in the back, I'm talkin' peering into the truck bodies, whooping like tourists, it's not fuckin' workin'."

"Listen, honey," said Artie, "your leather queens can be more like Jesus for a night, okay? We talked about this. If you're going to be the one place, it's gotta be live and let live, at least till we get a few more places open, then you can go ahead and have your fucking grotto from hell or whatever."

"I dunno, the way this thing is going," Leo grumbled. "That new hotel, all piss-elegant. Didn't see no place for the Harleys in the plans. Tell you, brings out the juvenile delinquent in me. We'll have the whole fuckin' East Side up here prissin' around. Gets me cranky."

"Look, what do you want, a tractor pull?" Artie blew smoke at him. "Go easy, this thing's working, better than we figured. Let it work. Down the road, you can have your water sports, I don't know, live torture shows, whatever—we'll get there, but one step at a time."

AFTER YEARS of counting down to the day when he could leave Long Spit to go off to college, Anthony now found himself torn. Wendell showed up with his pickup to help him move. His mother hovered fretfully in the kitchen as the cartons of CDs and sneakers went out the back door. She dabbed distractedly at the spotless counters, as though, if the kitchen were only a little cleaner, he might decide not to get on with his life. Then, settling in on campus, through the freshman mixers, registration fair, meeting his unpromising suitemates, he kept feeling the pull of his real life—back home, of all places. It wasn't homesickness, though, in the usual sense. Rather, he felt panic at the fizzling first taste of being a star— so unexpected, and now had he blinked it away?

He sneaked back for his shifts at Angleton's, vague with his mother, sometimes not even stopping home. He no longer wore drip-dry shirts to work, so this meant having to go to a Laundromat and buy an iron for the first time in his life. Midweek, when he did stop in before work, his mother noticed. She wasn't going to say anything, but he insisted on knowing why she'd gone so quiet.

"Nothing, I'm fine," she said, reaching for the dishrag. "It's just your shirt."

"My shirt." Caught, he tried to make it ridiculous. "And? Meaning?"

"Well look at this." She gave his upper sleeve a bitter little yank, displaying a crushed crease. "I could do that for you. . . . I mean, what's the point?"

"No point. I'm not here anymore, is all." He sounded sensible.

She turned away. "Don't I know it."

He gave her a long-suffering look. "I gotta go." He waited in hug position. After a moment, she turned half toward him, impassive, making one cheek available.

By this time, the Wednesday, he already felt an unprecedented buzz in the town. The end of the straight tourist season, the departure of the summer people, the building stream of boys arriving, added up to a demographic lurch that made the village seem seen through a surreal lens, everything tinted gay. Primness about public affection vanished. Boys strolling Front Street with hands in each other's back pockets were as common as golden retrievers leashed to parking meters. Frankie's patio had a minor dance party going shirtless all afternoon, until the drift toward the Sand Box kicked in later on. An "art show" arrived in a van from Derek and Tracy's gallery in Boston and set up in the park along the front, selling framed Rittses, Webers, and Mapplethorpes, and charcoal drawings of men lounging together naked. Anthony saw Derek giving Helen Boothroyd a personal tour, pointing out possible decorations for the new rooms she was building. She looked game, but rationed her glances at each one, turning her head aside with a finger on the chin and a nervous titter.

Anthony floated along toward the restaurant, harvesting greetings from summer regulars, at play with eye contact like a hummingbird sampling stamens, feeling more like he belonged on his own main street than he ever had before. His friends had all gone off to college, which put him even more at ease. Right in front of Stevie Lund's shop, he exchanged acquaintace embrace and air kisses with Eggie, who was immediately the gossip columnist. "Saw you at tea dance with that young—scholar. Are you—happening?"

"Wellll . . ." Anthony feigned bashfulness.

"Aren't you just! Well, listen, honey." Eggie tapped him on the wrist bone. "Gonna tell you something. Love's great, sure, but remember, it's just like gorgonzola—keeps getting better and better, right up to the moment it turns to garbage." He peered over his sunglasses. "You heard it here."

Anthony gave him a big grin. "Noted."

Angleton's had a line all day and night now. At Anthony's suggestion, Lattie had donated several additional benches and trash bins for the park across the street, which had now become the takeout annex for picnics, especially with the art show on. Anthony had also warned her not to lay off staff, as she always had after Labor Day. Some of the kitchen help were not pleased, looking forward as they had been to their annual sojourn on unemployment benefits.

She cut him a tense look from her perch behind the chrome cash register. She'd grown more and more agitated as his departure neared, the end of her buffer zone.

"How much more you gonna give me?" She tapped her hair hat nervously with a ballpoint pen. Lattie was already taking her enormous hike in income for granted—three days a week now at the hairdresser's, a raw silk tunic instead of the navy cardigan with the shells—and had settled into regarding the avalanche of business as an annoyance.

"Once my classes really start, I guess next week, that's it," he said, "but this should trail off pretty soon, don't worry." She shook her head peevishly.

A heavy-duty hurricane fence went up around the Ocean and, on the Thursday afternoon, Arnold Prendergast looked out his windows to see two dozen portable toilets crowding along the property line. That was it. He called the police station.

"I'm afraid they've got all their permits, sir," said Jim Priestly.

"Well, how the hell long are they going to be there?" Prendergast roared.

"Oh, just till Sunday," Jim said. "Guess they want to have some sort of a party after they unhook the sewer line."

"That's the damnedest thing I ever heard." Prendergast slammed the phone down.

On Friday afternoon, *Nighthawk,* Simon Whetstone's gunmetal-colored motoryacht, grumbled into the harbor with its decks deserted, turned in place, and bow-thrusted sideways into a berth on the town dock, three uniformed crew appearing from the wheelhouse at the last minute to handle lines. A gunmetal Bentley Turbo with a "W" plate idled at the dock gate.

Late afternoon saw a steady buildup of cars, buses, and boats; impromptu scenes blossomed here and there, a boom box on a balcony, the iron-pumper chambermaids dusting the horses on the antique carousel, and a new element, the first circuit-party pilgrims, an abrupt uptick in the numbers of physically tweaked, harshly confident men in whiter-than-white T-shirts, roaming in packs, dishing everything in their path. Suddenly they were everywhere, sharp-faced, startlingly honed, having paid major attention to dental and body-hair decisions, the lay of certain veins; some sported what were evidently trademark accessories, sunglasses with feathered wings, lucky whistles, garments with strategic holes offering peeks at tattoos, abdominal definition, or other attractions, about them all the heady aura of an in-group joyfully reconvened after far-flung stints among the masses.

But the weekend was truly galvanized into life when the first of Artie's little cruise ships arrived. It was the one from Providence, so its approach brought it through Long Spit Passage, right past the Sand Box, where tea dance was in full cry, music pumping and a few hundred boys flailing. Hundreds more were making their way over the dunes to Mel Cleveland's biggest clambake ever. When the crowd on the ship saw the hordes ashore, a mutual cheer broke out across the water, music on both sides got turned up, the whole landscape undulated with boys waving their arms over their heads in time, like anenomes on a reef, yipping and howling for joy, many feeling the first beneficent surges of their Ecstasy tabs, but many coming honestly by their tears. And it was just beginning.

By the time the first ship wound its way through the dredged channel to the anchorage, the lights of the Boston ship were visible off Point Judith to the east, and a few minutes after that, the lights of the first New York ship appeared through the sunset over the Sound. Watching and buzzing at their approach, the spontaneous party-vigil grew larger and larger along the ridge of the dune, infused with the fresh ranks coming ashore from the first ship, until the charged throng stretched solidly from the Sand Box all the way to the colored lights of the clambake. The fading sun gave way to the gentle light of a quarter-moon high in the sky. Everywhere boys exchanged looks of wonderment at something quite unexpected that was happening: looking to get laid, they'd somehow stumbled on a moment of transcendence.

FLORIAN HAD insisted that Hollis move the telescope out onto the open part of the porch; they were taking turns peering at the scene. Hollis was at first uncomfortable, didn't know whether Florian understood he'd been spied upon with this very instrument. But, as with so many things in these past few days, Florian's blithe energy propelled them both through it.

"Umh! Gonna be *bad* tonight!" Florian exclaimed, training the barrel on the dunes with stroking motions. "Boys on the loose! Nobody safe!"

As much as it had smoothed the way at times, Florian's lightheartedness had a heedless quality—outwardly at least—that had kept Hollis in turmoil ever since he'd arrived, as though, from the start, it had never occurred to Florian that the grounds for his being there needed discussing. Hollis had veered from hope and secret arousal to sour self-pity, from resignation to bereft emptiness, and now was careening, several scotches the worse for wear, toward more trouble, as Florian merrily prepared to head out alone. Of course that was the only plan that made any sense, but did it have to be so assumed?

When he was ready to go, Florian presented himself, in black jeans and a white tank top. He flipped up the shirt to bare his silky tummy. "Gonna give us a tickle? Come on. She's all nervous, give her some confidence, just kidding . . ." He clutched the shirt around him. "Well, home by Monday! No . . ." He touched Hollis on the sleeve, looked him in the eye for half a beat. "No, I'll be back before too long," He skipped down the steps.

Hollis looked after him, took a gulp of his drink. "Heartless slut," he muttered. He realized in the instant that he hadn't muttered aloud to himself in weeks, and was reminded in a rush of how his rage was multiplied by letting such words escape his lips. He wished he could retract them: too much to lose—or was there? Maybe nothing at all, just making a fool of yourself anyway, and on around again . . . Despite all that he had overturned of his former, peep-show life, it seemed at this moment that he was worse off. He had lunged so much closer to the mark—the actual paragon, right here in his rooms—but was still shy of it, Florian as unavailable to him as if he'd been an etching in the collection. Glum, woozy, he stared. . . . It's a verdict that's been handed down, he thought: guilty of prurience, and the sentence: having Florian here but just out of reach, and sick. He stood abruptly to shake off the thought, and went up to prepare for bed.

As the floss found its automatic way among the yellowed teeth, he came to his senses. How in hell can you think such a gorgeous man would even consider you in that way? He's come to live in your house, available to your senses and open to becoming a real friend. What on earth more could you wish for?

RAY AND Sibley decided to leave the Sand Box open into the evening, since the impromptu rave in the dunes showed no signs of letting up. The boys had their own stupificants out there in the sand, and just needed a dance floor to repair to when the energy hit and the world suddenly became a benign place, all about loving your fellow man. So the Sand Box jumped on and on, boys hooting and groping in the Upper Reaches, spilling off the lower decks, shouting encouragement to clenchers in the dune grass shadows all round. It became one steamy pearl in a string that stretched from the ruins to the ships to the clambake to the egg crate, to Frankie's, Sully's, and the Crab Hole.

Nonetheless, by Saturday noon, the circuit-party regulars

were already not happy: there was no gym, there were no tan-ning beds, no decent restaurants, and hardly any shopping; the best-looking antique shop was closed, the sand was too big, and—shuttle buses? We don't think so. Artie and his minions worked intently, putting out brushfires. One of the ships had a gym, get it open to all, round up a convoy of ethnic food vans—Vietnamese, Indian, Japanese, Mexican, Thai, double the bus runs, add drinks (the Indians won't have to know for one night) and the sand? Well . . . Plus his cell phone rang every few minutes with a new crisis at the Ocean, where dem-olition crews were tangling with lighting and sound crews, all flat-out preparing for the upcoming night's events. The riggers were running practice quick breakdowns; the laser software guy was fine-tuning, calibrating. Artie and B. J. Gelson teased each other: "Stress monger!" "Stress glutton!" "No, you!" "No, *you!*" And they were supposed to have lunch on *Nighthawk.* What could he have been thinking of? But twenty-four hours, and it would all be over till next year.

ADMISSION TO the Wrecking Ball was twenty-five dollars, but that wasn't why Anthony informed Wendell that they would be sneaking in. As a townie, he couldn't think of paying to get into the Ocean, where he had stolen peppermints from the lobby as a small boy, had moved on, at ten, to buying cigarettes at the front desk, saying they were for his mother, and ended up scrubbing pots in the kitchen for his first working summers. The imminent destruction hit him in mixed ways, all of them a bit proprietary. It was erasing part of his eight-year-old scamp's domain, but it was relieving his new world of a frumpy throw-back. Not gonna pay. Wendell was bemused by his determina-tion, but was getting used to Anthony's occasionally iron will.

"Oh—and," Anthony added, "I'm underage."

The party was slated to begin at ten P.M. By eleven, with no soundproofing to stop it, the dance music trod the dark hilltop like a stomping boot. The dance floor was in the main dining room; from there, the party opened onto the vast, recently shored-up porch, and spilled down the broad pair of stairways to the stone terrace. As Anthony and Wendell, both in black, made their way up the hillside from the beach, through the tangle of beach roses, jagged strobe and laser darts shot out of the dining room's hundred-foot wall of windows to play over their heads and on out to sea, arousing curiosity on Block Island and Montauk. Mixed with the insistent engine of the music was the roar of the crowd, fifteen hundred and still pouring in, stoking themselves into high party mode.

The chain-link fence, intended to keep people at a safe distance from the blast, had simply been run into the prickers and terminated. But any self-respecting local boy knew all the narrow paths, some overgrown into tunnels, that ran through the beach-rose and poison-ivy jungle.

"Don't touch anything," Anthony said over his shoulder. "P.I."

"Oh, great, so am I going to erupt in blisters on the dance floor?" Wendell panted after him.

They crossed the kitchen staff parking area, directly below the windows. Wendell snagged Anthony by a belt loop for a hug. Anthony glanced around, but was too busy being in charge. "It's right over here," he said efficiently. The freight entrance had been torn open to the foundation to get the fixtures out. They entered the dark, cavernous kitchen, lit only by patches of moonlight on the rubbly floor. Here and there dangled loops of the blasting wire.

"There used to be a whole wall of sinks, there"—Anthony pointed—"where I worked. And those were the dumbwaiters, up to the dining room. We used to ride them." The party was surprisingly muffled, the nearest sounds occasional squawks from the floorboards. Again Wendell tried to break Anthony's momentum for a second, but he dodged slightly aside with an exaggerated look around. "We can't get caught down here. We've got to get all the way in. Come on. There's a stairway over here."

From the minute Anthony pushed open the basement swinging doors, the roar grew with each step they climbed. There was no one who looked like security at the top of the stairs, just stragglers recovering from the dance floor across the hall. The two plunged through the archway into shattering noise, rambunctious jostling, all conversation impossible; meaning to observe, they were instead drawn into the whorl and swept slowly along under the salvos of strobes, like water at the perimeter of a draining bathtub, hands passing shirtless, sweaty-and-oiled bodies along, whiffs of pot, poppers, pits, and hair gel, the music a brutal sear on top overloading the eardrums to twangs of intercranial feedback and, on the low end, a chewing gut-crunch like being on a catwalk alarmingly close to violent, full-tilt machinery that if you touched it would crush you to a smear. But the boys all round were blissful, as though it were Palestrina they were savoring, and eerily polite; more than once the words "Excuse me" were mouthed by a beatific gym bunny as he chested his way through or squeezed Anthony's buns in passing.

Anthony barely recognized the place. Overhead, the rank of tarnished brass chandeliers had been cut down and in their place hung aluminum spaceframes studded with clusters of hundreds of motorized lights that swept the room in synchronized batteries, their beams piercing the artificial smoke like the tines of a rake. A self-propelled scissor platform loomed as the command-and-control center at the end opposite the windows, glowing with turntables and sound and lighting panels—prepared, at the final moment, to drive out the front door towing all its cables behind. On cylindrical platforms here and there, boys volunteered to have their bodies adored—precisely the plan, after all, that had drawn them from Palm Springs and Vancouver. Anthony and Wendell were slowly spiraling closer to the dance floor, their extremities already starting to twitch.

Once the music had invaded his physical being and swamped his receptors, Anthony was surprised how quickly he got used to it, driven to a sort of detached internal observation post he'd never known. Before long he was letting his body start to bounce in time. He became an even more disembodied consciousness, entranced, borne along by a sensor-equipped conveyance down there somewhere, its feet getting stepped on. Wendell smiled encouragingly at him (Who is this young man I hardly know?), reached around him, and clutched his hipbone. A joint materialized, passed to Wendell with a wink, making its erratic way through the press along with the hundreds of other charitable contributions to the psychoactive seepage gradually permeating the throng. Passing it along, Anthony noted lipstick on the end. In a reverie that took all of two seconds, quiet amid the relentless crash and jolt, he thought of all the handsome waiters he had spied on from his pot-scrubbing post down in the kitchen, how extraordinary it was that these hundreds of men were working themselves into a paroxysm over precisely what had been so forbidden to him then. He came to as their propelled drift brought them to a lower-profile hummock in the fleshscape. Security personnel, spectral in the smoke, were crouched around someone on the floor—"K-hole," a voice said. The casualty was hauled to his feet and conveyed by a security wedge toward the chill room, the dancers opening a path with hardly a side look. A passing daisy chain of bumping boys tried to scoop Anthony in; the two feinted aside, not quite there yet, but, a moment later, they let go hands and finally let themselves be sucked into the maelstrom of the dance floor, beginning to move in earnest. Anthony's shirt came off; his lean, pale torso bobbed in the smoke and flash, became the destination for reconnoitering fingertips from all sides, and for determined, slithery collisions, so that Wendell needed to keep fighting his way back to proximity. At one point, they found themselves surrounded by an arms-laced scrum that seemed bent on crushing them, and struggled free through the legs.

For the next hours, the party was a seamless mêlée, unbroken by anything that could interfere with getting lost in it. Time taffied, now surging, now stuck, as the DJ built the music in quarter and half-hour waves to higher and higher peaks, sometimes triggering the most intense bedlam by suddenly shutting down to just the punching bass drum, letting the crowd feel its own seething intensity in a moment of suspense before the crashing return of the wall of sound unleashed a howl of release. Boys came and went from the porch, the terrace, recuperating, cruising, topping up their buzzes before plunging back into the raving crush, maybe pausing to look at the starry sky and be reminded of where they were. It was only as the end drew near that things started to go wrong.

With the grand finale coming up, nobody was leaving. At a quarter to five, another collapse on the dance floor, and this time the emergency staff could not revive him. They phoned the town ambulance, which had been on standby all night. At the firehouse, Sam Jenkins shook himself awake and started the engine. A minute later, he and his EMTs, Ron and Stephanie, backed up to the Ocean's door. While Stephanie pulled out the stretcher, she glanced over at Sam, who already had on a surgical mask and was pulling on latex gloves. "Not with a ten-foot pole," he said grimly. "You don't care?" She and Ron shook their heads.

They headed inside, Sam wielding a powerful flashlight. Seeing them, the head of security radioed the control center and the music abruptly faded; a grid of worklights came on, capturing hundreds of blinking, frazzled, drenched, and dis- pleased partyers. The man was propped, unconscious, with his head in another man's lap, surrounded by security and produc- tion staff, a doctor who had come forward, and by a circle of onlookers, some now snapped alert, some staring addled, still behind the curve, idly groping their boyfriends. Sam moved in, head down, leading with his elbows, made room to set the stretcher down as though the encroaching feet and legs were furniture. Stephanie checked the man's pulse with a worried shake of the head, and they began to move him onto the stretcher. "Keep his head raised!" blurted the doctor, then more diplomatically, "So he doesn't aspirate—you know, vomit?" Sam turned to him with a look of utter contempt laced with grim satisfaction. "I'm in charge here." Stephanie and Ron exchanged a glance; the three hustled away the laden stretcher.

There were a few yips and cries to get the music going again, but the freight train's momentum had abruptly waned. It was five A.M.; sunrise would be at 6:18. A production decision was made to start the move outside. So music returned, but now moody, tempo-less synthesizer washes, a backdrop for porten- tous announcements urging everyone to "prepare for the com- ing dawn."

"Beware if anybody offers you Kool-Aid," said Anthony. They stood amid a drug- and dance-stunned flock behind security lines watching the motorized scissor platform grind across the lobby and bump clumsily down the ramp onto the front lawn, techies close behind untangling its trailing trunks.

The music, still interplanetary, gradually shifted to the speakers outside. The groggy stream was herded out through the fence, past the gate tally clickers. Inside, the riggers began tearing down the lighting trusses and sound towers and hauling them on dollies out to the staging area; the demolition crew started through the structure from top to bottom, placing the dynamite charges in the auger holes. A few of the village's earliest joggers and dog walkers were amazed to come upon a scene of two thousand haggard, mostly shirtless men, milling around in the dark street. Drawn by the eerie waves of music and the low hum of voices, neighbors who had endured the hammering all night now came to their windows in bathrobes for the spectacle and saw the old building, seemingly licked around its foundation by slowly billowing flames of purples, greens, and blues, projected by programmed banks of lights. Bedside phones began to ring here and there about the village, and gradually a contingent of hastily buttoned townspeople assembled to one side of the crowd of men. The town's two fire trucks arrived as the first hints of a rosy glow appeared in the east. A few people noticed the sound of a light plane in the dark sky overhead.

Finally the riggers and wreckers emerged for the last time. The flames had crept up the facade and become orange and gold curtains like aurora borealis, making the entire building seem an undulating hallucination. A voice, deep and slathered with echo, came over the speakers: "Gentlemen. And ladies. We have a perfect count. All are safely out. Zero hour will be in ten minutes." The music resumed.

It took a few seconds for this to register on Anthony. Suddenly, the hair on the back of his neck stood on end. "Oh, my God!" He bolted toward the control center, leaving Wendell behind in confusion. The platform was now crowded with production people, B.J., Artie, Leo, a video crew, photographers, a couple of reporters, the head of the demolition crew, who was going through his final check of the electronic detonator. Just as Anthony reached the stairs, a security cordon was escorting Simon Whetstone from his Bentley. "Sorry, kid, back off," said a giant wearing a headset.

"But it's an emergency!" cried Anthony. "Don't do it!"

The man shielded his mouthpiece, barked into it: "Artie, hang on, got a problem here." He turned to Anthony. "What the fuck's up, kid?" Artie appeared at the railing.

"I—we—snuck in?" Anthony said. "My friend and I? Your head count's off."

"Oh, Christ . . ." said Artie. The demolition man looked over at Artie questioningly.

"I can't fuckin' believe it, there's people in there," Artie said.

"Goddammit!" the demolition man exploded, slamming down his clipboard. "I told you this is not the way we do things. Jesus fucking Christ, I never should've—"

"Listen, we'll find them." Artie turned to Anthony. "It's how many?" Anthony coweringly raised two fingers.

"You're not going in there, no way," said the demolition man. "Insurance. That building's ready to blow. My crew's the only ones allowed in there."

"Whatever," said Artie, checking his watch. "But let's get on it."

"And anyway, if you let two sneak in, how many others are there in there?"

"We'll make an announcement, whatever," Artie pointed to the sky, "but we don't have much time."

The demolition man was heading down the stairs. "This is the last fuckin' time I get involved with a bunch of . . . Eddie! Pete! Come on! We gotta go in! People in there!" Artie trailed them up the front walk until the boss turned on him: "You! Stay the fuck back! Asshole . . ."

Just then two men appeared in the hotel doorway, looking dazed and sheepish. The demolition man trained his flashlight on their faces. They both had on overalls, the bibs unhooked and dangling. "Well, now, where in Christ's name have *you* been?"

"I guess we sort of fell asleep," said one of the men, "down in the basement. Found what looked like a walk-in—"

"Meat locker," put in the other, giving his friend a dopey smile. "We, like, woke up when it got so like quiet."

Anthony made his way back to Wendell. "Guess we got away with it."

A minute later, an announcement boomed out: "Ladies and gentlemen, please listen carefully: this is a matter of life and death. This is the last warning. Everyone must be out of the building. If you know of anyone who may have entered the event without passing through the admission gate, please come forward now to the production platform. There will be no questions asked. We must be sure no one is left inside." For several more minutes, the announcement, the music, the waiting.

"I'm telling you," said the demolition boss, "we should wait till it's light, do a full search, it's too risky."

"We're going ahead," said Artie. "The upper floors were all barricaded. It'll be fine. I'll take responsibility." He nodded to B.J.

The familiar music began, the lone trumpet, the opening of Richard Strauss's *Also Sprach Zarathustra*, the music from *2001*. The front and sides of the building were hit with a dotted line of two hundred purple lasers, making a beam ceiling over the crowd, each dot seeming to ignite a patch of smoldering red and orange on the tired clapboards. With each building climax and its residue of timpani, more intense and spreading color, until the final climax: A blaze of white light, and, deep in the building, a muffled *CRRUMP*. The cupola dropped straight into the collapsing core, walls toppled inward, and a sharper *WRRACK* of perimeter blasts shattered the walls to tumbling rubble with a roar spiked with deep splintery crunches like one rogue wave full of wooden boats hurling itself on a stony beach. It was all over in seconds.

Then, applause, cheers, the fire trucks playing their hoses into the plume of dust, smoke, and steam, and the first break of sun over the horizon catching sky-writing directly overhead: SIZE MATTERS.

"What the—!" Artie cut a look at B.J., equally shocked, and beyond him: Leo, palms-up, don't-ask-me shrug, big smile.

Wesley opened one eye at the distant thunder, wondered sleepily why, out of a clear dawn . . . ?, saw the boat safe at the dock, and went back to sleep.

Hollis padded from his bedroom in the back to Florian's room—door ajar, the bed still made. He entered—trespassing, it seemed, and looked out at the new gap in the dawn silhouette of the village.

Anthony cocked his eyebrow at the skywriting and said dryly to Wendell, "Kinda makes you proud, doesn't it?"